ISLE OF HUGH

A LACHART ISLE ROMANCE

JESSICA BURNLEY

LOVE, ZERTEX

ISLE OF HUGH

ISBN: 978-1-912767-65-6

Published worldwide by LOVE, ZERTEX, an imprint of Zertex Media Ltd.

2

www.zertexmedia.com

1

SCOTTISH ILL

*H*ey, hey, it's Summer Rose, coming to you all the way from off the western coast of Scotland, cruising around the beautiful Hebrides! It's a beautiful day here, across the pond! The scenery is so beautiful! It's so...

Summer frowned at the screen, her finger hovering over the "delete" key. She'd gotten so much use of that key lately, the little backwards-facing arrow printed on it had almost faded away.

'Beautiful?' Come on, Summer. You can do better than that.

She thumped her skull, then raked a hand through her auburn curls. There'd once been a time when she could wax poetic for pages on the virtues of the perfect avocado, or the benefits of oat milk over soy. Now?

Nothing. Blank slate.

Summer sighed and looked around the near-empty inside passenger area of the ferry. Raindrops pelted the windows, and beyond that, nothing but a thick, soupy fog.

She shivered, pulling the anorak she'd bought specifically for this trip tighter around her. Until that moment, she'd thought 'chilled to the bone' was just a saying.

Right then, her bones were practically screaming in rebellion, longing for the warm Santa Monica sunshine. Or any sunshine, for that matter. Everything around her was gloom, doom, and then a bit more gloom again, like something out of a gothic horror novel.

Beautiful?

She looked down at her latest blog post and groaned. How was it possible to have used to many exclamation points in so few words?

She'd long-since suspected other bloggers overused exclamation points as a crutch, to hide their less-than-perfect existences. Now, here she was, living proof of it.

Delete. Delete. Delete. She hadn't been able to write a single usable word for her blog, *Summer All Year Round,* in weeks. Not since—

She shook her head to force the thought away. Noooo. *So* not going there. She'd ventured halfway around the world from the comfort of home precisely to forget about that. And that was precisely what she planned to do.

Shifting in her seat, she squinted through the window, trying to see something positive, something inspiring, through the layers of white mist. She'd hoped for bracing air, sweeping, breath-taking views, not this. She half-expected to see Heathcliff wandering out of the murk, or a lonely graveyard full of broken headstones.

Not for the first time, Summer wondered if this was a mistake.

Relax. When you get to Lachart Isle, you'll get everything you want. A change of scenery, beauty, adventure—and your muse will return.

Snapping the lid of her laptop closed, she caught an old man staring at her from the bench across the small cabin. He was wearing a flat tweed cap, and had a gnarled wooden walking stick propped between his legs. His kind face gave her grandfatherly vibes. Not that she ever knew her grandfather, but if she had, she imagined he'd have a face like this one.

Albeit with a better skin care regimen.

"You're no' from around here, are you, lassie?"

She pulled her anorak tighter. "No. I'm from the States. L.A."

The old man gazed blankly back at her.

"Los Angeles," she explained. "California."

"Oh. I see." He stared past her for a moment, his eyes glazing over like he was deep in thought. "Hollywood, you mean?"

Summer tilted her head from side to side. "Uh, yeah. Kind of."

"Right. Oh, well. You'll know that, eh, what's his name? Robert Redford, then?"

"Robert Redford?"

"He lives in Hollywood," the old man said, and there was a note of suspicion to his voice, like he suspected she was lying to him.

She smiled. "Sure. I know Robert Redford." It was easier than explaining the truth—that in all of her thirty years in California, she'd never quite travelled in those rich, fabulous circles.

Not like *some* people she knew, who she preferred not to think about...

Her new friend held up a paper shopping bag. "I was just picking myself up a new pair of Wellies on the mainland. Do you have Wellies?"

Summer looked down at her feet, like she might find a pair there. "Uh, no," she admitted.

"Well, God help you, then," the old man muttered. "What is it brings you all this way?"

"Well, I actually used to travel to Scotland a lot when I was young. My dad was Scottish. From Edinburgh. And I just wanted to shake things up a little. I was in kind of a rut, you know?"

He stroked his grizzled chin. "No. No, I can't say I do."

She'd been traveling since last night, the most she'd gone without speaking to anyone, since the man next to her in the window seat on the flight to Glasgow had insisted on sleeping the whole way. It felt good to finally be communicating again. Her sister, Indigo, always said that once someone found Summer's "on" switch, it was hard to turn her off.

Indigo was not wrong.

"Well, OK, so, you see, I was due to get married. It was going to be a whole big thing. Total showstopper. Except, my fiancé had a little change of heart. Told me on the big day that he wasn't sure he knew himself well enough to give his whole heart to me. I know. Can you believe that?"

Summer laughed, and ruefully shook her head.

"*But,* when he said that, I realised there's so much about myself that *I* don't know, either! You know? Who even am I? I'm Summer Rose, yes, obviously, but who is Summer Rose? That's what I found myself asking. So, I figured if I came out here, maybe I could discover myself. So, I guess it's like a metaphysical, reawakening trip. I think it was Thoreau who once said—"

She stopped when the man's head, which had been slowly drooping against his shoulder, collapsed entirely. He fell still—unnaturally so.

"Sir?"

There was no response from the old man. She loudly and emphatically cleared her throat, and tried again.

"Sir?"

Once again, he didn't answer. He just sat there, slumped forwards, not moving a muscle.

"Oh, good job, Summer," she whispered. "You've finally succeeded in actually boring a man to death."

She reached a foot across the aisle and jiggled his corduroy pant leg with her toe.

He jumped up suddenly, let out a long, loud snore, then wiped at his nose. "Milk, two sugars, thank you," he mumbled, and drifted off again.

"Well, at least he's not dead," she muttered, but her relief soon gave way to more gloom.

You need to level with yourself, Summer. Saying Brad had a 'little change of heart' is like saying Mount Everest is a 'little hill.' He dumped you for your best friend.

She stuffed her laptop in her carry-on as the ferry swayed. Her stomach swayed with it, then her head, then the rest of her, until all her insides felt like a spinning carousel. At the same time, all the oxygen seemed to leave the cabin in one big *whoosh.*

Air. I need air.

She jumped to her feet, pulling the sliding door open. Cold wind slapped her cheeks as she stepped onto the deck of the small ferry. Icy tendrils of mist licked at her skin. She rushed to the rail and leaned over, peering at the black waves swirling with white foam as she sucked in the frigid air.

Pull yourself together, Summer.

Her anorak did a poor job of stopping the chill from seeping in. She tucked her hair into the hood and fastened the extra button on the collar. Holding onto the cold, wet railing for dear life, she pitched back and forth on the tide as she made her way to the captain at the helm.

Water—or maybe snot—dripped off the edge of her nose as she looked up at him. He was wearing only a thin thermal shirt, and chewing on a cigar. He didn't look wet or miserable at all, which mystified her.

Her teeth chattered and her voice wobbled. "W-we almost there?"

"Aye."

She strained to see anything through the thick fog. Overhead, seagulls screamed. It sounded like a warning to turn back.

"Are you sure? I was here before. I mean, it was a long time ago, sure. But I remember, like, a Helter Skelter." When he eyed her dubiously, she said, "Not Charles Manson or The Beatles Helter Skelter. Just as in the fairground ride. At a fair? Like a carnival? It was like, all swirly. You know?" She made a twirling motion with a finger. "Sort of, swoosh, swoosh, swoosh."

She could hear herself babbling now, something she always did when she was nervous. And from his expression, he clearly *didn't* know anything about a Helter Skelter, swooshy or otherwise.

Ignoring her, he stepped from the bridge and motioned her out of the way.

"Dropping anchor."

"What? Here?"

"Aye."

She looked around. Had she missed a dock somewhere? Nope. Angry sea, in all directions. The kind of uninviting water people only went into to drown.

She followed after him, her ballet flats slipping on the slick deck. "Uh, sir. I don't see land. We're kind of in the middle of the bay, or the ocean, or whatever body of water this is. I hope you aren't expecting us to swim for it, because I paid a fare to..."

He finished working the crank, then pointed into the distance.

The mist parted like a curtain, and almost as if he'd summoned it, a rowboat appeared, cutting surely through the dark water towards them.

She stared at it, and at the huge figure working the oars, his longish, curly hair tossing about in the stiff wind.

"What am I looking at here?" she asked, dumbfounded. "I see a random guy in the world's smallest boat."

She gasped. Surely, he didn't mean...?

The captain cracked his first smile, almost as if it gave him great pleasure to say, "You're not going ashore in this boat, lass. You're going ashore in *that* one."

Oh, so he *did* mean that.

She squinted, hoping the boat only looked small and rickety from a distance, but was, in fact, a seaworthy vessel that was nowhere near in danger of sinking.

But no. The closer it got, the more convinced she was that someone was playing a cruel joke on her. The dinghy looked older than Scotland itself. And while history wasn't her strong point, she was pretty sure that Scotland was *ancient*.

The small boat skimmed up against the side of the ferry and the man at the oars nodded curtly at the captain. He was wearing a kilt. How very Scottish of him. Summer couldn't be charmed by the fact, though, because the man's strapping body seemed to take up almost all of the real estate inside the boat, leaving very little room for anyone else. And it also looked like his feet were submerged in about an inch of saltwater.

Fantastic.

She wiped at her nose, wondering if it was too late to turn back.

No, Summer. You want to be the type of woman who makes life happen, instead of letting life happen to you. Here's your chance.

"That's... *great*. Bring it!" She clapped her hands together. "I can totally do this!"

Even if it kills me, she thought. *Which it very well might.*

2

IN THE DINGHY

Twenty feet below where Summer stood gawping at him, the man let go of the oars and stood up in the boat. Summer admired his balance. The sea was tossing about angrily underneath him, but he didn't seem to have noticed.

"Incoming!" bellowed the captain from right beside her, and she ducked as something went *whumming* past her ear. It passed so fast, she didn't see it until it hit the water with a splash, and immediately started to sink beneath the foamy water. The guy in the kilt reached down to scoop it up, but it slipped from his fingers and disappeared beneath the waves.

"*Ocht*," was all he had to say on the matter.

"What was that?" she asked, turning to the captain. Her heart leaped into her throat when she saw that he was holding one of her suitcases in his hands. "Wait. What are you—?"

"I thought you'd have recognized it," he said. "It was *your* bag."

Her jaw dropped. She spun around to find another four of her suitcases piled up behind him. She'd gotten the very expensive collection as a wedding present from Brad, and they'd planned to use them for their honeymoon to Hawaii before...

Well, before plans had changed.

There were four cases on the deck, and one more currently being hoisted above the captain's head. That made five. Her cosmetics case was missing, which must mean...

Oh, no. No no no no no!

A sinking sensation overcame her, and the bile in her throat fought its way up, making her gag. She gripped the railing tight, as the deck rolled and spun beneath her feet.

No makeup. No hair dryer. No frizz serum, which was a *must* for her rat's nest in this weather.

This was not good. Not at all. When she'd pictured this trip, she'd imagined all the selfies she'd take for her blog, all the people she'd wow here with her L.A. sophistication.

Actually, there was only one person she *really* wanted to wow, and he certainly wouldn't be stumbling around on a boat in Scotland, but that was beside the point.

Necessary to her plan to impress the locals was her assortment of the latest Sephora colours. Her straightening iron. Her fresh mist setting spray, which all the best fashion bloggers had called *this season's absolute essential.*

"Fire in the hole!" the captain bellowed.

Before she could extend a hand to stop him, he hurled another, larger suitcase over the side. She clutched her head and screamed as she watched it fall, sure that all the fancy, stylish new clothes she'd bought were about to become fish food, too.

This time, though, it landed securely in the arms of Mr. Kilt. He placed it at his feet on the bottom of the rowboat, then reached his hands out for the next one.

She grabbed the bag from the captain. "Give it to me. I'll do it!"

She tried to lift it, but this was one of the bigger ones. She toppled over and nearly face-planted into the rail, her cheeks going bright scarlet. The captain just watched her with amusement.

"How's that working out for you?" he asked.

"Okay, I guess I could use a little help," she admitted.

He clamped a calloused hand around the handle, and lifted the case like it weighed no more than air. She watched, teeth gritted, as he tossed that bag down, too.

"Catch it, catch it, catch it!" she whispered, then she almost cheered when Mr. Kilt grabbed it in the nick of time.

"Good grief," he called up to her. "What's in this bag? Rocks?"

Summer leaned over the railing. "I, uh, I like to collect them from the different places I go. You know, like souvenirs? Like... heavy souvenirs."

She smiled, like she thought he might be charmed.

She thought wrong.

He gazed at her like she'd just announced she collected the heads of her enemies. Then he said, "And how many more of these do you have?"

"Just four more. There's six in total. Including the one that's currently submerged." She peered into the waves. "Which isn't going to stay that way? Right? You're going to get that back?"

He ignored the question. "What the hell do you need all this..." He shook his head. "Forget it. None of my business. Just get chucking before the tide turns."

One by one, she watched the captain feed the bags down, still not quite able to believe this was happening. She wasn't going in that boat. Of course she wasn't. That would be ridiculous, not to mention incredibly dangerous. She was here because she wanted to make *life* happen, not death.

She couldn't say she was particularly impressed by the welcome, either. The man in the boat had so far shown none of that famous Highland hospitality.

Of course, it was likely that he was just the luggage service. Once he collected all of her bags, and fished her cosmetics case out of the water, they'd ease the ferry to the dock, which she was sure was just out of sight in the mist, and let her off onto blessedly dry land.

She watched the man in the boat as he caught the bags and dumped them on the floor. What was it with these guys? This one was wearing a flannel shirt, too, rolled up at the sleeves, buttons undone to reveal a swirl of cinnamon-coloured, masculine chest hair.

He probably wore nothing under that kilt, either, if the rumour was true. There was a lot of bare skin going on, and some quite impressive muscles popping under the exertion. It made her shiver just watching him. Did the concept of *freezing one's butt off* mean nothing to these men?

When he finished securing the last bag, his piercing blue eyes fastened on her. She might have swooned, if the rest of his expression didn't suggest that he wanted to toss her into the sea.

"Now you," he said.

She cupped a hand around her ear and leaned forward. "I'm sorry, what?"

On the deck, the captain moved closer to her. She looked at him. If he was going to pick her up and heft her over the railing like a suitcase, she was going to show him just how obnoxious American tourists could really be.

Thankfully, he didn't even try. Instead, he pointed to a ladder attached to the side of the ferry.

"There you are, lass. Just you climb down there."

She looked at it, grimacing. It was more rust than metal.

The wet salt air had corroded it so badly that she expected her foot would slice right through it like a knife through warm butter.

In America, a thing like that would have *Wrongful Death Lawsuit* written all over it. Here, though? Clearly, the rules were different.

"Yeah, no," she said, shaking her head. "I'm not doing that."

"It's easy enough," the captain told her. "You just sort of, you know..." His gaze flitted to the ladder, just for a moment. "...climb down it."

He made a climbing motion with his hands to demonstrate.

"Like that."

"No, I get the concept," she said. "But, I'm not doing it. It doesn't look safe."

"Of course it's safe!" the man in the kilt bellowed. He grabbed the bottom rung and pulled heartily on it, as if that was supposed to convince her. "Get your backside down here, or this boat's going on without you. And I can promise it's no' a pleasant swim."

She scoffed. "You *are* going to go in and get my cosmetics case, right?"

He simply stared at her, his eyes narrowing slightly.

Okay, I'll take that as a no.

Summer peered through the waves, hoping to see the case bobbing about nearby. It was nowhere in sight. She had loaded it so full of stuff that it had taken almost an hour to get the zipper closed, so it made sense that it would sink straight to the bottom.

"My fresh mist setting spray..." she murmured, forlornly. She'd sprung for the large size, figuring it was a must for this kind of weather. At forty-five bucks, it hadn't been cheap. Brand new, not even used once.

The captain shoved his cigar in his mouth and said, "Come on, lassie, we've no' all day. I need to get a shifty on."

"Fine! Fine, OK, fine!" Summer said, sighing heavily for dramatic effect. "Just give me a second."

She took in a few deep, salty breaths, bracing herself, then stepped back from the railing, trying to gauge whether she could make it over. Her legs weren't exactly stubby, but they didn't go on for miles like her best friend, Audriandra's. Audriandra could've hurdled the railing without missing a step. For Summer, however, it was going to prove more of a struggle.

Gripping the metal bar, she lifted a leg as high as she could, and hooked it over the railing.

"Nope," she said, when she saw the waves swirling below her. "Nuh-uh."

She unhooked her leg again, performed a few star jumps on the spot for reasons she couldn't quite explain, then gritted her teeth and tried again.

"Right. This time. Here goes! Shoot for the moon, Summer! Shoot for the moon!"

"I'd maybe shoot for the ladder first," the man in the boat called up.

"Aye, I'd maybe stick with that for now," the captain agreed.

Summer lunged at the railing, and this time swung one leg all the way over the top, so she was straddling it. With the cold metal rail between her legs, she glanced down at the angry water that churned in the gap between the boats.

"I'm going to die, aren't I?" she said, and she sounded surprisingly matter-of-fact about it.

"No. You're all right," the man below her said. His voice wasn't exactly encouraging, and she got the impression that he'd be just as happy if she sank into the waves and was never heard from again.

The toe of her ballet flat found the first rung of the ladder. Holding the railing with white knuckles, she slowly brought her other leg over. It was as she was swinging that leg down that her first foot slipped on the slick rung.

She yelped and threw her body forward, clutching onto the side of the ferry like a barnacle.

Summer hugged the railing tight, shaking her head. "Nope. No. Not going any further. I'll just stay here."

"You can't stay there," the captain told her.

"Oh no? Just you watch me!"

Beneath her, the man in the kilt let out a growl that was audible even over the cry of seagulls and the crashing of the waves. Suddenly, she felt something slip around her thighs, lifting her up and away from the ferry.

Nessie, she thought. *Oh my god, I'm being eaten by a sea monster!*

Try as she might to hold on, she had no choice but to loosen her death grip on the railing, and then she found herself bending forward at the waist, her legs held immobile. She started to scream.

"Easy now," the man in the kilt said. She looked down and saw that he was halfway up the ladder. She froze when he wrapped an arm around her waist, and it was only when she was settled on the seat, her feet in the ice-cold sea water, that she realised he'd fireman-carried her down into the rowboat.

Safe on the seat, she let out a breath of relief. "I thought I was going to die."

"Well, the night's still young," he muttered unencouragingly, motioning to her luggage. "That's a lot of bags you brought with you. Better not all be rocks." He glared at her accusingly, then gave a jerk of his head. "Shift over."

She blinked. The seat was already cramped enough as it was. "What? Why do you want me to—?"

"Well, that's where the oars are," he told her. "I'd have you row us, but we need to balance out the weight of all your... belongings."

"Oh. Uh, yeah. OK."

Reluctantly, she shimmied sideways a little. Then, when he glared at her, she moved a little further along.

He motioned for her to move even farther until she was practically sitting with one butt-cheek in the sea.

When he sat down beside her, he was squeezed in close, their thighs and arms pressing together. She could feel the warmth of his body next to her. It might have felt comforting if she weren't absolutely mortified at being so close to this total stranger.

"Shift back a bit," he barked.

He didn't exactly have the tact and hospitality she'd been hoping for when she started this trip. But she was too cold to argue with him. She shuffled and leaned back as he commanded, and he took hold of the oars.

He used an oar to shove them away from the ferry, and Summer almost jumped out of her skin when the larger boat blasted its horn to send them on their way.

The man in the kilt began to row, and with each broad, powerful stroke, his elbow came dangerously close to slamming into her chest. She tried to remind herself that every stroke was also getting her nearer to Lachart Island, where she could finally get a nice hot toddy, relax, and start this vacation off right.

Without her makeup bag.

She cringed at the thought. As she did, she realised how much her back muscles ached. She might've pulled something lifting that suitcase.

"I could seriously do with a massage. You know if the hotel has a spa?" she asked as she squirmed yet again to avoid the swinging of his arms.

He grunted a little as he pulled the oars through the water, this time smacking his pointy elbow straight between her boobs.

"Ow." She rubbed the spot and waited for his answer to her question.

Time stretched out. She hated pregnant pauses.

Wait. Had the grunt been an answer? And if so, was it a yes? A no? An I don't know?

"How about a store? I at least need to replenish my mist spray."

Another grunt.

So that *was* an answer? OK, this was progress. Unfortunately, she didn't speak Grunt.

Maybe she just needed to work on him. Get him to open up. Some people were like that.

"It's been a long time traveling, you know?" she said, her teeth chattering. She shifted out of the way at the last moment, avoiding another boob-related injury. "I just want to get somewhere so I can unwind and relax and maybe have a drink. I'm really looking forward to some good Scottish food. You ever have haggis? You know if they make a vegetarian option?"

Another grunt.

He did speak English, she knew. She'd heard him before.

"My father was Scottish, but he died a long time ago. I didn't really know him. He was a botanist. You know, flowers and stuff?"

"I know what a botanist is."

"OK! Cool! Uh... good job! So, anyway, my mom's kind of a California hippie, and she met him while she was backpacking through Scotland. I say backpacking, she was more sort of...

wandering, I guess? You know, like, in a spiritual sense? They bonded over nature, or whatever. It's been a really long time since I've been here. None of it looks familiar. Of course, I was around five when—"

"You talk a lot."

She smiled. "Why, thank you."

"It wasn't a compliment."

Her smile fell. She pressed her lips closed. The boat pitched back and forth on the waves, unsettling her stomach again. She tried to suck in air to calm herself, but the motion made something bubble in the back of her throat, and she let out an unladylike burp.

"If you're going to chuck your guts up, aim it over the side of the boat," he said in a low voice. "I don't want to have to clean up after you."

She swallowed. "I'm fine, actually," she said, determined that there would be no 'chucking up' of anything, guts or otherwise. "Don't worry about me."

A second later, land came into view, and her lips popped open, quite of their own accord. "Ooh. I see the dock."

He shot her a sideways look, and a sarcastic, "Congratulations."

The only problem was, that was *all* she saw. Other than the long, rickety dock that looked like it was about to be swallowed by the sea, there was nothing else. Just a line of pine trees, disappearing into a cloud of white mist.

"Uh..." she began, feeling goosebumps popping out underneath her anorak. "There *is* a hotel here, somewhere in the fog, isn't there?"

Another grunt.

This time, she grunted with him.

Well, isn't that just great?

3

CASTLE PANIC

Summer sat in the boat, craning to see anything through the curtain of fog.

Where were the other tourists? The opulent hotel overlooking the ocean? The tour guide, waiting to see to her every whim?

Where was her freaking hot toddy?

Please, please, please don't let this be another mistake.

She'd certainly made enough of those lately. And maybe this was just the latest in a long line. She'd been in a bit of a rush to book something, *anything*, after the disaster that was her wedding. She couldn't escape the thought of it: Brad, springing from the altar as she made her way down it. At first, she'd thought, *How sweet! He loves me so much he doesn't want me to make the trip on my own!*

But then he'd stopped, hung a quick right in the front pew, and dropped to one knee in front of her maid of honour.

Audriandra. Her best friend.

She'd said 'yes.' People had clapped. Some had gone,

"Awww!" and dabbed at their eyes, like it was the most romantic moment ever.

It wasn't. At least, not from where Summer was standing.

Now, the whole thing played on a non-stop loop on the projection screen inside her head.

And not just there, either. The worst thing was that, because it was L.A., there'd been no shortage of social media accounts broadcasting the tragedy to the world. She got to see it from all different angles. Again and again. Within hours, her ugly, twisted crying face, mascara flowing, only half-hidden by the veil, had been transformed into a meme that said, *WAHHHHH! DON'T YOU LOVE ME?* as a caption.

Escaping the country was the only thing she could do to save her sanity.

She winced for the thousandth time at the memory. Yes, her escape had been rather rash. Alone in the bridal suite, still wearing her wedding gown, she'd gone on Travelocity and booked the first flight to Glasgow she could find. Then a hotel, a charming, remote little converted castle on an island she dimly recalled from childhood, where she could effectively close herself off from the world. She'd only emerge to post on her blog about how amazing and happy her life was. How perfectly things had turned out.

And she really hoped she wouldn't have to lie too much about it.

But now, as Mr. Kilt tossed up a line, mooring the boat to the dock, she looked around and wondered if this place was the same Lachart Isle she'd remembered as a kid. Had she gotten the name wrong? Where was the fairground?

This ladder was quite a bit sturdier than the one on the ferry, so after standing and pitching back and forth, she managed to grab it and hoist herself onto the dock as her guide tossed her luggage up to her.

"Careful with that!" she said, noting a scuff in the pink brocade. "It's expensive. Do you know if there's a luggage cart?"

Of course, the man didn't respond. *You might as well stop asking him questions, Summer. He's caveman-grunting his way through life.*

And he seemed to be throwing the bags even harder now.

"You know, if you spoke a little more, instead of making sounds like a wild animal, you might not be so miserable," she said as he threw the last case onto the dock. She sighed. Then she looked along the wooden pier, as far as she could, to where it disappeared into the mist. "Is there a bell somewhere that I need to ring for the bellboy, you think? Or do you...?"

He pulled himself up next to her, and the sheer size of him took her breath away. She'd known he was broad in the boat—the lack of room on the bench had made that abundantly clear—but he was tall, too. Six-four, maybe more.

She swallowed, then flinched as he reached past her and grabbed four of the five remaining suitcases—one under each arm, one in each hand—then he turned and headed off along the pier without a word.

So apparently, he was not only the transportation manager, but the bellboy, as well? The website for this place had failed to mention how downright unfriendly the staff were. No wonder the castle had no reviews.

"So, I guess that means you want me to follow you?" she called after him, and wasn't surprised when only the wind answered back.

The one remaining case was mid-size and had wheels, so it was manageable. She extended the telescoping handle and pulled it behind her.

Well, I guess it's okay if it's just him, she thought. *Because then I'll only have to tip one guy.*

The wheels clattered along the wooden planks as she pulled her case down the long pier. She walked behind him, the gap between them growing because he moved impossibly fast, with long, sure strides.

She didn't bother to ask him to slow down because she knew he wouldn't answer. She saved her breath, and moved as fast as her shorter legs could carry her, trying to remember the conversion rate for the US dollar to pounds sterling, when she suddenly felt something jerk her back.

She looked behind her and realised she'd left the pier and was now on land. And not just any land. Not *nice* land.

It was mud. And her new luggage was getting stuck in it.

Summer yanked. That only dragged the suitcase an inch, before it got stuck again. She turned and called, "Actually! Mr. Man with the Kilt! Uh..."

Her jaw dropped when she realised she was standing at the start of a long set of narrow, earthen stairs carved into the hillside. Once again, the long, winding path disappeared into a cloud of white, like a stairway to heaven.

Mr. Kilt had disappeared into the fog, like vapor.

Grumbling, she yanked her case out of the mud. It was a little better once she reached the first step, but not much. Without the wheels, the case was so heavy it threatened to pull her down with every yank. The steps were dangerously steep, too, and covered in uneven stone and wet grass.

"Oh, well, this is just awesome!" Summer grunted as she made her way up the stairs.

She had to stop every two steps or so, but eventually, with sweat pouring down her forehead, she made it to the top of the steps.

There, she saw it.

The photo in the Travelocity picture. The thing that had made her fall hopelessly in love with the island. Like something from a dream, that fairy-tale castle loomed above her, sad, and stoic, and yet whimsically romantic, all at the same time.

It was a massive, sprawling pink sandstone castle covered in thick moss, with arched doorways and chimneys spread out along its sides. The thing stretched on, long as a football field. Summer gazed up at it, with its many stately battlements of various sizes looming over her, hardly able to believe she was standing before it. It was so... what? She fumbled for the right word. Inspiring. Yes, that was it.

Quite what it was inspiring her to do, she wasn't sure, but it was definitely inspiring her to do something. She couldn't wait to look inside.

Her eyes drifted to the doorway. Still no tourists. Still no bell-hops with gleaming brass carts willing to tote her luggage off to her suite with a smile, a tip of the hat, and a cordial, "How was your flight?" And there probably wouldn't be lemonade, or gluten-free cookies at the reception desk, either.

But it didn't matter. She was here! Gazing up at the castle, she felt for sure like her luck was *finally* turning around.

Then she looked toward the entryway. In front of a massive wooden door that was about twice as tall as she was, she noticed a flash of pink.

Kilt man had dumped her luggage *there*, in a heap in front of the entrance.

Perfect, she thought as she neared it. *If he's gone, then I don't have to tip him at all.*

She climbed the stairs, wondering if the term "luggage cart" was foreign on this side of the Atlantic. As she climbed, she noticed the massive stone planters full of weeds. There were two stone lions, too, on either side of the doors.

Well, one and a half, technically, since one was missing a head.

Leaving her suitcase with the others, she waved up at the door, then stared at it, wondering why it hadn't *swished* open automatically. Maybe there was a button? She looked around for one to push that would open the door, since it looked far too heavy to open the old-fashioned way. Finding none, she grabbed the handle and pulled it, hoping it was lighter than it first appeared.

No, it was *heavier* than it looked, and when it was open about six inches, it jammed. She pulled again, harder. No luck.

She blew a lock of wayward hair out of her face and squeezed through. The odour was what she imagined a grandmother's old coat closet smelled like—musty and old, pine with a hint of mothball.

It was dark, too. She blinked, trying to get used to the lack of light.

Then, she screamed when she saw the eyes, snout, and lethal-looking antlers of a stag staring back at her.

"Whoa! Whoa! Back up, easy! Easy!" she ejected, before concluding that the deer hadn't moved an inch.

Her eyes, which were now adjusting to the gloom, found other deer lurking in the gloom. They were all staring at her, glaring in her direction, as if demanding to know who had dared disturb them.

No, not other deer, she realised. Just their heads, mounted to the walls on wooden plinths.

She shuddered, and turned, taking in more of the gloomy room around her.

There was a fireplace so big she could probably stand in it. Animal skins. Faded, threadbare tapestries, coats of arms, and weapons like battle axes and swords hung on the walls.

This *was* a hotel, wasn't it? Because it wasn't exactly the height of luxury and relaxation. It looked more like the Hunting Lodge from Hell.

She took a deep breath of dust and *Eau de Mothball,* and choked as she let it out. Then she noticed the front desk. It was hard to see, as there were a plethora of stuffed birds, wings stretched in mid-flight to perched on the counter. She approached the desk, noting the mail slots behind it and keys on hooks, and then found what she'd been looking for. A bell, sitting in the centre of a yellowing doily.

She rang it.

Ding.

Nothing.

She tried again—*ding-ding*—more impatiently this time, as she looked up and down the halls. No gift shop. Things were not looking good on the spa-front, either. Heck, at this rate, she'd be lucky to get a room without a shared bathroom. Instinctively, she massaged a knot in her upper back.

Kilt man appeared behind her, seemingly out of nowhere. "You rang?"

Summer jumped ceiling-high and squealed. "What the...?" She collected her breath and scowled at him. "I'm sorry, is your name Igor, or something? I didn't realise I signed up for the Scare You to Death package."

He stared at her, his expression unchanging. He still looked like he wanted to kill someone, and she was the only person within grabbing range.

"Yes, I did ring," she said, her voice tripping over into the snippy realm. "I have a reservation here for seven nights, and I need help with my luggage, obviously, since somebody—naming no names, but we both know who—dumped it all outside. Can you take it to my room?"

He leaned against the doorjamb. "What did your last slave die of?"

She stared, agog. So now Mr. Killer in a Kilt was trying to be funny? "Seriously? You do work here, yes?"

"Aye."

What a lazy jerk.

She thrust her chin up. "I don't think the manager of this establishment would be very happy with your attitude."

The corner of his mouth quirked up in a smile. "Oh, don't you now?"

"No. So, I guess I have no choice but to lodge a complaint." She turned and punched the bell hard, again and again.

He walked around the counter, pulled up a wooden divider, and slipped behind the desk. Then he pried the bell out of her grip and slammed it back down on the desk. "You rang?"

Summer scowled. "I want—"

"Management. I understand that. You're looking at him. I'm in charge, here." His smile broadened. "And I'd appreciate it if you stopped ringing that bell like you're the Hunchback of Notre Dame."

Her scowl deepened. There were a lot of things she wanted to say to the man—a *lot* of things! Unfortunately, she couldn't currently think what any of them were.

"Let's see," he said, paging through what looked like an old recipe holder. "You say you booked a room for seven nights?"

She stared at him, ready to turn on her heel and march away. That was when she remembered the torture it had been to get here. She couldn't just hop on a plane and make her way home. She couldn't even hop back to Glasgow.

"You know what? I'll find another hotel on the island. One that actually has—"

He snorted. "Good luck with that."

She froze and ripped her hood from her head. He wasn't serious. "What, there's nowhere else?"

"Nope. This is your lot."

Summer looked around, nostrils flaring. "But, but... look at it! I mean, does it even have running water?"

"No. But for our VIPs, it's a scenic walk to the cludgie. Just back the way you came and over those hills." He pointed randomly. "Just watch your step so you don't fall off the cliff."

She stared. She had absolutely no idea what a 'cludgie' was, and no desire to find out. Still, from the way he said it, she had her suspicions. He was pulling her leg. He *had* to be pulling her leg.

"Don't listen to him," a small voice said. "He's talking mince."

A little person in a flat cap and tweed jacket jumped out from behind the counter. Though wearing the outfit of an old codger, her size said 'child' of around eight or nine. Enormous teeth stuck out rather adorably, and freckles studded the bridge of her pert little nose.

"Hello, ma'am," the interloper said, tipping a hat in her direction. "Don't pay any attention to this eejit. We do too have indoor plumbing, and it works pretty good, most of the time. Sometimes the loos get backed up, but that happens even at the Four Seasons and the Waldorf Astoria. Not that I've ever been to either, but so I've been told."

Summer smiled, glad to hear it. She caught the man glaring at the diminutive guest. Was she seeing things, or was that slight amusement on his face?

"Thank you," Summer said, nodding graciously. "I appreciate that."

"And this here is the best establishment on the whole of Lachart Isle, I promise you that. The hospitality and service are the best you'll find anywhere."

Summer wanted to believe that. She so badly wanted her stay in the castle to work out. "Well... great!"

"Not that you're exactly spoiled for choice, mind, but still. I'm Lola, the Lady of Lachart Castle," the little girl said with a proud grin. "And this is my da, Hugh MacGregor." She dinged the bell with almost as much enthusiasm as Summer had. "Now, Dad, quit being so crabbit. Do what the nice lady says and take her bags to room twelve. Our best accommodations, for our best guest."

He rolled his eyes, bowed low and with great flourish, then piled the bags in his arms and did exactly as she said.

Summer laughed as she watched him walk away, wondering if all Scottish men looked good in kilts, or just him. She hated herself for noticing, and even more for thinking so, but the fact that he carried it so well wasn't debatable—it was simply a fact of life.

"Well, now I know who to complain to if I want something done."

"That's right. He knows no' to argue with me." Lola climbed underneath the divider and appeared by Summer's side, then said, with all the finesse of a grown woman who'd been in the hospitality business all her life, "Might I take you on a tour of our amenities?"

"I would like that very much," Summer replied, glad to have someone, finally, with a friendly face to talk to. "But I'm a little hungry. I haven't eaten since before my plane took off. Do you have a restaurant on-premises?"

"Do we!? We have the *best* restaurant on the whole island! Again, competition's pretty thin on the ground, but it's great!" She took Summer's hand and smiled. "Come on. Tour first. I'll end it at the dining room where you can get the best meal you've ever had in your life!"

4

LACHART LASS

"All right!" Lola rubbed her hands together and walked confidently toward the large room with the vaulted ceiling and massive fireplace.

As she followed, Summer had to smile. The girl was wearing boy's trousers that seemed a bit too big for her; she had a piece of rope at the waist, to keep them up.

"This here is the common room, where you can stop and relax in front of the fire in the winter, and have yourself a whisky, if you like that sort of thing." She ran her hand over the small credenza, where there were several old, crystal decanters of various amber liquids. Then she lifted an aluminium jug. "Would you like some water? You must be thirsty?"

Summer shook her head as she gazed up at the massive wooden chandelier, noticing the thick cobwebs draped over it. "No, I'm fine."

"All right, continuing on our tour," the girl said in a theatrical voice that echoed in the cavernous room. "Through those doors is the ballroom. In Lachart's heyday, they had quite the parties there. So they tell me, anyway. Before I was born, which is a shame. I'd love to have seen it. It's closed off now, because we have to close up the rooms we don't use. Which is pretty much most of this place. Keeps the heat in. But it's so grand and lovely! Sometimes I can't help it, I have to sneak in. Anyhow, I'll take you down this way, to the courtyard."

"How many rooms does this castle have?" she asked.

"Oh. Thousands," the girl said, entirely serious. "Even I haven't found them all, and I've been here my whole entire life."

"All forty years?"

She giggled. "I'm actually only eight. But that's a common misconception. Everyone says I'm wiser than my years, and much more precocious."

"Imagine that."

Lola lowered her voice to a whisper, like she was sharing a secret. "Between you and me, I don't even know what precocious means. But I like it. It's a great word. It sounds important, and I find it fun to say. *Precocious.*" She elongated every syllable in a musical way.

"It is, definitely."

"But as for this castle, there are all kind of hidden doors, secret passages..." She gasped and looked back at Summer. "Oh! You know, one weekend, I found a passage behind a bookcase and took it all the way out, for what seemed like miles. And do you know where I ended up?"

Summer shook her head.

"A cave! It took me right to the beach! I kept walking and walking and suddenly I was splashing and splashing and then I was underwater! I had to swim out of it."

"You did?"

She nodded. "I'm a good swimmer. You have to be, living on an island. I'm good at lots of things. Except maths." She wrinkled her nose. "I *hate* maths. Dad insists I spend every day working on my multiplication. It's *so boring!*"

"I agree," Summer said with a laugh. She couldn't actually imagine that big, kilted guy as a father. He'd seemed so rough around the edges. But then, she'd seen a touch of him softening up when Lola had ordered him around. It was surprising, and she had to admit, a little endearing. "You live here with your dad, all alone on this island?"

"Not *all* alone," she said matter-of-factly. "There are other people here, about fifty or so people live in the village on the other side of the island. Not many, but they're all the friendly sort. They're all like family to us. You should go in while you're here."

"Maybe I will, is it far?"

"Have you seen the size of the place? Nothing's far. There's nothing on this island you can't walk to. Which is a good thing for me because I don't think I'm ever going to learn how to drive a car."

"Why not?"

"Because there aren't any. On the island, I mean! No real ones, anyway. People use quad bikes and things to get around. But that's all. We don't even have a traffic light. I've only seen them in movies." She smiled, picturing one in her head. "They look pretty."

"But surely you'll need to know how to drive for when you get off the island..."

Lola wrinkled her nose, as if the thought had never occurred to her. "I suppose so, aye."

She guided Summer outside, to a damp, closed-in square with a few empty tables that glistened with raindrops, and damp-cushioned wicker chairs. There were a few lawn games set out, but the place was empty. "Er," Summer said, looking around, "are there any other guests here?"

"At the moment?" Lola smiled. "No. You're the only one."

"Oh, but you *do* get guests, right?"

She nodded. "Oh, of course. We had an elderly couple here just last autumn. Although, I think they got themselves lost on the way to Rum."

Summer spun around the rectangular courtyard of the massive castle, with all the windows peering back at her. They stretched off into the distance, hundreds of them, disappearing into the mist. If each one belonged to a room, then... "Then, it's just you? For all this?"

"It is quite a lot, isn't it?" she said, looking around with a mysterious smile Summer couldn't comprehend. "Come this way."

The French doors they went through to another long hall got stuck, too. As skinny as she was, Lola had no trouble nudging it open. "All the doors and windows stick in this place when the weather's like this. And the roof's got more holes in it than a fishing net. Not to worry, room twelve is dry. Mostly. That's why I put you there. It's our only bedroom that doesn't smell like something died when it rains. Most people think it rains here all the time, but it doesn't. We have lots of sunny days."

As she chattered on, Summer listened intently. Normally, she was the one doing the talking, but here she could barely get a word in edgeways. She didn't mind. Here was a girl who talked almost as much as she did. By the time they'd made it past more than a few rooms with closed doors, Summer had learned quite a bit about the place.

"Most of these doors are closed, you see, because the rooms through there are an absolute wreck! We don't have the money to fix it, Dad says. You're welcome to explore, but if a door is closed, you might want to leave it that way and stay out so you don't get hurt. And the East Wing is completely off-limits."

"The East Wing?" What was this, *Beauty and the Beast?* With the way Lola's father had grunted at her, she didn't put it past him. But she was far from fairy tale material. Fairy tales only happened to people like Audriandra.

Not thinking about that, Summer.

"Some of the floors there have collapsed. It's not safe." She shrugged. "Or so Dad says. He's always telling me to watch this, watch that. He's very careful."

"He's your dad. I'm sure he just worries about you."

"He's only really happy when he's grumpy," she explained. "He only has one mood. Bad."

So, she'd noticed. "That's sad."

"No, it's a pain in the bahookie, is what it is. How hard is it to just decide to be in a good mood? Am I right? I know, it's easy for me to say, I'm just a kid with no real responsibilities. But things aren't *that* bad. Look at me. I don't go to a proper school, because there isn't one on the island. I've got no friends my own age. But it's a nice place, this. Don't you think? I think so, I wouldn't want to grow up anywhere else."

When Lola stopped for a breath outside the double doors to a library, Summer was finally able to wedge a question in. "It's a little spooky here, isn't it? For a young girl like you?"

"Oh, no. I'm not scared," she said bravely, pushing open a door.

The library was one of the brighter rooms. It had a two-story-high ceiling, with several windows across from the door. Every available wall was covered with books. There were balconies and sliding ladders, and of course, another giant fireplace. Summer went in and pulled an old copy of *Macbeth* from the shelf, then choked on the dust that puffed out as she did.

"Careful," Lola said with a grin. "Pull out the wrong book and the wall will spin around on you, just like in the movies! And we might never get you back."

Summer laughed, though she couldn't quite tell if the girl was joking. There was a playful mischievousness to her tone.

"But feel free to take any book you like, to read while you're here, if you're looking for something to pass the time." She giggled. "That's one thing we have oodles of, here—time."

"That's good. I was so busy in L.A., it'll be nice to slow down."

The girl's jaw dropped so wide that Summer could see her molars. "You're from L.A.?"

Summer smiled. "Yes."

"Oh, my gosh. Do you know Robert Redford?"

Summer frowned. "What is it with you people and Robert Redford?" she muttered, then she shook her head. "Truthfully, no. I don't know any big stars. People always think that, though."

"Well, the castle will probably be boring for you, considering you're so glamorous."

"I'm not that glamorous," Summer said, thinking of some of the people she'd left back home.

Her wedding? Now that had been glamorous. The sparkle and dresses and fanfare had been like a red-carpet *Oscars* event. Summer had done everything possible to tone it down, so the whole thing didn't become a complete circus. But her circle of friends? Just by being there, they automatically made it that way.

"I want to go to Hollywood one day and see all the famous movie stars," Lola said, a little wistfully. "You sure you don't know *anyone* famous at all?"

"Some of the people I know are social-media famous. Does that count? They're not in movies, but—"

"Oh, you mean, like on Instagram?" She wrinkled her nose.

"I've seen about that on television. But I don't have a phone. My dad won't—well, you know."

They stepped out into the hallway. Lola took a step, but stopped suddenly, as if she'd forgotten something.

"I don't really have a reason to be creeped out. I'm not afraid of the ghosts in here," she announced, rather loudly.

"Ghosts?"

Lola nodded. "Of course. You do believe in ghosts, don't you?" The girl was entirely serious, her voice now lowered to a soft, tinkling whisper.

Summer shook her head, but decided to humour the girl. "Well, I've never seen one. Have you?"

"Oh, aye. Loads of them. All the time." She froze, and then leaned into Summer's ear and whispered, "Especially in this hallway."

Summer looked around the darkened hallway. The stone walls were covered with Gothic iron sconces, draped in cobwebs, and the lights above flickered. She realised her breath was coming out in white clouds. It had been cold before, but now, it seemed positively frigid. *What the heck is going on?*

There came a soft creaking sound, the shifting of floorboards up ahead. Summer squinted, trying to get a better look. The sound grew louder, and was joined by another one. A low, unearthly moan.

Without warning, the walls around them started to clank loudly, as if someone was striking a cymbal, again and again. Summer looked up to the ceiling, trying to gauge where it was coming from. But it seemed to be coming from everywhere, from deep within the bones of the castle.

Then a figure in a long, flowing white robe glided around the corner and stood at the end of the hallway, watching them.

5

GHOST HOST

Summer stifled her gasp and instinctively took a step in front of Lola, fanning her arms out. She'd never before had a reason to believe she had a maternal instinct, but was nice to know that, at thirty, it was finally kicking in.

Okay, so ghosts really *did* exist. That was interesting.

Although, not nearly as frightening as she'd thought.

The apparition just stood there, shifting from foot to foot as if standing in front of a vending machine, wondering what candy bar to get. The moan grew louder, but now it sounded less menacing and more like it'd stubbed its toe.

"Oh, it's the horrifyingly evil ghost of the castle!" Lola wailed in fright behind her. "Make it go! Make it go away!"

Summer raised a finger, trying to decide how to make that happen. She'd never been faced with this predicament before. She turned to the swaying ghost, then spread her arms out wide and shouted, "BEGONE!"

The apparition jumped in fright. It headed off in one direction, bumped the wall, then turned and headed the other way.

Wait. It bumped the wall? Weren't spirits supposed to be able to pass through those suckers?

Now that she'd gotten a better look at it, it didn't seem all that wispy either. Rather solid. Amidst Lola's giggles, Summer finally noticed a few other things—this apparition had buckskin shoes and a walking cane.

"Dad, cut it out, you daft auld bugger," a male voice grumbled behind her, and Summer jumped once again.

Kilt man stood there, hands on hips, rolling his eyes. For a big guy, he was very quiet on his feet. He reached forward, grabbed the fabric of the white robe, and yanked.

The ghostly figure swatted his hand away, took off running, and disappeared behind a corner, robe billowing out behind it.

Hugh shook his head. "Lola, quit filling this daft lassie's head full of nonsense."

Summer blinked. "Daft lassie?"

"There are no ghosts in Lachart Castle. Evil or otherwise," Hugh said. "Because there's no such thing."

Lola stuck out her tongue at him. "I bet there are some."

Summer gazed down the hallway, attempting to get her bearings. The temperature dropping like that? The odd clanking sounds? After all that, she had a hard time believing the place wasn't haunted.

"What about, um…" she pointed in the direction the robed figure had gone. "…him?"

Lola grinned. "That's Duncan MacGregor. My grandfather, and the Laird of Lachart Castle." She giggled after him and called, "Grandpa! Come say hello."

They waited a moment, but he didn't reappear.

She shrugged. "Oh, well. That was Grandpa. He's a wee bit deaf."

"And a wee bit mental," Hugh muttered.

"You'll meet him later," Lola concluded.

Still astonished by the whole thing, Summer shook her head in wonder. "Oh. Wow. That was quite a production. I don't know how you did that. All those clanking noises, and the air suddenly getting so cold that I could see my breath? Well done. I'm impressed"

"That was no production," Hugh said in a low voice. "My father probably just woke from his nap. He gets a bit bewildered when he wakes up. Starts to wander."

Lola smiled sheepishly. "And the clanking was the castle's heating system. Grandpa invented it!"

"He invented a whole heating system?" Summer said. "That's impressive."

"Clearly, you haven't seen it in action," Hugh scoffed. "It's unique, antique, and mostly broken. A bit like himself, in fact."

Lola punched his arm. "Grandpa says it's worked for us for years and years, through decades of life here at the castle. You can't ask for more than that."

"Oh aye, it works so well, we can see our breath half the time."

Summer looked up and realised his blue eyes were on her. It made her feel a little self-conscious. She hadn't noticed before, with all the grunting and posturing, but his face wasn't too terrible a thing to look at. He wasn't her type, obviously. Nothing like Brad, who was so polished and Hollywood-like that he practically glowed in the dark. Hugh MacGregor was gruff and rough around the edges. But his stare was enough to make her bite her lip and tuck a lock of hair behind her ear.

"Right, get a shifty on. Dinner's about ready," he said.

Lola cleared her throat and shot him a very deliberate look.

"Oh, for..." he muttered, then he bowed, stepped aside, and

gestured along the hallway. "Ms. Rose, if you'd care to step this way, dinner is being served in our dining hall."

He shot his daughter a sideways look, and she gave him a thumbs-up of approval.

Summer opened her mouth to reply to him, but her stomach spoke for her, gurgling obnoxiously.

She clamped a hand over it in alarm, embarrassment heating her face.

Lola giggled. "I hear a hungry beast that must be tamed," she declared, pointing down the hall. "We won't make you wait any longer."

"Thank you," Summer said, blushing as she set off along the hallway, and Hugh fell into step beside her.

At first, they walked as a threesome, with Summer and Hugh at the front, Lola slightly behind. But from his brisk pace, Hugh soon took the lead, and wound up several paces ahead of her, just like he'd been on the walk from the boat. The hallway turned this way and that, and before long, she'd lost him entirely.

She slowed a little, frowning. Then she hugged herself, rubbing the chill in her arms. *He's more than grumpy. He's a big, fat jerk. What did I ever do to make him hate me?*

Lola hooked an arm through hers. "Don't worry. My Dad isn't very friendly, but the rest of us are. Even the ghosts. We'll make sure you arrive safe and sound."

"I appreciate that."

The walk was a bit of a marathon. Summer hadn't remembered walking this far away from the front doors, but then again, she'd had a very entertaining guide. When they arrived at the front lobby, they kept walking directly past the reception desk to another hallway. There, at the end of it, stood Hugh MacGregor, hands on hips, tapping his foot impatiently.

"Where've you been? What kept you?" he asked as they approached.

"I hadn't realised this was a race," Summer muttered back. "I got lost."

"You did?" He seemed surprised.

"Well, yeah," she said, eyeing him. What did he expect? "That sometimes happens when you visit a giant castle with a thousand rooms that you've never been to before. But don't worry, your daughter showed me the way."

He stared at her for what felt like a beat too long, like he wanted to say something, but in the end, he didn't bother. Instead, he pushed open the double wooden doors and stood back so she could enter.

"About time she made herself useful," Hugh said, and there was that suggestion of a smirk again when he caught Lola's eye. "Anyway, I'm sure it's no' as fancy as the sort of thing you're used to, but welcome to our dining hall."

6

HAGGIS HAGGLING

Summer blinked in wonder as she stepped into the enormous dining room. The walls were the same pink sandstone as the outside and covered in ancient Celtic tapestries, the rafters so high that they disappeared in cobweb-covered shadows. There was another impressive, giant stone fireplace, but this one had a roaring fire in it, setting the room in a cheerful glow.

But the most impressive thing in the room, by quite some margin, was the enormous dining table.

She'd expected a dining room like any restaurant, with plenty of tables and chairs scattered about. What she hadn't been prepared for was a single, dark oak-slab table, stretching from one end of the giant hall to the other.

There were throne-like wooden chairs with high backs set around it, enough for forty guests. There were large, ruby-coloured goblets and pewter plates at each setting. It looked like something out of a royal banquet. She half-expected a court jester to come in, juggling, or joking around, or generally just making a nuisance of himself

"Wow," Summer said, taking it all in. "This is..."

"A wee bit over the top?" Lola asked with a laugh.

"No! It's beautiful," Summer said honestly, already feeling cosier and more at home. Funny how a warm fire could do that.

Hugh seemed a little confused by her reaction, then gave his daughter a nod. "Lo. Why don't you..." He walked his fingers off to indicate that she should scram.

"Oh, right!" She gave Summer a little wave, then she took off, her little soles making a racket on the stone floor, even long after she'd disappeared.

"It's very nice," Summer said cheerfully, taking a step further into the room. "Where should I...?"

"Anywhere you like. But the kitchen's over there," Hugh said, pointing to a door. "So if you want to..."

"I get it." *If I want to make it easier for the staff, I should sit closer to it.* She went to the chair at the very end of the table, closest to the kitchen door.

"Are you sure you want to—"

"What? I thought you said—"

"Aye, no, that's grand." He shook his head. "I just thought you'd sit somewhere more, you know, awkward."

"Why would you think that?" Summer asked, but his only reply was a shrug of his shoulders, and another of his trademark grunts.

Hugh dragged the heavy chair out so she could sit, with what seemed like some reluctance. Then again, Summer felt like he did everything reluctantly, where she was concerned. When she sat, he pushed the chair in so abruptly that her backside hit the hard seat before she was ready.

"Oh, uh, thanks."

She waited for him to sit, but he didn't.

"Aren't you going to eat, too?"

Hugh shook his head. "Staff doesn't eat here."

"Why not?" She gazed over the never-ending line of chairs. "It's not like you don't have enough—"

"Because we don't. We don't mingle with the guests."

OK, that was odd. So, did that mean she'd be condemned to wander this Scottish isle alone the entire time she was here?

She'd come here to discover herself, of course, but she felt a little pang of disappointment at the thought she'd be discovering herself *all by herself*.

"Uh... but you don't have any other guests here," she pointed out.

He stared her down, his hard expression not softening in the least. "Aye, well, someone has to serve you the food."

She blinked. "So, bellboy, concierge, waiter... You're a true Renaissance man, aren't you?"

It was as if she hadn't even asked the question. He muttered, "What'll you have?"

Have? I'll have a host that doesn't treat me like he absolutely hates my guts. Then she looked down at the plate and realised he meant food.

"Don't you have a menu?"

"No."

"Then how do I know—"

"We serve the regular Scottish foods."

"That doesn't help. I don't know many Scottish foods. Except haggis. Do you have haggis?"

He nodded. "Is that what you want?"

"Yes." She took the napkin from the plate and spread it over her lap. "Is it vegetarian?"

Hugh looked back at her, eyes narrowed. "In what sense?"

"In the sense that it doesn't have meat in it," Summer said, wondering what other possible sense there was.

Hugh puffed out his cheeks. "Well, I don't know if you'd call it 'meat,' exactly."

Summer hesitated, not quite sure how to respond to that. "Is it made out of animals?"

"Bits of animals," Hugh told her. "The more purple, knobbly sort of bits generally found on the inside. Those are then rammed into a sheep's stomach and cooked."

She swallowed, trying not to dwell too much on the description.

"But I looked it up before I came here," she said. "There's a vegetarian option, made of oats and—"

"We don't have that. We only have real haggis. For real people."

She stared at him. That sounded like a thinly veiled insult. "Fine. Can you ask the chef what he recommends for a vegetarian?"

"I am the chef."

"Oh, of course you are," she said. "Then what would you recommend?"

"Meat."

She sighed, her fingers tightening around the napkin on her lap. "That's not very helpful."

He shrugged. "Well, I don't know what you like, do I? Besides *not meat*, I mean."

"OK, well, maybe you can tell me what *you*'ll be having?"

"Whatever you don't. It all needs to be used up. Some of it's on the turn."

This was getting exasperating. Finally, she said, "Do you even *have* a vegetarian option?"

He stroked the salt-and-pepper stubble on his chin. "Well, not officially. But I can scrape the tatties off the Shepherd's Pie if you'd like."

She grimaced. "I don't know if I want to know what a *tattie* is. Sounds dirty."

"Ah, of course, I'm sorry. I meant the Po. Tay. Toe."

Her grimace deepened. "You expect me to eat some mashed potatoes that have been marinating in god-knows-what animal grease? That's not an option."

"Aye, it is."

"Trust me, it isn't."

He shook his head slowly. "This is Scotland. Not someplace where people eat sprouts and twigs all day like a bunch of cattle waiting to be led to the slaughter."

Her mouth opened. OK, the last one *had* been thinly veiled. This one wasn't veiled at all. "Am I a cow in this scenario?"

He grunted and gave her a look that said, *If the shoe fits...*

She threw her napkin down on the plate and tried to push the chair away from the table. It was even heavier than it looked, though, and kept her caged.

"Where are you going?" he asked, then he corrected himself. "Where are you *trying* to go?"

She pushed and flailed like a fish on the deck of a ship, groaning a little. Shoving with all her might, she inched the chair back far enough for her to extricate herself from its clutches. Straightening, she met his eye and stuck out her chin. "I guess, since there's no food here for me to eat, I'm going back. Home. I can't just starve here."

His eyes narrowed. "Fine by me. But you're going to have to swim, since the ferry only runs once a day."

She wavered on her feet. She'd forgotten that she was on an island. That was the nice thing about L.A., when things went wrong—and with her luck, they often did—she could just walk out. Now, she was a captive.

She sat down in a huff. "Fine. You have anything I can eat? Sourdough?"

"What's that when it's at home?"

"Bread. Sourdough bread."

"Oh. No."

"No sourdough?"

"No bread," Hugh said.

"No bread? How can you have...?" She sighed. Now she had the distinct feeling he was just messing with her. "How about oyster crackers? You have those?"

"Again, I don't know what that is, so I'm pretty sure we don't have them." His tone was only slightly snarky.

"What about salad?" When he stared at her like he'd never heard the word, she said, "Fruit?"

He crossed his arms and stared blankly at her.

No doubt about it, now. He was *definitely* messing with her.

Before, she'd just been exasperated, but now, she was well on her way to flaring like a hot volcano. *Zen, Summer. Do what Mom would do. Channel your inner peace. Find your Zen.* The next time she spoke, she was calmer.

"If I took that cruddy old dinghy of yours," she mused with a sly smile, "would you be stuck on the island without a way of getting off?"

Not that she would. On a rowboat, in the middle of the sea, miles from the coast of Scotland? Sounded like a fate worse than death. Actually, it probably would lead to death. But that wasn't her intent. She'd hoped that it would get some kind of rise out of him, or at least he'd reconsider and offer her something vegetarian to eat, if only to avoid having her certain doom on his hands.

But he simply shrugged. "Do what you will. But if I were you, I'd bring a torch. It's dark out on the sea at night."

She picked up her phone. "I don't need a torch," she said, shining the flashlight in his eyes. "Unlike some people, I live in the twenty-first century and have this."

He simply held up a hand, blocking the beam of light from his eyes. "Are you quite finished?"

She tutted, then sunk back into the chair and sulked like a child. "Just so you know, I'm not going to give this place a very good review on Travelocity."

"Aye, well," he said, forcibly pushing the chair back under the table and trapping her again. "No surprise there."

Her eyes snapped to his. "What does that mean?"

"It means you've done nothing but whinge and moan since I've met you."

Her jaw dropped. She scooted to the edge of her chair. "I'm sorry. Should I have thanked you for drowning my cosmetics in the ocean? Or for elbowing me in the boobs so much that I'm pretty sure I have a bruise? Or for making me sit with my feet in two inches of seawater? And that was even before we got to *this* place, which, by the way, looks nothing like what's online."

He folded his arms over his chest. "Maybe if you just took the stick out of your arse, you'd—"

"Dad!" a voice called from the doorway leading to the kitchen.

He stopped at once, and they both turned to look at Lola, who was wearing a chef's hat and apron, her hands stuffed to the elbow in oven mitts. Her eyes were wide.

"She's our guest. You don't shout at our guests," she admonished him as if *he* was the child. "What is wrong with you?"

He pointed to the kitchen. "Lo, you need to—"

"No, *you* need to. You're acting like a proper headcase. Away you go outside and count to a hundred. I'll take her order."

He opened his mouth to speak, but then let out a grunt,

shook his head, and stalked off, slamming the doors behind him.

Lola turned to Summer, smiling.

"I thought *he* was the chef?" Summer said, unable to keep the bitterness out of her voice.

"Oh, he thinks he's a lot of things around here. I'm the real brains of the operation. Now, what can I get you?" She leaned in close. "I hear him talking about the Shepherd's Pie. I wouldn't go near it. I think it's taken a turn for the worse."

Summer gritted her teeth. Leave it to Hugh to try to pawn it off on her. Did he really hate her that much that he wanted her up all night with food poisoning? Or worse?

"Actually, I was just trying to explain to your father that I don't eat meat. I'm a vegetarian. Do you have anything vegetarian in the kitchen?"

The girl's eyes widened. "What, really?! I've never met a vegetarian before!" Lola looked her up and down. "An *actual* vegetarian?"

Summer realised that she might as well have said she was an alien from Mars. "Yes. So, I guess that means you don't have anything on the menu I can eat?"

"No, but..." The little girl's nose scrunched so that all the little freckles joined hands. Her eyes lit up. "I have an idea!"

She zoomed off to the kitchen and returned five minutes later with a silver tray that was almost bigger than she was. "Fancy some cereal?"

Summer sprang up. "Oh, let me help you with that!" she began, before she realised she was still caged in by the chair. By the time she groaned and pushed her way out, Lola was standing next to her.

Lola handed the tray over and motioned toward the giant

stone fireplace. "I hate this stuffy old table. Let's eat in front of the fire!"

Summer carried the tray over to the plush animal-skin rug in front of the fireplace. She wasn't sure what kind of animal it was. Though she didn't really like the idea of sitting her butt on a dead creature's skin, as she knelt there, an odd sense of déjà vu settled over her. She felt so comfortable and cosy that she fully settled in. Lola poured her a bowl of cereal with milk and handed it over.

"*Coco Pops*," she said proudly. "I eat them every morning. They're magic!"

Summer laughed. "I thought all you ate over here was porridge."

Lola stuck out her tongue and waggled it, her face screwing up. "Oh, no, I don't like porridge. But if you want it, we probably have some."

"No." Summer dug her spoon in and took a bite. Because she was so hungry, it was the best bowl of cereal she'd ever had. "You're right, this is magic. What kind of milk is this?"

"Horse," a voice boomed behind them.

Without warning, she spewed the entire mouthful into the fire. Sputtering, she swallowed, trying to erase the image from her head. "Horse?!" she wheezed.

"Dad!" Lola cried, patting Summer's back and shaking her head. "What are you trying to do, kill her? Stop being such a numpty."

"Wait, so it isn't horse milk then?" Summer asked, eyes watering.

Hugh tapped his chin. "You're slittering cereal down your jumper."

She wiped the dribble of milk that had slipped down her chin. "I'm what?"

When he came near, Lola smacked at his pants leg. "It's not horse milk. It's regular cow's milk."

Summer let out a breath of relief.

"I mean, I'd prefer a non-dairy alternative, but I'll take cow over horse."

Hugh came over, pulled out a chair from the dining table, and sat there, facing the fire. "Of course it's not bloody horse! What do you take us for?"

Lola shot her father a scathing look. "Don't listen to anything this eejit says. He likes pecking at people. Like a silly rooster." She dunked some Coco Pops with her spoon and said, "You do use cow's milk in America, right?"

"Yes, of course. But I like soy milk. Or almond milk. Sometimes I use coconut milk to—"

"That's braw!"

Summer froze with the spoon half-suspended between the bowl and her mouth. "It's what?"

"America's amazing! I've seen it on TV. You don't have just one choice of anything. You have a million. Everything there's just bigger and better. And so glamorous!"

A fleeting thought of Audriandra invaded Summer's mind. Audriandra was glamorous, even when they'd met in first grade. While the rest of the kids in the classroom were just having trouble opening their milk cartons during lunch, Audriandra was practicing her modelling poses, that vacant, pouty-lipped expression on her face.

"It can be pretty glamorous," Summer admitted. "You've really never been?"

"Ha!" Lola glanced over at her father, who was sitting there quietly, fingers laced together on his lap, staring deeply into the flames. "I've never been anywhere. Not even to the mainland."

"You've never been...?" Summer blinked, shocked. "But it's only like, two miles to—"

"I know."

"Don't you want to go explore the rest of the world?"

"Of course." She shrugged and looked carefully at her father, until Summer got the feeling that this had been a topic of discussion before. She said, softly, "But Dad says I'm better off, here."

Summer looked over at Lola's father, wondering what he was afraid of. She hadn't known the girl long, but she already could tell that her personality was bigger than the castle. Bigger, even, than the whole island.

"And why is—?"

"Because I said so," Hugh barked, in a voice that said, *conversation over.*

He didn't look at either of them. He simply reached over and pulled the tray toward him, piling the empty bowls onto it.

"Dinner's over," he said, lifting the tray and standing. "Lo, say good night. It's time you were in bed."

Lola's lips pressed together into a pout, but she did as she was told.

"Good night, Summer, Good night, Dad," she said. She gave Summer a reluctant look that said she had so much more she wanted to ask about the outside world.

The world her father wouldn't let her see.

A flame of indignation sparked inside Summer as she watched the girl leave, but she squelched it out again. She didn't know them. This wasn't her family. She had no business butting in. She stood up and wrapped her arms around herself, anticipating the chill when she stepped away from the fire.

"Well, thank you for a delightful dinner," she said to him, not attempting to disguise her sarcasm. "Seriously, five stars."

Either he didn't sense her sarcasm, or didn't care, because he gave no reaction. He set the tray down on the table. "Follow me. I'll take you to your bed."

"After one date?"

She cringed at the joke, which had slipped out of her mouth all on its own. Any other guy she knew would've chuckled, just to humour her. Once upon a time, before Audriandra, Brad would've gazed at her adoringly, like she had said the wittiest thing in the world.

Hugh, though? He frowned, and awkwardness hung between them like a living, breathing thing.

"I'm kidding!"

She laughed too loudly, and as she went to take a breath, she burped so loudly that it echoed around the dining hall.

His gaze went to her, more surprised than disgusted. That was something, at least.

Still, she cringed and patted her chest.

"Whoops. Excuse me! Must've been the dairy. Went straight to my head." When he still didn't react, she said, "Don't worry, I'm not going to... How did you describe it? *Chuck my guts up?*"

He simply nodded as if that was a relief, and took a step toward the door.

Wow, she was really knocking 'em dead tonight. *Quit while you're behind, Summer, and you might be able to survive this night with at least some of your dignity intact.*

She clapped her hands together and smiled, trying to pretend none of the last few seconds had happened.

"Alrighty, then," she declared. "Lead the way!"

7

ROOM WITH A HUGH

Just as she'd feared, the moment Summer left the light of the fire, the ice seeped back into her bones. She could see her breath again. It might've been a great accomplishment for the Laird of the house to come up with that heating contraption, but it would've been a lot more impressive had it actually *worked*.

She stepped carefully across the vast dining room to where Hugh waited impatiently for her, trying not to trip into him on the way. Now that night had fallen, the place was even creepier than before, and her thoughts turned to what her bedroom might be like.

Would there be deer heads, cobweb-covered chandeliers, and creepy paintings with eyes that followed her around the room?

Would it be as frigid as the rest of the house?

Hugging herself, she opened her mouth to ask him if her room had central heating, but then closed it again. He'd said all she did was complain, and as much as she wished she didn't care what he thought, she did. She didn't want to come across as that annoying American tourist. She wanted to be the smooth, glamorous L.A. socialite, like Audriandra, though she suspected she'd already smashed that image to bits before she'd even left the ferry.

She'd done other things, too.

Like burp in his face.

Oh, God. I really did that.

She tried to shake the memory out of her head, but it was already wedged tightly in there. Great. Something else she'd probably relive again and again for the rest of her life.

She had built up quite a library of those cringe moments over the years. She'd never been exactly smooth around men, especially good-looking ones. She'd first introduced herself to Brad by tripping over his feet while on the way to the ladies' room in a crowded bar.

She half-expected Hugh to grab a candelabra and escort her, limping and hunch-backed, up the stairs. But, standing there with his kilt and his whisky-barrel chest, Hugh MacGregor looked nothing like a castle troll.

And that was a problem.

If he had been one, she likely would've dismissed his attitude and pushed him out of her mind. But no, instead, as he walked, she couldn't help taking in his strong, muscular legs. His broad shoulders. The way he glided over each step as if he knew the place by heart. She found herself wondering just who Hugh MacGregor was, and whether he'd always been such an insufferable jerk.

No, it was no use, she realised. She was a goner. It didn't matter how much of a jerk he was to her, she'd probably continue to fumble like an idiot around him for the rest of her stay.

To her relief, they didn't have to rely on an old candelabra, either. There was electric lighting on the stairway, albeit in the form of just a single overhead bulb.

Shadows lingered everywhere, and she shivered again as she grabbed the railing, trying not to trip on the narrow, unfamiliar steps.

He paused at a plain, non-descript door. "This is you."

She looked up and down the hallway. There were dozens of doors on each side of the corridor that looked exactly the same, and none of them numbered. If she left this room to use the bathroom, she'd never find it again. "Uh, OK. Thanks."

He seemed to hesitate there, almost as if embarrassed. Maybe it was because he thought she was a spoiled brat and he was bracing himself for her complaints. She decided to hold her tongue.

Well, she'd hold her tongue *for a little while*, at least. Wait until they were inside, give a compliment or two, and *then* she'd lodge her complaints. Ask for air freshener. Demand that the creepy paintings and animal heads be banished from the room, maybe even ask for all her money back and demand he send for a helicopter to take her home.

Hugh pushed the door open, standing aside to let her pass.

The first thing she felt was a wall of comfortable heat. It hugged her, making her sigh with contentment. Then she saw the warm glow of the fire. The fire he must've spent time, building for her while he was away from the dining hall.

She stepped in, sniffing the wood of the crackling fire, and looked around. No creepy animals were staring back at her. There was a large, four-poster bed in the room, made up with a fluffy tartan blanket and matching pillows. Tasteful curtains and furniture. A little sitting area with a table and a pile of books. A corner vanity. And, ensconced in a bay window, an enormous free-standing metal bathtub.

She wasn't generally one to be speechless, but this time, she came pretty close.

"Oh!"

"Toilet's through there. Towels and what have you, are in there, too."

She followed his pointed finger to a door. A private bathroom.

"Breakfast starts at seven. If you need to find the dining hall, just keep making lefts at the end of the hall and you'll get there." He made a weighing motion with his head. "Eventually. If not, just shout, and I'll come find you."

Summer felt herself become excited by that thought, but quickly pulled herself together.

Hugh motioned to the bed. "There's a bell pull, if you need anything."

Summer glanced around the room, and noticed all her luggage was neatly stacked on a rack near the fire. "Uh, a bell pull?" she asked.

Her host strode to the bed and turned a tiny lever built into one of the posts at the pillow end. "Rings down to the servant's quarters. One of us is always there."

"Oh. Thank you," she said. "Cool." She clicked her fingers, dancing from foot to foot on the spot. "Cool, cool, cool."

Her eyes were drawn to the large, floor-to-ceiling window. She thought it looked out over the courtyard, but she wasn't sure. All she could see right now was the sky. True to what Lola had said, it didn't rain there all the time—the sky was clear, and while the sun had dipped below the horizon, it painted orange and purple fingers across the heavens, which the sea reflected like a mirror.

It was so breathtakingly pretty, the first thing she thought was how she'd like to snap a photograph.

The second thing she thought was that she had plenty of photographs of sunsets. Hundreds of them. And yet, she had very few memories of anything amazing that she'd ever actually done under one.

After a moment, she realised how quiet it was, and she turned around.

Her eyes went to Hugh, because his eyes were on her. Waiting.

He probably didn't care what her complaints were, but she honestly didn't have a single one.

No, he had to have been waiting for something else.

Oh, right. A tip.

She rummaged through her bag. "This is lovely. Thank you," she said, handing him the one crumpled note she'd gotten at the airport.

He didn't make a move to take it. She stood there, holding it out for a little while. Then jiggled it a bit, like she was trying to entice a dog.

Still, he made no move.

Finally, he said, "I don't want that." He moved for the door, putting his hand on the knob, then hesitated in the doorway. "You best get to bed. You've got an early start tomorrow."

She rolled her eyes, put her hands on her hips, and fixed him with a stare. "I'm not swimming back, if that's what you mean."

"No." He hesitated, looking down. "What I meant is that you're booked in for activities. The full package."

"The full..." She winced. "I did? When did I do that?"

He shrugged. "When you made the reservation."

"And what does that include?" she ventured, almost afraid to ask.

"Accommodation, food, and activities."

She played the list over in her head. The food hadn't been much to write home about, but the accommodation—this room, anyway—was decent. "Activities like... a spa?"

He shook his head slowly. "No. Not a spa."

Well, that was a big downer. Or maybe not. Considering Hugh was just about everything around here, she wasn't sure she'd be able to survive the awkwardness if he were her masseuse, too. But...

"Activities? What activities?"

"You'll find out tomorrow. But again—and I really can't stress this enough—you'll want to get plenty of rest."

Thousands of questions swarmed her brain, but he closed the door before she could ask even one of them. The truth was, she wasn't much of an 'activities' kind of person. She'd never played a sport, even for fun. She had been cursed with two left feet.

Where Brad had insisted on booking himself snorkelling sessions, zip-lining, and water-skiing for their honeymoon, Summer had booked herself into the spa. Not because she loved pampering herself, but because she thought it'd be safer that way. For her, and for everyone around her.

So, she really hoped those activities were gentle, and laid back. Croquet on the lawn. Seashell-collecting. Needlepoint lessons. A nice, leisurely golf-cart ride around the island, maybe.

But he'd told her to get plenty of rest. You didn't need rest to crochet a doily.

Then again, it probably depended on the size of the doily. But no, she didn't see Hugh as an arts and crafts kind of guy.

I'm quite possibly going to inadvertently kill myself tomorrow, she thought, wishing she had Lola there so that she could ask her more.

Instead, she wandered about the room, running a finger over every surface, looking for dust, but finding none.

She went to the bed. It was on a platform, so she had to climb a step to get in. She sat on the edge, expecting it to be either hard as a rock or so soft that it swallowed her whole.

But it was surprisingly comfortable, firm and yet yielding, even nicer than the one in her apartment back home, and she'd spent thousands on that. She slipped her ballet flats off and pulled her legs up, then lowered her head onto the most luxurious tower of pillows. She grinned up at the ceiling.

Ah, now this is what I'm talking about. I can get used to this.

A sudden idea sprang to mind. She reached into her purse and grabbed her phone. *A few photos for the blog. And nothing beats this scenery. This amazing room.*

Her charge was quickly fading. She held the phone up to get a selfie, then blinked at the face staring back at her.

That wasn't her, was it? When was the last time she'd looked in the mirror?

Her hair was flat, her face a weird, sickly pale shade of green. And wait... Was there something black between her teeth? She hadn't even had anything to eat but cereal! Prying a soggy, squished-up *Coco Pop* out with her thumbnail, she sighed.

And lucky you, Hugh saw this version of you in all your glory.

The second the thought flitted through her mind, another one followed: *What do you care what Mr. Killer in a Kilt thinks?*

Groaning, she threw down her phone and looked around for her cosmetic case. She could just touch herself up a little, snap off, say, three or four hundred photos, then pick out the best, and post away.

She got up and went to her stack of bags, imagining the look on Brad's face when he saw she was out living her life, not holed up in her bedroom pining over him. OK, yes, she might have been doing an awful lot of that up until now, but today was a new day. Time to prove to him that he didn't make her world go round.

She stood there in front of her bags, momentarily confused.

Oh. Right.

Her cosmetics case was at the bottom of the sea.

"Great."

Sighing, she went to the vanity mirror and peered at her reflection. She looked exhausted. Puffy. Like an old, harried housewife, not like the young, thirty-year-old up-and-coming lifestyle blogger with the fantastic life she tried to show the world.

She looked like what she truly was.

A fraud.

There were some things even the greatest photo filter couldn't fix.

Stop getting down on yourself, Summer. Relax, take a shower, and then you'll be ready for anything tomorrow.

That idea settled into her mind, and she smiled as she went to the bathroom. She flipped on the light to find a rather frightening, steampunk-like contraption, with a bunch of black gears and pipes. There were half-a-dozen showerheads, all pointing in different directions, and about as many levers and controls.

This was a shower, right? It wasn't something from some James Bond villain's underground lair?

It made her tired just looking at it. Knowing her, with all those controls, she'd only screw it up.

So instead, she changed into her silk PJs and climbed into bed with her laptop. As she sat there, waiting for her computer to boot up, she pouted, feeling defeated.

Really, Summer. Some kind of adventurer you are. You can't even turn on a shower.

No. She could save this. She could take photographs of the room without her in it. That tub was legendary. And this bed? Oh, yes. Then she'd post it all online with a little write-up, minus her ugly mug. In fact, that might even be better. Lend an air of mystery to the trip.

Smiling, she powered up her computer and sat back to watch it warm up.

It was taking a while, so she moved it to the dresser and started laying out the shots, taking pictures from various angles. She added a filter, and voilà. Not bad. Definitely something to make people drool with envy.

She really didn't care about all of those other people, though. Just one person in particular.

"All right," she said aloud, heading to her computer. It was on the login screen. She hooked her phone up to it to download the photos and navigated to her blog page so she could write the prose that would make people weep.

All she saw was a blank screen.

She jiggled her fingers on the track-pad, trying to bring it up again.

No dice.

Then she noticed the little notification in the corner of the screen. *You are not connected to the internet.*

Well, of course. She wasn't in Glasgow anymore. Even so, she tapped the icon, hoping it'd magically connect.

Nope.

I need WiFi.

Groaning, she sat back and looked for that little piece of paper that was usually left on a night table in a hotel room, explaining how to access the WiFi, and the password for guests.

Nothing.

A little niggle of doubt started to nibble away at her. They did have WiFi here, right? Surely? It was only a couple of miles from the mainland, not on the other side of the world.

She stared at the empty screen and sighed. It figured. So much had happened to her today that her fingers itched to write about it. And she had other descriptive words in her head besides 'beautiful'—Gothic, charming, haunting... The list went on.

But she couldn't write a thing with this damn blank screen.

Dragging a hand down her face, she thought about her site sponsors back home. Well, sponsor, now, singular. She hadn't posted on the blog since before the wedding, and then, it was all excitement about her upcoming nuptials. If she didn't do something soon, she could kiss that last sponsor goodbye, as well.

And where would she be then? Broke and humiliated.

Although, to be fair, she was halfway there already.

She rolled onto an elbow and looked at the bell pull. Hugh had said that all she needed to do if she needed something was turn it.

And no, she didn't want to be a pain, but in any other hotel, she'd have phoned down to reception. Easy. So why would this be any different? She was paying for the full-service treatment, after all. And he'd said someone was always there.

She leaned over and turned the tiny lever. She waited for something to happen. A sound. A faint ringing, somewhere. Then, unsure if she'd done it enough, she did it again.

Then again, for good measure.

No wonder the telephone was invented, she thought, glaring at the thing.

She sat there for a few moments, waiting for a knock at the door. But there was nothing. She yawned and grabbed her phone, opening it to Brad's Instagram.

She didn't even care about the blog update anymore, really.

Her readership had been taking a nose-dive for a long time, ever since the wedding-that-wasn't. The chances of Brad checking it were slim to none.

But she always checked his social media right before she went to bed. It had become a dirty little habit of hers. The morning after the wedding, he'd posted a video of him with Audriandra, roller skating at the Santa Monica pier. So much for wallowing in his loss. Audriandra was a roller-skating queen, and she'd been wearing nothing but a skimpy bikini. Her former best friend had a penchant for wearing as little as possible, and Summer couldn't blame her with a body like that.

The one and only time Summer had gone skating, she'd been banned from the rink for a particularly bad wipe-out, where she'd levelled a number of skaters like bowling pins. A few had gone to the hospital for their injuries. One man had died.

Fortunately, they'd been able to revive him.

She couldn't help poking around in his Instagram. It was no longer just a habit, it was a compulsion. She simply *had* to know what Brad was up to. Because though it hurt, he'd been a part of her life for so long that she couldn't simply extract him from her life the way he'd extracted her from his. She wanted to share in his life, even now. And if that made her pathetic, so be it.

But now, when she tapped the app, it brought up a blank screen.

No WiFi, stupid.

Her eyes went to the door. So much for the bell pull working.

Curiosity spiked in her, making the hand holding the phone shake. She had to know what he was doing.

She had to punish herself with his happiness.

Pulling herself out of bed, she found a pair of fluffy slippers and her robe, and headed out in search of the password.

8

NIGHT TIME WANDERINGS

The moment Summer stepped into the hallway, she wondered if venturing out was a mistake.

Her room had been so nice and cosy. But outside her door, it was cold, dark, and uninviting. Hugh had turned out the lights, probably to save money, so she could see nothing in any direction, except her breath, puffing out in front of her in a cloud of white.

Even after the stunt earlier that day, Summer didn't believe in ghosts. But that was easy, in sunny L.A. where her apartment building was only two years old. Here, in a place whose walls had seen countless generations of Scots? Maybe some of those old inhabitants had stuck around.

Not to mention that the walls were dungeon-like with cold, dark, uninviting stone. That awful clanking noise seemed to shake the ground beneath her, too, vibrating through her feet and traveling all the way up her spine.

Calm down, Summer. Just get down to the lobby and get the password. It'll be five minutes. Tops.

She scrolled through her phone to turn on the flashlight and shone it in both directions, half-expecting to see glowing eyes staring back at her. To her relief, she did not. The place was empty. Still, it was spooky. There was just something very *The Shining* about long, empty hallways. If a couple of twin girls walked around the corner right now, she knew *for a fact* that she'd drop dead on the spot.

She'd never been particularly good with directions. Once, she'd gotten lost in a Target, looking for Excedrin. But that wasn't a problem in this instance. She had directions.

Turn to the left, Hugh had said. *Just keep turning to the left and eventually, you'll reach the dining hall.*

And close to that, from what she remembered, was the lobby. No problem. She had this.

Taking a deep breath, she turned to the left and headed down the hall. Her footsteps thudded hollowly on the stone floor, and every so often she stopped to look up at a painting.

"Creepy eyes following my every move?" she whispered. "Check."

She decided to stop looking at the pictures, and kept her eyes fixed on the route ahead.

The next time she reached a T-intersection, she took another left. It only went a few paces before heading off toward the right.

A right? Why was there a right? Hugh hadn't mentioned a right.

She followed it, because she had no other choice, then took another left. Each time she made a turn, she felt less and less confident.

She came to another T and, as instructed, took the left. It finally led to a spiral stone staircase, but it only went upwards, not down.

Peering up, she saw nothing at the top but a deep, murky black.

This couldn't be right. Where was the staircase going *down* to the dining hall?

She turned around, retracing her steps. But for some reason, going this direction, everything looked different. At the next intersection, she decided to go right.

Arcing the flashlight about, she didn't see the giant black statue of the man with a hawk on his arm until she nearly walked face-first into the bird's metal wing.

She screamed at the menacing look on the statue's face and backed away, heart pumping madly.

"Oh, well, that's nice," she muttered out loud, skirting around it and continuing on. "Décor that can kill a person. Lovely. Who decided to put that there? I'd fire that decorator."

By the time she reached the next intersection, she decided she was never going to find the stairs leading down, and turned back.

But as she passed the statue again, she realised she had no idea how to get back to her room.

"I should've dropped breadcrumbs," she moaned, now wanting nothing more than the comfort of her bed.

After all, who cares about WiFi? Don't torture yourself—you know his posts only show him having the time of his life. Now, he's having the time of his life, without you.

Still, if she was ever going to get over him, she needed to keep posting on her blog. Continue to post, to show everyone she'd moved on, and worked through the hurt.

And the shame.

And the humiliation.

Really, Summer? Do you really think Brad will be won back by a picture of an old bathtub? He has Audriandra and her place in Malibu, which probably has six bathtubs, all overlooking the Pacific Ocean.

She turned a corner, feeling miserable, and froze when she spied a light up ahead. A real light, silhouetting a closed door.

It was her bedroom. It had to be.

Her heart skipped. For a moment, she wanted to drop to her knees in gratitude. But she broke into a run, tripping a little because she forgot she was wearing slippers, and rushed to it.

She stopped when she realised the door was slightly ajar.

And then she heard the voices. A child. Lola.

She moved closer so that she could see their shadows moving on the opposite wall, and listened. "Correct me if I'm wrong, Father, but it's sounding like you're saying that I can't have a pig for a pet."

"That's exactly what I'm saying, aye," Hugh confirmed.

"Why?" Lola asked, with absolute sincerity.

"Because pigs are for eating. Not for any other purpose. And they eat a lot, themselves. And we barely—"

"Aye, OK. I get it," Lola said in a small voice. "We barely have the money to feed ourselves."

Summer leaned in and saw a small bed. Hugh was sitting there in profile, a beaten copy of *Charlotte's Web* on his knee.

"Right. Good. I'm glad we got that sorted," he said. "Now, may I continue?"

The little girl was wearing a nightgown that looked like a giant white sack. She had pulled her knees into it so that only her bare toes stuck out on the bed, pillow behind her, arms folded over her knees.

"You may," she confirmed.

Hugh smiled, then read on. He only made it a sentence before Lola interrupted him.

"Do you think they have any farms in L.A.?"

Hugh lowered the book. "I doubt it. It's a city."

"But Disneyland is there, isn't it? And that big Hollywood sign? And that street with all the stars, like I see in the pictures?"

He nodded. "Aye, but they're not farms, are they? Nobody's harvesting Mickey Mouse." His brow furrowed, just for a moment. "At least, I hope not."

"Have you ever been there?" Lola asked. "To America?"

"No. I have not."

He raised the book to read, but she made a humming noise that made him lower it again.

"I think you're right," she mused. "I think L.A. is far too glamorous to have pigs and slop and mud and any of that. They get their milk from nuts, so they don't even need farms. They're very clever, aren't they? How do you even think they make milk out of an almond?"

He shook his head. "I don't know."

"They don't have nipples," she said.

He blinked, and stared back at her in silence for a few moments. From what he could gather, though, she was being deadly serious.

"No. They don't," he confirmed. "But I don't think it's that sort of milk. I think they probably just squeeze them, or mash them up, or something."

Lola nodded emphatically. "I bet they do. I bet that's it. Because they're cleverer than us. They've got everything all figured out. That's why they can look and smell so good all the time."

He jiggled the book in his lap. "Can I finish this—"

"She's *so* pretty, Dad. And did you smell her? Ah!" She fell back on her pillow. "I think that's why her mum and dad named her that, because she even smells like summer. She smells like, I don't know... Like happiness, or something!"

Summer blinked at the mention of her name. No one had

ever called her pretty, but that was usually because she'd been standing next to Audriandra, the sun who blocked out the rest of the stars. It was the first time she'd ever been noticed on her own, and she felt her cheeks flare.

"Don't you think she's pretty, Dad?"

He neatly dodged the question.

"I don't go around smelling people, and if you don't want to get into trouble, you won't, either." He closed the book. "It's too late to talk about this, though. You should—"

"Och, come on, man, finish the book!" the girl instructed.

"Finish it?" He chuckled, a sound that Summer hadn't known he was capable of. She liked it. "I only just started."

"All right. Just the chapter. Please?"

"All right, all right. Fine. Just the chapter. Now, where was I?"

Summer found herself smiling as she listened, and then suddenly remembered where she was. Here. In a castle in Scotland. In a dark hallway. Eavesdropping on a private conversation.

She pulled away and started to tip-toe down the hall. As she walked away from the light, into a pool of pure blackness, she felt more lost than ever. She'd certainly never been in this hallway before.

At least, she didn't think she had.

She turned to go back the way she'd come, wondering if it was possible for her to get so lost that she wound up being found a dozen years later in a dusty corner somewhere, nothing but a pile of bones and a disappointed expression.

Trying to block that cheery thought from her mind, she took another step around a corner. All the air rushed from her lungs as she ran straight into a wall.

Or a chest.

A very broad one.

A ghost?

She put a hand up to feel. No, this was very much alive. Warm. Hard. Nicely contoured.

Then she looked up, up, up, and found two very confused eyes peering down at her.

She realised she was petting his chest like it was a lap dog, and quickly removed her hand.

"Uh. Hello," she said. It came out incredibly high, so she quickly tried again. "Hello." This time, her voice dropped so low she sounded like an old jazz singer in a smoky bar. And a male one, at that. She shook her head and flinched. "Sorry, that was worse."

Hugh looked back at her with his eyebrows raised, then spoke in a whisper. "I thought I heard something. You're not in your room?"

"I know, well—" she started, but he quickly put a finger to his lips, silencing her.

He motioned to the door a few feet behind her. "Lola is sleeping."

"Oh, sorry," she said, anxiously tucking a hair behind her ear. Why did he make her so nervous? "Where is her mom?"

"Her mum is dead," he said, without emotion.

Summer winced. *Way to bring the conversation to a screeching halt. Not that it was much of a conversation. Still, it was better than grunting. Now, you'll be lucky to even get those from him.*

"Oh. I am so sorry."

Now she felt even more self-conscious. She cursed herself inwardly for bringing it up. But her burning cheeks didn't seem to matter to her mouth, which had always had a way of betraying her brain. She clenched her teeth to stop herself from asking the inevitable follow-up question that burned inside her. *What happened to her?*

He shrugged in a dismissive way. Of course, he didn't want to talk about such things with her. *Abort. Abort. Do not ask. Change the subject, idiot.*

"Do you have the WiFi password?" she blurted, so obnoxiously that even in the dim glow of her flashlight, she saw spittle fly from her mouth.

Oh, great. Really perfect. Way to go, Summer. First you burp, then you spit on your host. Why not just squat down and pee on his feet, too, so you can complete the trifecta?

His frown deepened. "WiFi? Eh, no, we don't have that at the moment."

"Oh. But you will?"

"Well, no, we won't. Not officially. But sometimes, if the wind's blowing in the right direction, we'll get a signal from the mainland. It's rare, though."

Summer tried not to groan. That was a disappointment. All this for nothing. She should've known, though. It wasn't like this place had been updated in the last century. "That's too bad."

He was still staring at her, so she clapped her hands together awkwardly.

"Thanks! Carry on!"

He didn't move.

At first, she didn't understand why, but then she looked down and realised she was standing on his toe.

She let out a hysterical laugh and covered her mouth, both to silence herself and to avoid covering him in her saliva again. She glanced at Lola's bedroom door. "Sorry."

With that, she turned and carried on her way.

A moment later, she stopped and turned back.

He was still in the same exact spot, watching her leave.

"You wouldn't happen to...?"

He pointed behind him. "If you're looking for your room, it's that way."

"Ah. Thanks," she said sheepishly, heading past him.

"A right. Two lefts. Then another right, and all the way down. Stop before you get to the stairs."

She'd lost track of that even before he finished. "Is this the same as your *Just always make a left and you'll get there,* set of directions? Because those, frankly, sucked."

"What? No, they didn't. Any eejit could follow them."

Summer jabbed to thumbs back at herself and said, "Not *any* eejit."

She realised that this was less of a critique of his direction, and more a commentary on herself.

Hugh smiled. It was a little lop-sided, like he was trying to fight it off.

She liked it.

"I think I know the problem," he told her. "I bet you went left out of the room."

"Like you told me to, yeah."

"Well, *obviously* you don't make a left straight out of your room. You make a right and head the way we came, toward the stairs. *Then* you make the lefts."

"Oh, well, you could've told me *that* vital piece of information!" she responded, still whispering, but awfully close to not.

He opened his mouth to argue, but she waved him off.

"I'm tired. Just—which way? Left? Right?"

He threw up his hands in surrender, and in an annoyed voice, said, "Forget it. I'll take you."

"It's not like I asked you to donate a kidney!" she whispered hoarsely. "Don't bother yourself. I'll go on my own."

She went striding past him, head held high, lips pursed. He easily kept pace with her along the hall, then corralled her as she attempted to go left by placing both hands on her shoulders and guiding her right.

"Hey, watch it!" she protested.

Sparks of... something... travelled up her arms, which was strange considering she was wearing a fluffy robe. Electricity? Why? Just because he touched her?

Get a grip, Summer. It's probably static from the throw rug you're walking on.

She shook out of his grip and he quickly dropped his hands. "You go that way and you'll wind up in the East Wing," he explained. "Trust me, you don't want to go there. For your own good."

All right, so she did need him.

"*Ooooh.*" She mock-shuddered. "Not the dreaded East Wing. I heard the Beast doesn't want anyone going there and touching his rose."

"I have absolutely no idea what any of that means," he told her.

Summer rolled her eyes. "Beauty and the Beast."

"The book?"

"The movie."

Hugh frowned. "They made a movie? When?"

"Like, five lifetimes ago," Summer replied. "So, you know, it'll probably reach here in a couple of decades."

He ignored her comment as they reached the next intersection. Again, she tried to go left, and he went right. They collided, and he stepped on her slipper.

"Ow!" she wailed, pulling it from beneath his foot. "You weigh more than—"

"A suitcase full of rocks?" he asked, lifting an eyebrow.

She glared at him, then kept walking, still unsure where she was going.

"Left!" he called after her as she hit the intersection and attempted to go right. She reversed direction.

He easily caught up with her. "Sorry for standing on your baffies."

"My what?" she asked, not stopping.

"Your baffies." He pointed down at her feet.

"You mean, my slippers?" She paused and looked down. It only occurred to her, just then, that not only did she look like hell, as confirmed by her photo-taking failure, but that she was wearing pink jammies and fluffy slippers.

Oh, God.

She turned and tried to speed up. Of course, he kept up with her, easily. It was so dark in these hallways that she could barely see anything. "Why don't you get good lighting here?" she accused.

"Why should we? We know it like the backs of our hands."

She stopped. "Yeah, but for guests?"

He shrugged. "Don't get many of those."

"It's a wonder why not, considering... Oh, forget it." She waved him off and hurried down the hall. He easily reached her again and moved in front of her.

She took a step back, offended. "What do you think you're trying to—"

This time, he didn't move to touch her. He simply pointed behind her. She followed his finger to a door.

Her door.

"Oh. Thank you." She reached for the doorknob, and then said, "It's probably no use. I won't get to sleep, since I can't get online."

He stared at her, hands on hips. In this non-lighting, she couldn't help but think of romance. A man. A woman. In the dark. Alone.

If only the man weren't a complete jerk.

"Won't you, now?" he asked. "It's really that important to you?"

She nodded. "Tell me you do get internet service here sometimes? Like when the weather's nicer?" she asked hopefully.

"Occasionally, aye. Stranger things have been known to happen."

"Oh, good," she said. Then, because he was just so handsome and she was keenly aware that she looked like a total dweeb in front of him with her pink jammies, she continued, "I always check Brad's Instagram before bed. He has such a fascinating life."

She waited for him to ask the inevitable follow-up. *Who's Brad?* That's all he had to say. The answer to it was on the tip of her tongue. Obviously, anyone who was interested in her as a person would ask it.

Unfortunately, Hugh was not one of those people, because he just nodded. "Good for him. All right. Sleep well, then."

"Like I said, I won't, since I can't check…" she said, pushing the door open slowly, giving him plenty of opportunity to question her on the subject, if he so chose.

Nope. He simply walked away.

She went into her room and closed the door, then leaned her back against it, thinking. *Way to completely humiliate yourself, Summer.*

The fire in the hearth was still going, somewhat smaller now, but it was still warm and comfortable in the room.

Pulling off her robe, she sat on the edge of the bed. She stared at her computer and then shoved it over and climbed into bed, turning out the light and pulling the blankets up to her chin.

There was no way she was getting to sleep. No way. She

hadn't checked Brad's Instagram, her mind was still buzzing with everything that had happened that day, and there was still the lingering dread of death from whatever 'activities' Hugh had planned for them tomorrow.

She yawned.

No way she was sleeping. No chance.

Her gaze fell on the dancing flames of the fireplace. The burning wood crackled and spat in the hearth.

And then, still convincing herself there was no possible way it was going to happen, Summer's eyes closed over, and she drifted off into a deep, dreamless sleep.

9

WAKE-UP CALL

Summer dozed, comfortable and happy, in the four-poster bed. Lights danced across her eyelids, but she didn't open them. She'd had one of those rare, satisfying bouts of sleep that had made all her worries evaporate during the night.

Thwack! Thwack! Thwack!

She scrunched up her nose and pulled the covers more tightly around herself, choosing to ignore whatever the heck that sound had been. She could worry about that later.

Right now, in her head, she had no troubles. The wedding was still a few weeks away, and she and Brad were going out to breakfast to plan their honeymoon. Cards and calls from well-wishers were pouring in, and she couldn't wait for the rest of her life as Mrs. Brad Swash.

Okay, it was a big joke among her friends, whenever they realised that her married name would be Summer Swash, but she didn't mind. Not at all. She'd be Fried Okra or Ripe Kumquat for all she cared, as long as she got to be with the man she loved.

Thwack! Thwack! Thwack!

Yes, life was going to be good once she was married. Things were finally going to—

Thwack! Thwack! Thwack!

Oh, for goodness sake!

Summer sat up straight in bed, and was puzzled for a moment by her unfamiliar surroundings. Where the hell was she?

It all came back to her as she spotted the metal tub, and the sunlight streaming in through the leaded-glass windows, and the ash-choked fireplace that still lightly warmed the air around it.

Scotland.

Lachart Castle.

Thousands of miles from Brad, and another day away from the life that could have been.

Thwack! Thwack! Thwack!

Her eyes fastened on the door. Someone was trying to beat it down.

She grabbed her phone and stared in disbelief at the time. 5:12 AM.

Who woke up that early? And hello, didn't the Scots know of a thing called jetlag?

Thwack! Thwack! Thwack!

Apparently not.

"Hold o—" she started, until she inhaled and smelled smoke.

Was the castle burning down?

She'd been reaching for her robe, but suddenly she decided it wasn't worth it. Not if she was about to be burned to a crisp. She hopped out of bed, skipping the platform entirely and landing with her bare feet on the stone floor. Then, she rushed for the door, pulled it open, and went barrelling through.

She was a rocket, all power, no off-switch, so though she saw what she was about to do far ahead of time, she couldn't stop herself. She ran nose-first into Hugh's broad chest.

My, he smells good, was her first thought, despite her fear of imminent death by fire.

There were no flames that she could see, though. No plumes of thick, black smoke. Her instinct to flee screaming from the castle was quietly dialled down a notch as she stepped back into her room.

"Is it normal for you to wake people up before dawn?"

He squinted at her. "Sun's out."

"Well, that may be, but it's still *really* early. Insanely early. I don't ever wake up—"

She froze as she took him in. He was wearing a rust-coloured sweater and jeans, and looked rather like the cover of a menswear catalogue. She could just picture him, axe over his shoulder, hand tucked in his pocket, back from a rugged day of chopping wood.

Wood. Which reminded her... "Uh, is something on fire?"

He looked her up and down, for far longer than she would've liked. "No. Breakfast is almost ready."

"Oh. Is it going to be burned or smoked?"

He stared at her, once again mute.

She felt her heart skipping a beat, and felt an urge to either get closer to him, or much, much farther away. "Is that all?" she asked.

He nodded. "Aye. Why? Did you want more, like?"

"Yes, actually. A nice, 'Good morning, Ms. Rose. Breakfast is available in the dining hall, whenever you care to partake of it.' That might've been better. And, you know, maybe not in the middle of the night."

He stared at her like he had no idea what she was talking

about. "It's no' the middle of the night, it's the start of the morning."

"Same thing."

Hugh shook his head. "Opposite things, really, if you think about it."

She sighed. There was no point trying to argue, the man was insufferable. "I have to get ready."

"Aye," he said, already at the steps. "Then you do that. And remember, take a right out of the door."

She rolled her eyes to the ceiling and muttered under her breath, "And you can take a long walk off a short pier."

"What?"

She looked up to find him staring at her from the top of the staircase. With those blue eyes, it really was quite a piercing look.

She swallowed. "What?"

"You said something?"

She started to shake her head, her mind blank. Then, she said, "No kilt today?"

He looked down at himself, then back to her. "Evidently not."

"I, uh, I like your sweater," she said.

Her eyes widened, just a fraction. Why had she said that? Why was she trying to prolong this conversation, when he clearly didn't want to?

"My what?" Hugh asked. He tugged on his rust-coloured top. "You mean my jumper?"

Summer shook her head. "*That*, sir, is a sweater."

"It's a jumper," Hugh insisted.

"Oh. And does it jump?" Summer asked. She rocked back on her heels, like the argument had just been comprehensively won.

"No, but it doesn't bloody sweat, either," Hugh said.

"We'll agree to disagree," Summer said, deciding that this was not the hill she was going to die on.

"Aye, well, fair enough," Hugh said, turning for the steps. "Just get down here before breakfast gets cold. Don't forget. Keep making lefts."

"After the first right."

"Obviously after the first right, aye," Hugh confirmed, then he headed down the stairs.

Summer returned to her room, shaking her head. *Keep making lefts.* He talked to her like she was some kind of eejit. She blinked, and gave a little shake of her head. Where had that come from? Some kind of *idiot.*

Just because she'd gotten turned around her first night in a building that was as big, confusing, and—frankly—as scary as the ingredient list in Audriandra's favourite foundation? What had he expected, when he kept the place so dark?

Well, if he thinks he's going to rush me, he's out of his mind. This is my vacation.

She wandered over to the window and looked out, stretching her arms over her head. Sure enough, a lovely day was dawning, with bright sunshine spilling out over the courtyard. She was pleased to see that she had been right, and the picture window did look out that way. She could see the lawn games and patio tables down below. A few squirrels scampered among the trees.

Maybe it would be a nice day for *activities*. Gentle activities. Ones that wouldn't involve her dying while she was at it.

She smiled, but it quickly disappeared from her face when her eyes trailed over to the vanity mirror.

Wait. That isn't what I think it is....

She dashed over to it, horrified, and confirmed that it was. Drool. Crusty and white. On her bottom lip.

She winced. She'd had a feeling Hugh was staring at her with more disgust than usual. Now she knew why.

Unfortunately, that wasn't even the worst thing. Her hair had somehow worked itself up into a triangle-shaped rat's nest atop her head that was an architectural marvel to rival the Great Pyramids. She pressed it down, just to make sure it was real, and almost sliced her hand open with the point of it. It sprang back up, undaunted. How had that happened?

There was no question, now. She needed to tame the monster on her head.

With water.

And that meant dealing with the over-complicated shower in the bathroom.

She marched into the bathroom, determined to figure out how the contraption worked. Stripping down, she stood warily outside the shower and stared at the different levers. One had a faded blue tinge to it. One a red. Another said ON/OFF. The others didn't say anything. But that was okay. The important ones were there.

The only thing was, she had to get into the shower to reach them.

She climbed in gingerly, shivering in the cold, moving some of the jets so they'd be pointed away from her, once the water started.

Standing out of the trajectory of the spray, she turned the middle lever from OFF to ON and waited for some water to come out.

Nothing happened.

Okay, well, I just have to turn these temperature levers up, she thought, turning the red one up, as far as it could go.

Nothing like a really hot shower, she thought.

Behind the walls, the pipes groaned loudly. Unfortunately,

the only thing that dribbled out was a little bit of water, sliding down the shower walls and swirling around the drain. A lot of noise and fuss, for that?

She dipped a finger in and felt it. It was warm. Hot even. Steaming a little. Only there wasn't nearly enough of it.

She turned the blue handle slightly, and water started to drip out of the shower head attached to the far wall. She ran a hand under it. Cold.

She turned it off.

All right, well then, Mr. Jumper. There is no way I'm stepping out of this room with the Hanging Gardens of Hammurabi on my head, so no shower, no activities.

But at that moment, she had to admit that she wanted a nice shower. Desperately. Her skin felt slick with oil. All that travelling from the day before had made her feel gross.

She grabbed a little glass bottle and opened the lid, sniffing it. Shampoo. Oh, that would make her hair smell so good.

Then she thought about what Lola had said last night, about how she smelled good. *I'm not going to for long, if I can't get this thing to work. They'll be able to smell my stink from the mainland.*

She had a fleeting thought about using the bell pull, not that it had helped her much before. And Hugh had called her an *eejit* last night. She didn't exactly love the idea of driving the point home by asking him how to work the shower.

"Please work," she pleaded, twisting the levers indiscriminately, trying to get them to do something. Anything.

Just more dribbling.

She pounded a palm against the tile. "Fine!" she shouted at it. "If that's how you want to play this, let's do it the hard way!"

With a brief but maniacal cackle, she started throwing all the levers, like some mad organ player, lost in his music. Her fingers flew across the controls, twisting, tweaking, spinning, and swiping at them.

When she was done, she stood there, breathing heavily, watching the water continue to dribble pitifully down the walls.

She sighed. "OK. Fine. You win," she told the shower, turning to leave.

She stopped when she heard the groaning. It seemed to come from all around her—the walls, the floor, even the ceiling overhead—and the air *hummed* like it was coming alive.

And then—*whoosh*! A thunderous cascade of Arctic water hit her, seemingly from every direction at once, the pressure as hard and unrelenting as the blast from a fireman's hose.

She screamed, wasted a few seconds trying to stem the flow from all the various shower heads with her hands, then her survival instincts kicked in and she launched herself, naked, out onto the bathroom floor.

She slid on for a couple of feet, leaving a slug-trail of icy water behind her, then she lay there where she stopped, soaking and shivering and trying to catch her breath.

Her teeth chattered as she fumbled around, trying to find a towel, and she realised that her earlier thought had been correct.

That was *nothing like* a really hot shower.

10

THE LAIRD OF LACHART

It turned out that the *turn left* advice actually worked.

Once Summer hung that right out of her room, she followed those instructions and soon found herself in the hallway leading to the massive double doors. They were open, and when she saw the giant banquet table, she sighed in relief.

She'd managed to scrape her unruly hair into a tight ponytail, and she'd also found a tube of pink lip gloss and some roll-on perfume in her purse. That was the extent of her beautification. The two seconds of water torture she'd gotten had blasted at least some of the dirt away—and possibly some of her skin with it—but it had also left her never wanting to take another shower for the rest of her life.

Even though she'd lost all of her cosmetics and her styling tools, she'd been impressed at how well she'd made do. She'd put on a casual outfit and a jean jacket and thought she looked rather cute, considering. If she could stretch her arm out *really far* to take selfies that weren't too close up, and if she could find the right filter, she might even be able to put some pictures of herself on her blog.

As soon as she arrived at the threshold of the dining room, she smelled it. Some sort of cooked meat, with a lot of spices. It was thick and greasy and pungent. Her stomach turned as she tried, and failed, not to think about the purple knobbly inside parts of a sheep.

She stepped into the dining hall, finding it empty, the fireplace cold, a thin stream of early morning sunlight slashing through the leaded-glass windows. She went to the chair she'd sat in the night before, but hesitated there. Lola was right. It was all so excessive. Especially just for her.

The windows in the room had wide ledges, so she perched on one of those, and found it overlooked a garden. Beyond the branches of some thorny rose bushes, down a cliffside, she could just make out a white-sand beach, and the sea.

"Pretty," she murmured, taking out her phone and trying to capture it, but it was hard to get nice photos through a window. She'd have to go out there later.

"It's about bloody time," a voice said behind her.

She turned. "Good morning to you, Mr. MacGregor," she said, smiling widely and tipping an imaginary hat. "You've woken up on the cheery side of the bed once again, I see."

He ignored the comment. "Sit. I'll get you breakfast."

"I'll just stay here," she said, patting the ledge. "And what's on the menu today? From what I can tell, it smells meaty. Barbecue? Side of beef? Sloppy joes?"

"Sloppy what?"

"Doesn't matter."

"It's a traditional Scottish breakfast," Hugh announced.

"Of course it is. And what does that involve?" Summer asked. "Cows' eyes and pig hearts?"

Hugh grunted. "No. We're fresh out of those, actually."

"Don't you have something simple? Like Elderflower tea and a bagel?"

"A bagel? No. We have toast. And just regular proper tea."

Summer tutted, but forced a smile, trying to stay positive. "Fine."

Hugh started to walk away.

"But, I'm curious. What does that actually entail? A traditional Scottish breakfast?"

"All the good things that you don't have the sense to eat. Bacon, fried eggs, baked beans, fried tomatoes, mushrooms, buttered toast, tattie scone, and of course, black pudding."

"Black...?" She clenched her teeth. She knew that rice pudding was some sort of British dessert, but she'd never heard of a black variety. "That sounds ominous. Is it real pudding?"

He looked confused by the question. "No, it's imaginary. Of course it's real. You don't get much more real, in fact."

She wasn't sure what that meant, but if it was anything like Jell-O pudding, she was in. She'd been a junkie for that stuff as a kid. Plus, the cereal last night hadn't done it for her. She was starving. Too starving to eat nothing but toast. "Okay, fine. I'll take one of those and some toast."

"Ah! Good on you!" Hugh said, and for the first time since they'd met, he actually looked impressed. "Can I no' tempt you with a wee square sausage while you're at it?"

Square sausage? Wow. She really was through the looking glass here.

"No, that sounds... confusing," she said. "I think I'll just keep it simple."

"All right," he said, turning to leave.

Once he was gone, she took out her phone and tried to hold it up, hoping to get some kind of signal so she could check Brad's Instagram. No luck.

A moment later, as she was standing on the ledge, her hand thrust way up in the air, trying to get a few bars that way, Hugh returned with the tray.

"There's no phone service here," she said with a shake of her head. "I thought you said you sometimes got something."

"I believe I said 'rarely,'" he reminded her.

She clambered down, and studied the tray he was carrying. It actually smelled pretty good. The bread was tiny and thin, not like those giant American slabs, so she was glad that wasn't all she'd ordered. The pudding, though, wasn't anything like she'd expected. It looked like slices of black, round bread.

"Are those hockey pucks?" she asked.

Hugh looked down at the plate. "What? No. That's black pudding."

"It looks odd," she said.

"Ah, just wait until you taste it."

Summer had absolutely no intentions of doing that until she'd thoroughly tested it first. She prodded it with a fork and tore it apart. It felt dense, and a little dry, the black colour continuing all the way through.

"I'm used to... creamier pudding," she told him.

Hugh frowned. "I can't imagine what that would look like," he admitted.

He started to set it on the ledge next to her, then paused. For a moment, he just stood there, frozen like the Tin Man in *The Wizard of Oz*. And then, finally, he let out a soft sigh.

"I brought this out to you, but would you rather eat in the kitchen? It's not grand, and a little rowdier in there with my family, but—"

Summer felt herself start to smirk. "I thought you said I'm not allowed to mingle with 'the help'?"

Hugh nodded. "Ordinarily. But since there are no other guests, I suppose we can make an exception."

She studied him, noting the hardness of his face. It suggested this was the last thing he wanted to do. So why was he doing it? The answer came to her easily.

"Lola asked you to ask me, didn't she?"

"She may have suggested the idea, aye," he admitted.

Summer smiled all the way this time. Even though it wasn't strictly his idea, it was nice to see that softer side of him, and clearly his daughter was the way to that. She scooted off the ledge. "Well then, how could I disappoint the Lady of Lachart Castle?"

She followed him to the kitchen door and, since he was carrying the tray, reached out to open it for him. As she did, he said, "You might want to brace yourself."

"Why?"

The door was thick, and heavy. When she managed to heave it open, she heard giggles and the frenetic sound of a fiddle playing from an old CD player in the corner. Lola and an elderly man—the ghost from the day before, she guessed—were holding hands, dancing a lively jig together, and laughing their heads off.

"Grandpa, you're going too fast!" Lola cried as the old man, much sprier than he looked, whirled her around the room in a frenzy. They whizzed past Summer, making her take a step back to avoid a crash.

The old man—well-dressed in a dapper tweed blazer—finally brought his granddaughter to a stop, and they fell into each other, laughing. He had thick white hair, including a bushy moustache that framed his broad smile. He had his son's bright blue eyes, too, but there was a mischievous sparkle to them that Hugh's lacked.

"Help ma Boab! You're a natural, Lola," her grandfather said.

"Aye, but you're a good partner!" Lola replied, giving the man a warm hug. She pulled away and gasped, running a finger over the red, angry bruise on his liver-spotted forehead. "Oh, Grandpa. You've got a bump."

Duncan touched his forehead. "Ah, yes, we got a wee bit over-excited during that Strip the Willow earlier, as we are sometimes known to do." He pointed up to where several cooking pots hung from a rack above them. "Yon big frying pan clonked me out of nowhere."

Hugh went to the CD player in the corner and pressed a button, turning off the music. He crossed his arms. "Serves you right, I'd say."

The old man waved him away. "*Och,* away and boil yer heid." His eyes shifted to Summer. "Ah! A guest. Pleased to make your acquaintance. I am Duncan MacGregor, Laird of Lachart Castle."

He bowed, and Summer was amazed, given his age, how close to the ground he got.

"Nice to meet you. I'm Summer Rose. I just got in from—"

"*Los Angeles,*" Duncan said, like they were the two most exotic words on Earth. "So I've been hearing. Lola has told me all about you. Delighted to have you with us." He gave Lola's cheek a squeeze. "There's nothing better than a little morning exercise to get the old heart pumping, I say!"

"You were very good," Summer told him. "But I hear you're good at a great many things. You designed the central heating?"

Duncan beamed and breathed on his fingernails, buffing them on his tweed blazer. "Aye. A bit of an inventor. A bit of a dancer..."

"A bit of a pain in the arse," Hugh muttered.

Lola shot her father an angry look, then turned back to

Summer, all smiles. "You should see him shoot clay pigeons! He's so good at that!"

She mimed blasting targets with an imaginary gun, complete with sound effects, until her father took her by the shoulders and steered her away.

"Stop harassing our guest and let her eat. She's got a busy day ahead of her."

"Och, stop harassing our guest," Lola parroted. "Talking is not harassing, Dad. If it was, I could take you to the courts for neglect."

"Ha! You're a smart one, sweetheart." Duncan wrapped an arm around Lola and beamed at Summer. "It's very nice to have you here. But you crack on and eat. We can chat while you have your breakfast."

The kitchen wasn't much to write home about. Considering the grandeur of the dining hall, she'd expected a vast space with industrial-sized appliances, capable of producing enough food to feed a crowd. But the place was rather dark and cramped, with a pot-belly stove and a brick hearth, and a long wooden prep table. As well as the ones hanging from the ceiling, there were iron pots and dishes scattered over almost every surface.

She took a seat on a stool at the prep table and lifted her fork, ready to dig in.

Duncan studied her tray. "My lady here says you're a vegetarian, eh?" He pointed at the pudding. "You won't want that, then."

She poked it a little. "Why not?"

"It's meat," he said.

"I thought it was pudding?"

"*Black* pudding," Lola corrected. "It's made from blood. It's like a blood sausage."

Summer's nostrils flared and her eyes went wide. She stared down at the hockey pucks on her plate.

"Blood sausage?" The words came out as a whisper of horror. "You really eat it? And, you know, live? And you're not vampires?"

Lola giggled and held an arm up in front of her mouth, like she was hiding behind a cape. "I *vant* to suck your blood sausage!"

Duncan elbowed his son. "What I want to know is why this brute was giving it to you, if he knew your dietary requirements."

Summer was wondering that, too. Did he really hate her that much? Because that was downright mean.

He shrugged. "She asked for it. I try to give our guests what they ask for."

She glared at him and picked up the toast. "This is all right, isn't it? It's not *brain matter* toast? There are no hidden animal parts in this?"

Lola shook her head. "Butter. Not from horses but from cows," she said, grinning at her father. "If that's okay?"

"Yes, it is." Summer took a bite.

Duncan glowered at his son. "I think you owe the lady an apology for being such an obnoxious big arse."

She held up a hand. "Oh, it's not necessary. It's not like it'd kill me. I can eat meat. I just choose not—"

"No," Hugh said, bowing his head humbly and looking into her eyes. "Allow me. I do apologize, Ms. Rose. I was concerned about us being late and so I might have acted a bit rashly in my haste to get you to hurry up."

His gaze was so intense. She fought the blush she could feel climbing her cheeks. "Late? For what?"

"You'll see," Hugh said mysteriously. "You'd have already seen, in fact, if you'd gotten up when I asked you to."

She gazed at the other two standing around the table, hoping they'd spill the secret. But they just smiled mysteriously.

"Fine." She held the toast up. "I'll be done in a minute."

As she nibbled the toast, she caught sight of a painting across the kitchen, near the hearth. Unlike the others in the castle— portraits with haunting eyes that seemed to stalk a person across the room—this one was a painting of a simple blue flower with white edges. For some reason, it sparked a feeling of déjà vu in her, but that was lost just as quickly as it appeared.

"That's a lovely painting."

Lola followed her line of sight and smiled. "That's a lily. The Lachart Lily. It only grows on this island."

"Grew, lass," Duncan corrected, rubbing her shoulder. "It hasn't been seen on the island since before I was born."

"Some people say fairies planted them," Lola said, in an awestruck, breathless sort of whisper.

"Aye, well, some people talk a lot of old shite," Hugh said. "It's a fairy story, I'll give you, passed down from generation to generation. There's no truth to any of it."

Lola gave her father a doubtful look as he started the water to wash the dishes. She leaned in and said, "Grandpa says it's real, and there's a drawing of the lily in an old book in the library. I've seen it."

Duncan nodded. "Thousands of botanists have searched for it over the years, and none have ever found it." He smiled, but it was a sad, forlorn sort of thing. "They've mostly all given up now, of course."

"Because it doesn't exist," Hugh stressed.

"When you came here, I thought you were one of them!" Lola told Summer, ignoring her father completely.

Duncan smiled at her. "We used to house a lot of botanists

from the mainland in my youth. But, like I say, we never get them anymore. On the rare occasions one does come around, they tend to stay in the village."

Lola sighed wistfully. "I wish it did exist. If it did, and we found it, we could show it to everyone, and all our money problems would be over."

Duncan patted her hand. "Now, now, wee one—"

"It's true! It would! The botanical tourism industry is worth over *three-billion* pounds every year. There was a thing on the telly about it. That's a *lot* of money," Lola added, in case anyone wasn't sure.

Summer nodded, impressed at the little girl's enthusiasm. But she couldn't help feeling a little niggling in the back of her mind. She was sure she'd heard this story when she was much, much younger.

When her father was alive.

Her eyes lit up. "Wait. I think my father came here!"

Hugh turned off the water, and when she glanced up at him, he was gazing at her in confusion. In fact, they all were. Then again, it was quite a random thing to just blurt out without any sort of context.

"No, you see, he was a botanist. He died when I was young. But before he did, he came here, looking for that lily. I came with him. I was sure I'd visited the island when I was younger— I was *sure* of it—and I was right! And now I know why!" She jumped up and slammed both palms on the table excitedly, making everyone jump. "*And* now I know why, when I was planning my trip, I didn't choose Mexico, or the Bahamas, or somewhere, you know, nicer than here. No offence."

"Some taken," Hugh grunted.

"Something drew me here. To Scotland. To this island. *My*

father. It was the last place we ever travelled to together. It was the last thing we ever did together, before..."

Her burst of excitement faded, and she sunk back into her chair.

Lola put a hand on her arm, and Summer managed to summon a smile for her.

"Your father," Duncan said, "What was his name?"

"It was Callum. Callum Rose?" she asked, hopefully. "He's actually from Scotland. Edinburgh."

Duncan scratched at his temple. "Aye. It doesn't ring a bell, but these days, at my age, not much does. There were many names, looking for that lily—it's hard to keep track of them all."

She pushed down her disappointment. It had probably been too much to hope for. "Of course," she said. "I understand."

"Regardless of how you were brought here, we are glad to have you." Duncan bowed. "Now, if you'll excuse me, I have a phone call to make."

As he made for the door, Hugh called, "Who do you have to call at six in the morning?"

But the door slammed shut without an answer. Hugh growled something under his breath about a, "Stubborn old bugger."

Summer smiled. Duncan seemed to live to get under his son's skin. It was a nice thing to see, since Hugh seemed to enjoy doing the same to *her*. She looked down at the black pudding—blood sausage, gross—and nudged it as far away from her as she could.

As she took the last bite of her toast, she noticed Hugh standing poised to take her plate away.

"All right, all right. You keep a very tight schedule, don't you?"

She grabbed her tea, which by now was cool, and took a sip.

"Aye," he said, checking his wristwatch. "You'll need to get dressed for this morning's excursion."

"I *am* dressed."

"Not for this."

She looked down at her T-shirt dress, cropped denim jacket, and ballet flats. Chic, effortless, suitable for many *activities*.

But not, apparently, for this one.

11

MORNING ACTIVITIES

An hour later, dressed in her anorak, jeans, and sturdy shoes with non-slip soles, Summer found herself hugging the deck of a small sailing boat as it sliced through the water, a strong wind powering it along. Shivering, the wind smacking her in the face, she didn't dare move a single inch for fear of falling into the water below.

The ferry had been bad. But this? This was sheer hell.

"I hate this," she said into the wind.

"What?" Hugh called back.

She raised her voice to a shout. "I said I hate this!"

"Och, away with you, woman! This is the life, right here," Hugh laughed, striding about the deck like a master of his domain, taking deep, bracing breaths of air, totally in his element.

Meanwhile, Summer hunched in a ball, the wind pulling tears from her eyes. The gusts from the sea were so cold, she felt like her face was freezing solid. She could barely move her lips to say, "OK, that's enough of the full-service package, thank you. Can we go back to the fire?"

He was doing something with the sail, pulling a line. She didn't care to know what. He looked down at her and frowned. "You really don't like this?"

"It's hard!" she protested.

"Aye, of course it is! A little hard work never hurt anyone, though! Come on, you'll enjoy it!"

She shook her head, her teeth chattering. She pulled the bright-orange life vest around her to ward off the cold. It didn't really help.

"I'd seriously rather eat blood sausage," she said, motioning to the island, which seemed so far off in the distance. Rising above it, she could see the highest battlement of the castle. "So, can we go back now?"

He stared off into the distance. "Not until I've taught you how to sail. That's the package."

"Oh. Don't bother yourself. I've really gotten my money's worth. The boat ride was eno—"

He held a calloused hand out to her, palm upwards. "Come on. Get up. I'll show you."

She clung tighter still to the deck of the boat. Getting up was the last thing she wanted to do. In her mind, she could clearly see herself, pitching forward with a wave and falling head-first over the low rail into the ice-cold waves. He'd probably leave her there, too, like her poor cosmetics case.

"No." She shook her head frantically.

He rolled his eyes like he was dealing with a fussy child, then reached down, grabbed her hand, and hoisted her up onto her feet with a single tug. She didn't want to be so pathetically dependent on him, but she found herself clinging to his arm like it was the only thing anchoring her in place. Her knees wobbled, and she started to shake uncontrollably.

"Easy does it, now. Relax," he told her, and there was a

comforting gentleness to his voice that she didn't recall ever hearing before.

Not that she cared right at that moment.

"I can't!" she yelped. "I'm going to fall in!"

She felt a strong arm wrap around her waist. "You're no' going anywhere. Don't worry. I've got you."

He brought her toward the centre of the boat, away from the railings at the sides, and the water foaming just beyond them. That relaxed her a little, though her stomach pitched along in time with the waves. He showed her something with one of the lines, how to tie some fancy knot or other, but she only half-listened, because most of her concentration was focused on staying upright.

"Here. Now you try."

She took the ends of the rope and tied a regular knot, like she was lacing a shoe. "*Voila*. Can we go back—?"

He took the knot and undid it. "Were you even listening?" When she shrugged, he let out a deep breath and said, "Let's try again."

"This is hard!" she cried in exasperation after her third failed attempt. Her fingers were blue and numb. "Why do you have to tie a knot that way, anyhow? Can't you just do it the regular way?"

"Each knot serves a different purpose," he said, tying it himself effortlessly. "This knot—the clove hitch—is so you can move the fender. See?"

He demonstrated, and she watched, impressed, but a little embarrassed. It felt like he was speaking another language.

"It's an easy one."

"Easy? Well, don't show me any of the hard ones," she mumbled, looking out on the sea. There were other islands in the distance dotting the horizon, and she had to admit, it was rather breathtaking.

The wind had dropped a little, too, so the cold was no longer quite so biting.

A little surer of her footing, she reached for her cell phone. She aimed it at the islands in the distance and snapped a photograph. If she could just get service, she could post it on her social media.

"What are you doing there?" he asked, still securing the sail on a cleat.

She'd been playing with the filter to make it perfect, but she tilted into the sun and showed it to him. "Taking a photo for my blog."

"Your dog?"

Summer felt herself smiling at that. She raised her voice above the sound of the waves. "No, of course not my dog! My *blog*! It's a lifestyle site. Lot of written content. I know, I know, most people just hang out and make videos on Instagram and TikTok these days, but I love writing." She wrinkled her nose. "Or I used to."

"Blog," he mused, as if it was his first time saying the word. Maybe it was, although that was impossible, surely, since blogs had been around for most of their lives. "What's it for?"

"Oh, it's called *Summer All Year Round*. It's kind of like a sunshine-lifestyle, slice-of-life journal, with a sort of multi-faceted fantasy-come-mythological slant. But with recipes. And fashion advice. But not like *fashion* fashion. You know what I mean?"

He shook his head. "No."

She couldn't blame him. Based on that explanation, she didn't know what she meant, either. "Well, maybe I'm not explaining it in the best way—"

"All right." He sat down on the railing, a little too close to her liking to the frothing sea. "Try again."

"You're not really interested."

"Says who?" Hugh asked. He nodded for her to continue. "Explain it to me."

He was staring at her now, those keen blue eyes making her feel even less like she knew what she was talking about. And it was entirely possible, she thought, that she didn't.

She decided to give a simple, basic explanation and then hopefully the conversation would just blow over, even if he didn't really get it.

"I just write about my life and experiences so that people can read about it."

"Ah." A wrinkle appeared on his forehead. "Why?"

Damn. So much for letting it blow over.

"Why? What do you mean, why? So that people can read it and relate and—"

"Who are these people?"

"Just anyone. Not just in the US but everywhere. I have a reader in Abu Dhabi," she announced proudly, though she left out that she was reasonably confident it was just a search engine bot.

"Do you, now?" He stroked his chin. "And is that important to you, is it? Having strangers peer into your life?"

She squinted at him. "I'm not sure what you're getting at."

He shrugged. "Well, that's what they invented drapes for." He mimed drawing closed a pair of curtains. "Keep the nosy buggers at bay."

Summer did have to admit that it would've been nice to have drapes over some of her life lately. If she hadn't been so eager to be in public like all of her friends, the past week wouldn't have been nearly as humiliating as it had been. But she was used to that life. In L.A., everyone shared online. In fact, the second question people usually asked upon meeting you, right after, 'What's your name?' was, 'How many followers do you have?'

It was expected. It was *normal*.

This, being here, in the cold, dangerously close to icy waves? This was just the opposite. This was abnormal.

"Well, I'm just not explaining it the right way. It's not just for that. And anyway—I have sponsors. They put ads on my blog, and I make money from it."

His eyes went wide, finally interested. "You make money from it? Good money?"

Summer hesitated. Making money from blogging was difficult at the best of times. She used to make enough to cover hosting fees and a few nights out, but after the whole wedding humiliation, her blog numbers had become so dismal that she'd be lucky to be able to buy a sandwich with the revenue.

"It can be done," she said, slightly dodging the question.

"How many do you have? Advertisers, I mean?"

"Two!" Summer declared, then she winced. "Well, one, actually. A margarine company. I used to have a skincare line, but they didn't renew the contract after..."

After my humiliating trip down the aisle.

Her cheeks flamed. TMI. She needed to stop babbling.

"Forget it."

He looked her up and down, and she braced herself for further questioning. To her relief, he just sniffed, then shrugged, and got to his feet.

"Forgotten," he said, then he crossed to the other side of the boat and beckoned her over.

He spent the next few minutes showing her how to make another knot, and this one, miraculously, she got the hang of pretty easily. He gave her a length of rope to practice on, and watched her for a while in silence.

She could feel herself starting to blush beneath his gaze, so turned to face him.

"What is it?" she asked.

"Oh, nothing. Nothing," he said. "Just... I get it."

"Get what?"

"Your whole *blog* thing. I'd imagine your life in the States is something people want to read about. Ever since you arrived, Lola won't stop asking me questions about Hollywood."

She smiled. "It's not as glamorous as people might think."

He gestured around at the boat, and the choppy water. "No' as glamorous as this, you mean?"

Summer looked around and chuckled. "Actually, when we went out on the ocean, it was on a super-yacht. One that was so big, you didn't even feel the waves under you."

"Aye? And where's the fun in that?"

"Well, Brad made it fun. He's kind of..." She searched for the word. "Crazy. That's his personality. Go big or go home. There's no use doing something unless you can overdo it. That's his motto."

"Sounds like hard work," Hugh said. "Does he have a blog too?"

"No, he doesn't write. I mean, he can write. And read." Her forehead creased doubtfully. "I think. He's a TikTok and Insta-gram star. Has about a million subscribers, last I checked."

"TikTok? Is that like some sort of clock thing? So, he can read, write, *and* tell the time? Quite a catch."

He said it all so seriously and deadpan that Summer let out a high, lilting laugh. "Not quite. TikTok is a platform where people post short videos of themselves."

"Of clocks?"

"No! I mean, maybe, I guess. But Brad's is more just him doing stuff. Like, hanging out."

Hugh blinked. "And a million people want to watch that sort of thing?"

"Well, yes. If you are particularly entertaining, they do. And Brad is entertaining. He's a skateboarder, too. A really good one. One of his most-watched videos is him skateboarding naked on the upper deck of his yacht." She smiled at the memory. "And then there was this one time he sent a poor junior crew member out on a rowboat for a hamburger and fries because he had a hankering for an In-N-Out Burger. But it was too mushy, so he took one taste and threw it overboard. That one went viral, too." She laughed. "Then he would occasionally post videos of the hamburger's travels, around the world..."

Hugh nodded slowly, but she could tell it'd gone completely over his head. After a moment, he said, "He sounds like quite the character," in a way that didn't sound even remotely like a compliment. "He's your boyfriend, then, is he?"

She cringed, remembering when Brad Swash was her boyfriend. After so many years of living in her best friend's shadow, being noticed and loved by Brad was *everything*. Whenever Audriandra would complain about her many boyfriends and never being able to find the right one to settle down with, Summer would feel like dropping to her knees and thanking the heavens for Brad. She was so lucky to have found him right out of the gate. Unlike her best friend, she'd never had any boyfriends before him, but who cared about that when he was *the one?*

She couldn't bring herself to tell him about that horrible day at the church, so she waved a hand. "It's complicated."

"Ah. Sounds that way." He untied a line and wound it around

his hand. "Because if you don't mind me saying so, he sounds like an absolute roaster."

She wasn't sure what that meant, but it didn't sound like anything good. "What? Yes, I do mind, actually. Brad's a good guy."

A good guy who left you at the altar. Give it up, Summer.

But the words were hanging out there, and Hugh, though he looked doubtful, simply shrugged. "Aye, well. I'm hardly the best person to be offering relationship advice."

"Your dead wife," Summer said, then her eyes widened and she clamped a hand over her mouth, far too late to stop the words blurting out. "I am *so* sorry!" she mumbled through her fingers.

Hugh stared at her with one thick, bushy eyebrow raised, looking like he might be about to throw her overboard. And, to be fair, she couldn't blame him. Right at that moment, she was considering doing it herself.

Then, to her surprise and relief, he flashed her a grim smile, and waved a hand as if dismissing the apology.

"It's fine," he told her.

Summer risked uncovering her mouth. She'd already put her foot straight in it, and there wasn't much worse damage to be done.

"I'm, uh, I'm sorry for your loss. Was it... sudden?" she asked awkwardly, after a long pause.

"Aye," he said, looking ahead in the direction they were sailing. "It was."

She waited for him to say more, but he didn't. She added, "Well, that's terrible." then searched the recesses of her mind to find something from her own life to compare to it. The only thing close was her father, and all she had of him were scattered memories that sometimes seemed like dreams. The only sadness she ever had when she thought of him was because she'd missed growing up with a dad. She never really knew him, and so she hadn't mourned him, exactly. Just the idea of him.

Of course, she had the trauma of losing Brad. But though it'd completely sent her life into a tailspin, it wasn't nearly the same.

"I'm sure it's been hard."

"Aye," he said again, looking up into the rigging. He untied a rope from the mast and handed one end of it to her. "Here, hold this."

She shifted her phone to her left hand and grabbed the rope. Then, while his back was turned, she snapped a photograph of herself, hoping that just holding onto the rope made her look like a real sailor.

"At least you have your memories," she said. Then, when she realised that sounded like something from a sympathy card, she added: "And Lola. You have Lola."

She watched him closely, hoping she hadn't said anything to upset him, and was so wrapped up in his reaction that she didn't notice the faint buzzing in her hand until he pointed at it.

"You're bleeping."

Summer looked down at the phone she'd forgotten was in her hand, eyes widening. She had a few bars. She could post her photograph!

"Oh, my God," she said, opening up her email. She hadn't checked it in days. Predictably, the second she opened it, the counter on the bottom said that it was *Downloading message 2 of 398.*

She stared at the messages as they arrived, noting the sales emails from various stores she shopped at, a *Don't forget to update your wedding registry* email from Nordstrom, a couple of *A reader liked a post on your blog!* messages. All the regular stuff she was used to deleting the moment they came in.

Then the name appeared.

Brad Swash.

The emails were coming in fast and furious now, so if she hadn't been watching carefully, she might have completely missed it. She scrolled to it, thinking she must've misread it. After all, why would he be emailing her?

But there it was. Brad Swash. In all its glory. The man who she'd expected to spend the rest of her life with. Her true soul mate.

Right then, a thought hit her. *He's realised he's made a mistake and can't live without me. He's emailing to apologize and ask to get back together.*

Before she could click on it, a number of other emails came in, pushing that one off the screen.

"Ugh," she said, annoyed, scrolling through and trying to find it. She was ready. She flexed both of her thumbs, ready to post and tell him that yes, of course, she'd take him back. It was fine. People made mistakes. No point crying over spilled soy milk!

All was forgiven, all would be well, and they would be together forever.

Unfortunately, switching to two-thumbs mode meant letting go of whatever she was holding. Which happened to be the rope that Hugh had handed to her.

"Careful!" he barked. "What are you—?"

Before she knew it, the boom arm of the sail swung out wildly. She skirted out of the way, and Hugh ducked just in time, avoiding certain disaster.

"Oh my God! I'm so sorry! That could've been nasty!" she began.

She watched the arm swinging out, out, out, then felt a rising wave of nausea as it began to swing back, back, back again.

"Um," she began, but before she could continue with the warning, the arm hit Hugh on the back of his head with a hollow *thunk*.

She saw it all playing out in slow motion. One moment, he was upright. Then, like some superhero taking flight, he was launched into the air, and went sailing over the railing of the boat.

Unlike a superhero, he then immediately fell into the sea.

"Hugh!" she screamed, making it over to the side of the boat in record speed.

He was there, treading water, giving her a death stare through a curtain of hair that was matted against his eyes.

"You dropped the line," he said through gritted teeth.

"I had a signal," she said weakly.

Although now that she looked back at her phone, it was gone. She groaned, and only the sound of Hugh clearing his throat made her hastily stuff the phone back into her pocket.

"Can I help you up?" she asked.

"No, I wouldn't want to trouble you. You're clearly busy," he grouched, swimming over to the side of the boat.

She reached over, extending her arm to him. "Here, grab on!"

He shook his head. "You're no' strong enough. I'll pull you in. Stand back."

Not wanting to upset him any more than she already had, she stood back, waiting for him to hoist himself aboard. She saw his hand appear on the edge of the boat, heard him grunting with exertion, but the rest of him failed to appear.

He was having trouble. She couldn't just let him stay out there, drowning. After all, if he did, she wasn't enough of a sailor to trust she could get back to shore. Her mind flashed back to that image she'd had of the pile of bones the night before, only this time they slouched in the corner of the sailboat, being pecked at by hungry seagulls.

Looking around, she found a fishing net with a long pole. She slowly fed it over to him. "Grab this!" she shouted, just as he bobbed up. It *thunked* him on the top of his head this time.

"Ow!"

Summer winced. "Whoops. Sorry!"

Hugh spat out a mouthful of seawater. "Are you trying to bloody kill me here?" he demanded, but he took the pole anyway, and with some effort on both their parts, he managed to climb into the boat.

Once aboard, he stood there, dripping all over the deck, and trying very hard not to shiver in the biting breeze.

"Are you cold?" she asked sympathetically.

"I'll give you three guesses, and the first two don't count!" he said, his voice steadily rising.

He caught the trailing rope and tied it off, preventing any more unexpected head injuries.

"Stay right on that spot," he told her, once he'd finished. "Don't touch anything. I've got extra clothes somewhere."

His shoes slipped on the wet deck as he went to a locker and pulled out some fresh clothes. She grabbed her phone from her pocket to see if she had a signal, but the screen was black and unresponsive.

Great. The battery of her phone was terrible, and it was even worse when asked to download a bundle of emails. She'd have to get back to the castle and charge it.

If her guide would just get them back to shore as soon as possible.

Her pulse raced. She had to read Brad's email. She had to tell him all was forgiven. She had to get her life back on track, and she had to do it now. She couldn't wait a moment longer.

You catch more flies with honey, she reminded herself. *Be nice to him and maybe he'll do as you ask.*

As he started to unbutton the collar of his sweater, she called to him, "I'm very sorry about—"

Her breath caught in her throat as he pulled his shirt over his head, revealing washboard abs and broad pectorals, smattered with the slightest bit of cinnamon coloured hair.

"Good grief," she gasped, her jaw dropping, all thoughts of everything else temporarily tumbling out of her head.

"What were you saying?" he asked, and she realised he was staring at her.

She averted her eyes and sucked back a bit of drool that threatened to fall over her lower lip. "Uh..." God. What *had* she been saying? "I don't know. I forgot."

"I think you were in the middle of apologizing to me?"

"Oh, right. Yes! I'm sorry." She shivered and sneezed as she realised the front of her clothes were dotted with spots of seawater, too. "Can we go back now? I'm a little wet."

"Oh no, really?" He lifted an eyebrow incredulously. "What happened? Did you get thumped on the back of the head and knocked overboard?" He tutted. "Wait, no. That was me."

"Yes, I know, sorry again about that," she said. "I'd just... I'd like to go back."

"Oh, don't you worry about that," Hugh said, untying another rope and shooting her a glare. "We can't get to land soon enough for my liking!"

$\approx$

HUGH'S BOATING shoes made a peculiar *squick-squick-squick* noise, all the way up the stairs to the castle, but at least it slowed him down, so when they arrived at the front door, she was only a few paces behind him.

The moment they walked in, Summer heard a loud, joyous giggle. "Watch out below!" someone cried.

Summer looked up just in time to see two bodies flying down the banisters of the giant staircase, one on each side. Duncan reached the end first, and a laughing Lola followed just a moment after.

"I won!" the old man cried in glee.

"That's no' fair! You're heavier!" Lola climbed off the banister and threw herself at Summer's feet, laughing so hard she was clutching her stomach. "Best eight out of fifteen?"

Duncan climbed off the banister and clutched at his lower back. "I don't know, lass, I think I sprained something that last time." He straightened, then winced when something went *crack*. "Wait, no. I sprained *everything* that last time."

"You're lucky you didn't do a lot worse, you old fool," Hugh muttered. "Those banisters aren't for climbing on, Lola. You know that."

She pouted, but Duncan put an arm around her. "Oi, let the girl have some fun, now and again, will you?" he said. "And we weren't climbing, we were sliding. That's the opposite of climbing."

Duncan reached up as if to squeeze Hugh's cheek, but Hugh flinched away. "We've been over this, Dad. It's not safe."

Duncan threw up his hands in despair, then smiled at Summer. "You have a nice time?"

"It was... interesting."

Duncan looked his son up and down. "Aye, looks it right enough. You're looking a bit damp there, son. You go for a swim?"

Hugh ran a hand through his damp locks. "Something like that."

Lola crossed her arms. "Now who's doing dangerous stuff? It's freezing out there!"

Hugh didn't crack a smile. He wiped away a drop of water that had slid from his hair to the tip of his nose instead. "Aye. You don't have to tell me that."

Duncan laughed. "Let me guess. You were such a pain in the bahookie that our guest here pushed you in? Can't say I blame her, lassie, just wish I was there to see it."

Summer smiled. "Well, I did *kind of* push him in," she admitted. "But it was by accident."

"Good for you, I'd say!" Duncan cried. He squeezed her shoulder. "Remind me of your father's name again, lass?"

She blinked, surprised by the question. "Oh, uh, Callum Rose."

"Callum Rose," he repeated, and for a moment, she thought he might say that he remembered him. Instead, he tapped the side of his head and then walked out without another word.

Hugh clapped his hands. "Right, well, I'm starving after that dooking. Who's up for lunch?"

Summer looked down at herself. Then she thought of the email Brad had sent her, and a frisson of excitement went down her spine. She needed to read that email from him. Alone.

"I think I'd just like to get out of these clothes and relax. It's been a pretty busy day."

"Oh, right, those wet clothes of yours," Hugh said with a snort. "How trying for you. But, aye. If you must."

"I must," Summer said without another look.

She headed up the stairs, hoping that this time, she'd be able to find her room without his help.

12

AFTERNOON EXERCISES

Summer stood in the bathroom's doorway of her suite, staring at the shower. She could still feel the raw chill of the sea breeze. A cascade of warm water would really help put some heat back into her bones.

But, no. Too risky.

She'd already had enough trauma in the water today. She didn't need to add to it.

Instead, she towelled some of the moisture from her hair, changed into some comfy lounge pants and a tank top, and went to see if she could finally get a look at Brad's message.

As she was plugging the phone in to charge, there was a knock at her door.

"Come in," she called.

But nobody did. She went to the door and looked out, finding no one. Her eyes drifted down and found a tray from the kitchen. Looking up and down the hallway, she decided whoever had delivered it had now left. She crouched in front of it. There was a carafe of coffee and a serving dish covered with a silver lid.

She brought it in and reluctantly lifted the lid, bracing herself for more blood sausage, or some other inedible horror.

To her surprise and delight, she found a small salad with walnuts and berries. Perfect!

She nibbled on a piece of lettuce and poured herself the coffee, inhaling the strong aroma of the beans. She hadn't been lying to get out of his company when she'd told Hugh that she wanted to rest. The exhaustion was bone deep. And besides being a hapless passenger on a boat, she hadn't really done anything all day but worry. Then again, worrying took a lot of energy sometimes.

But the thought of Brad's email, along with the smell of the coffee, boosted her. She took a sip of the steaming hot black liquid and felt a little better. Then, she sat on her bed and powered up her phone.

She had a bar. One whole bar!

Yes! Brad, I'm ready for you.

It felt like fate that she finally had reception right at that moment. Right as he was about to confess he'd made the worst mistake of his life, and promised to love her, forever.

It was perfect timing. A real *Hallmark* moment.

Opening her email and navigating to his name, she felt her heart flutter.

"Yes, yes, yes!" she whispered when she found the email.

She frowned a little when she saw the subject.

'A Special Invitation for Summer Rose.'

That was a little strange. What did it mean? A 'special invitation' to take him back? She'd been hoping for something like, *'I love you, I can't live without you! Take me back, please?'*

But all right. It was from Brad, and Brad had never done things the conventional way. That was one of the reasons she'd fallen for him.

This was just another of his funny little quirks. That was all. Nothing to worry about.

A troubling thought nagged at her. She pushed it away, took a deep breath, and tapped on the message.

The first thing she saw was a picture. It showed an envelope. On it, in curly script, were the words, "Open me, please."

This was ridiculously formal for an 'I'm sorry I messed up' email. If there was one thing Brad wasn't, it was formal. But in her years of dating him, she'd learned to expect the unexpected from him. She wouldn't even put it past him to have a camera installed in the room to capture her response for a later TikTok video.

She checked herself in the mirror and grimaced.

God, please don't let there be a camera in this room!

Brushing her hair from her face, she tapped on the image, and the envelope became animated, opening and unfolding before her eyes.

The first thing she read were the words, "You are cordially invited to..."

I'm cordially invited to get back together with Brad?

Even for him, that was pretty cheesy. For once, she wished he was more of a traditionalist. He'd never been what she might describe as 'traditionally romantic.' He'd never done the sort of things people did in romance novels—buying her cartloads of flowers, bringing her on weekends to a log cabin in the mountains. Even when he'd proposed to her, he'd just pulled a ring out of his pocket and made sure his camera was rolling to capture her response. He hadn't dropped to one knee, like she'd dreamed, and when she'd accepted, he'd immediately turned to the camera and started addressing his audience, leaving her not quite sure what to do with herself.

The message continued to unfold on her screen, and as it did, her heart shattered into pieces:

You are Cordially Invited to
The Union of
Brad Swash and Audriandra Foxley
Come Party it Up Rockstar Style
At the Lahaina Palms Country Club
Maui, Hawaii...

SHE STARED at the words for so long her eyeballs started to burn. She couldn't bring herself to blink. The words just sat there, staring back at her, impressing themselves forever into her psyche. She could actually feel them, scratching their way into her brain.

Letting out a little yelp, she swiped at the message, trying to delete it. Trying to unsee it. But for some reason, her stupid phone picked that moment to freeze up. The fancy-scrollwork lettering seemed to get larger, taunting her.

"Party it up like a rock star? Really?" she cried. That bit had stung almost more than the rest, because that's how he'd pitched their own wedding reception to her.

He'd wanted to do something outlandish and expensive, with champagne fountains, tiny horses carrying drinks around on their backs, and the bride and groom skydiving to the altar.

It'll make a great video, he'd said. But she'd told him she wanted her wedding to be more private. More traditional. And at the time, he'd agreed. That's why they'd done the traditional church wedding. Although, the guest list had been comprised of so many brightly-dressed, fabulous people that the priest had practically been blinded.

But clearly, Audriandra had been all up for the flashiest wedding possible. That was just typical of her. The bigger the circus, the better.

She grabbed the phone and read the date. Three months. They were getting married in three months. It had taken Brad four *years* to propose to her.

Because you and Brad never would have worked, Summer, she thought. *You were only fooling yourself.*

She let out a cry and swiped at the email again with her finger. And this time, it worked. As the invitation flicked off the screen, she landed on her photos from earlier that day. One photo, in particular, she hadn't even noticed she'd taken. It was of Hugh, right at the moment when he fell over into the water. It was a little unfocused and out-of-frame, but his face—his mouth stretched wide and his eyes open in shock—was so unlike the calm, stoic man she'd come to know over the past day.

She let out a giggle she didn't know she had in her. Then she swiped through the rest of them, lingering on the ones that included him.

This morning, she'd absolutely dreaded the idea of sailing around a dark sea in the cold. She'd thought there was nothing she'd rather do less. But, looking back through the pictures, she realised that—despite all odds—she'd actually enjoyed it. Part of it was the scenery, part of it was the sea air and the sense of accomplishment that goes along with learning something new.

And part of it was the company.

It had all been so outside her comfort zone, too, which had made it even more enjoyable.

Summer scrolled to another photograph of Hugh, working the lines effortlessly. She imagined he was probably someone who did everything gracefully and effortlessly—unlike herself, who often tripped over her own feet in her own apartment.

No doubt, he was a handsome man, without even really making the effort. She had to wonder about him. How had he been with his wife? Had he been different? Had he smiled more? Been happier?

She jumped from her bed and went through her carry-on, finding her charging cable. Connecting her phone to her laptop, she downloaded the photos.

Tucked behind the bathtub was a little ledge in the bay window that overlooked the courtyard. She took her computer and tray of food over to it, so that the warm sunlight touched her face.

She still had no connection, but with a bit of fiddling, she was able to open up a blog window in offline mode, so she could type, but not yet post.

She took a sip of coffee. A nibble of salad.

And then, she began to type.

13

CURRY AND CONVERSATION

When Summer finished typing, she looked up, surprised to find that the sun was beginning to creep its way down the sky. The room was now growing darker as the light slipped towards the horizon

She smiled. It'd been a long time since she let her writing take her away like that. Since she'd been so inspired. She'd written an entire blog post about the excursion and hadn't used the word *beautiful* once. It felt good, like her old self might finally be coming back.

But then she thought of the invitation, and her insides twisted.

She tried to convince herself that it made sense. That this was how it should be. She and Brad were so different. Whenever they'd go places together, no one seemed to think they were a couple. Women would always post comments on his videos, like, *What are you doing with that plain girl when you can have me?* and, *She adds no dazzle to your videos. You need a star!*

Okay, so maybe she was plain. She'd always been that way, hiding in her best friend's shadow. But Brad had told Summer that he liked that about her. That among all the uber-stylish and elegant in L.A., she was a standout just for going her own way.

But the thing was, she'd never really wanted to be different. She hadn't ever set out to *go her own way*. Just like Audriandra, she wanted to be so sophisticated and elegant that people followed her in droves.

She just wasn't very good at it.

It was a miracle that her blog even had the ten-thousand followers it had. Though, this was well, down from eighteen-thousand, following the wedding-that-wasn't.

And now, there was going to be another wedding. One that would probably increase the happy couple's followers tenfold.

That invitation.

Ugh.

It was just like him to think that, even though he'd pulled her heart out of her chest and stomped on it, they were still on friendly terms. She'd been nice to him, yes, but only because she didn't want to turn up as some deranged ex-girlfriend character in one of his viral videos. She'd told him that if he paid the bill for the reception hall, she'd return the wedding gifts. They'd worked everything out in a very calm, organized, and cordial way.

But that didn't mean she wanted to go to his wedding!

As she was pulling on a cardigan to ward off the evening chill, someone knocked on her door.

"Come in," she called.

"Can you let me in?" Lola's chipper voice echoed from behind the door.

Summer crossed the room and opened the door to find a giant canvas basket of firewood with feet that looked like it was about to topple over.

"Good evening," Lola said, from behind it, sounding every inch the perfect host.

"Can I help you with that?" Summer rushed to grab it from her. "Poor thing. Your father made you bring that up?"

"Oh, no. I wanted to." When the pile was pulled away, it revealed her bright smile. "I'm getting good at starting fires. I told him I'd get yours ready, so it's warm and toasty for you tonight, if you'd like to go down. Dinner's about ready."

"Oh. OK," she said, scuffing into her ballet flats. "Are you sure you don't want some help?"

"Do you know how to start a fire?"

Summer shook her head. "No. But you could teach me."

"I could, but you should go downstairs so our guests don't get lonely. That's what Dad said—to send you down so you could entertain them."

"Guests? You mean you've booked more rooms?"

She laughed. "Oh, no. It's just the Campbells."

"The Campbells?"

"Our neighbours from the village. They're old friends of the family. You'll like them. We invited them over for their anniversary. So, you should go down there, and, you know, be American to them. They'll like that." She kneeled in front of the fireplace. "I'll be done with this, quick as can be."

Summer smirked. "Be American. Right. I'll try my best," she said, heading for the door. "Good luck!"

By now, Summer was very good at finding her way downstairs. She made it without a single wrong turn, and found the doors to the dining room wide open. Sure enough, an elderly couple was sitting at the end of the banquet table, chatting away with Duncan.

"Ah, you must be Summer," the man said, rising to his feet.

He had a full, round face, a ruddy pug nose, and wire-rimmed glasses. "I am Michael Campbell, and this is my wife, Isla."

She shook their hands as Duncan stood up to pull a chair out for her.

"It's very nice to meet you both," she said. She sat down and Duncan helped push her chair up to the table. "You live in the village?"

"That's right. All our lives. We used to run Campbell's, the old pub in town."

Duncan nodded. "Did the best fish supper you'll ever try. I wake up sometimes, mouth watering from dreaming about it. Isla's quite the cook."

"*Oi,*" Isla said, patting Duncan's hand. "You old flatterer, you. You come over to our place any time you want, and I'll make one special for you."

"What happened to the pub?"

Michael's face fell. "That, I cannot tell you, lassie," he said in a low, mournful whisper. "Sure, but it's too painful a memory."

Isla rolled her eyes. "Don't mind him. He's still sore about it because the pub was his baby. It was in his family for three generations, you see? But we couldn't keep it going. We were losing money, year after year."

"Hand over fist!" Michael added.

His wife comforted him with a pat on the arm. "Ever since tourism stopped, it's been hard."

"That's awful," Summer said, twisting her napkin in her lap. "I'm so sorry."

"Och, it's no' your fault, lass," the woman said in a motherly tone. "But even our year-round residents have been thinning out. All my sons moved off to the mainland. Couldn't keep them here if I tried."

"But it's so lovely and quiet."

"And it's dying," Michael said sadly.

"Oh, but enough about that!" Isla said in a sweet, chirpy voice. "I hear you come from L.A. Do you know Robert Redford?"

Summer smiled and shook her head. "Sorry, I don't."

"For goodness' sake, Isla." Michael groaned. "Los Angeles isn't like Lachart Isle. Everyone doesn't know everyone who lives there. Of course the lassie doesn't know Robert Redford!" He leaned in closer to her across the table. "What about Meryl Streep, though? Do you know Meryl Streep?"

"I do not. Sorry." Summer smiled, despite their obvious disappointment. "I don't know anyone famous."

The kitchen door opened and Hugh appeared, wearing a white apron. He was followed by Lola, who was grinning from ear to ear. "Told you I'd be quick, Summer!" she said with a smile. "You have the roaringest fire in all of Scotland, I promise you that! You'll be nice and toasty tonight."

"Thank you," Summer said. "I can't wait!"

"Aye, well, you won't want to rush off!" Lola skipped over to Summer and squeezed in between the big chairs. Then she whispered, "We've got some special vegetarian items on the menu tonight."

"Really?"

She nodded. "Yes. I picked them out of an old recipe book." She started listing them off on her fingers, "Cauliflower curry soup, carrot and parsnip pie, and some mushroom thing we're about ninety percent sure won't be poisonous."

Summer chuckled. "Sounds... great!"

"Personally, I think you'll like the curry soup. I had a taste. It was delicious, and I don't even like cauliflower."

"OK, then, soup it is," Summer said, a little astonished. "I can't believe you went through all this trouble for me."

Lola began to reply, but Hugh spoke over her. "Well, we can't very well let our guests starve, can we?"

Then he turned and marched back into the kitchen, with Lola following at his heels.

Summer stared after him. She'd thought he was starting to show some personality out on the boat, but now he seemed like angry Kilt Man again. Was he still upset over the whole sailing mishap?

Duncan must've noticed her concern, because he smiled at her. "Don't pay any heed to him. He's just trying to be difficult."

"He's succeeding," she mumbled under her breath.

"Oh, he just hasn't been the same since he lost Sarah." Isla leaned in as if imparting a secret. "Her death really threw the poor dear into a tailspin."

Summer really couldn't imagine that man married. "What were they like together?"

"They were good together. I didn't know her well. She'd only visited a couple of times before..." Isla shuffled uncomfortably in her chair, unable to find a suitable end to that sentence. "Well, you know, *before*. She was from Inverness. He met her when he went there to study. They lived there after they got married, didn't they, Duncan?"

Duncan nodded. "Aye," he confirmed. "Aye, that's right. Came back soon after she'd passed."

Isla leaned back in her seat and looked over to the kitchen door. "I don't think I've seen him smile once since he got back. Not really. Not properly."

"So, he did smile before?" Summer asked, hardly able to believe it.

"Oh God, aye!" Duncan laughed. "Wee bloody menace, so he was. His favourite thing as a wee lad was terrorizing the travellers from all over, back when the tourism business was booming on the island. He used to have them hunting all over the place for the gold he said had been left by some pirate ship."

Michael burst out laughing. "Or what about the Lachart Lion?"

Isla joined in. "That was a belter, right enough. He told some whoppers, but that was one of the best. He had a whole group of scientists trying to track it down."

"The Lachart Lion?" Summer asked, confused.

"Oh, aye," Duncan said with a snort and a shake of his head. "Hugh liked to tell stories when he was a kid. One summer, he invented this ferocious, man-eating beast that could only be found on the island. Half tiger and half weasel, or something. He drew up pictures of it. And he must've gone around creating claw prints in the mud, all over the island. Everyone was scared to bloody death of the thing. They all bought into it. I never saw tourists go so crazy looking for something that didn't exist."

"Like the Lachart Lily?" Summer asked.

"Well, that *did* exist, at one time," Duncan insisted. "Whether or not Hugh wants to believe it. It would do him good to, I think. To believe in a wee bit of magic. He's closed himself off since Sarah's death. All he does is mope around the castle, like he's waiting for death himself."

"That's sad," Summer said. It seemed sadder still that he'd changed so much. "It sounds like he used to be a lot of fun."

"Not just that," Isla said, sipping from her glass. "He was always a good man, too. A real asset to the community. Always helping people out in a pinch, putting others first. He was the life and soul of this island, always smiling, always positive, and now..."

Her gaze went to the kitchen door again, then quickly shied away, like it was too painful a thing to look at.

Summer looked across the table at the other woman in

shock. *Always smiling, always positive?* That was the exact opposite of the man she'd met.

She wanted to ask more, but before she could, the kitchen door swung open and Lola appeared, holding a bowl and smiling broadly. Hugh followed after her, shouldering a larger tray.

"Dinner is served," Lola announced, setting the steaming bowl in front of Summer. It was a white, creamy mixture, and smelled heavenly.

Hugh went around, setting down plates for the rest of the people seated at the table, but Summer noticed his eyes remained on her the whole time.

"It smells good," she said.

"Try it, try it!" Lola urged, watching her closely.

"Right, here goes!" Summers said, making sure that everyone else had their plates before she started. She noticed they had some sort of dark, meaty stew, though it appeared mercifully free of purple knobbly bits.

She picked up her spoon, dipped it in, blew softly, and sipped.

"Well?" Lola asked before Summer could even swallow.

"Lo, give the lassie a chance to breathe," Hugh said, though he seemed to be watching as well, waiting for her reaction.

Normally, she'd be too self-conscious to show one, since everyone around the table was looking at her. But her tastebuds took over.

"Wow," she said, scooping up another, larger spoonful. "This is amazing!"

"Seriously?!" Lola gasped.

"Seriously! It's delicious. I've never tasted anything so good." She shot Hugh a suspicious look. "This can't be your first time making it."

"It was," Hugh said. He shifted his weight from foot to foot, and there was something deeply endearing about it. "So, you like it, then? You don't think it needs anything?"

Summer swallowed the next bite, and immediately started loading up the spoon again. "I love it. It's perfect as is. I think you should make this part of your regular menu."

"Oh," Isla said, peering over her bifocals at it. "It certainly makes me want to try it!"

Hugh didn't smile, but for a moment it looked like he might at least be coming close. He seemed genuinely relieved that it had passed muster. He brought out the soup tureen and bowls for everyone to try it, and then, after a few moments of awkward hesitation, pulled out the chair next to Summer and sat down.

Around the table, everyone tasted the soup, and were soon raving about it, just like Summer had. Before long, the tureen and their bowls were empty.

They all chatted then, talking freely and fluidly about the island, America, and everything in-between.

After an hour or so, Isla and Michael announced that they had to return to the village. Summer realised, as they stood up to leave, that even though she'd been so miserable about the news of Brad's wedding, with good company, she'd actually managed to forget about it for a while.

She waved goodbye to the couple. "It was very nice meeting you," she said as Duncan walked them to the door.

"Likewise, lass," Michael said. "You come round our place in the village if you want a fish supper, all right?"

"Consider me there!" Summer said. She patted her stomach and smiled. "Though, maybe not right now. Kinda full!"

As they left, Summer sat back and wiped her mouth with a napkin, then she turned to Hugh, who was staring pensively into his wine.

"So, Recreation Coordinator, as part of the full-service package, do you have any activities planned for me this evening?"

She said it as if it would be a chore, but actually, she hoped he'd say yes. The last thing she wanted to do, after this nice evening, was to go to her room early and simmer in bed, thinking of Brad and Audriandra tying the knot.

Hugh lifted an eyebrow. "Why? You fancy something?"

She shrugged. "Well, the night is young. Maybe something a little more low-key would be my speed. And maybe not on the water."

"Aye, that's probably safest for all involved," he agreed. He stroked his chin for a while, then glanced at Lola, who was looking back at them both and smiling from ear to ear. "Let me get this one off to bed, and then I think there's something I might show you."

Lola pouted. "What? But I want to—"

"*Lola*," he boomed, in a voice that made her shrink a little. His voice became softer. "Remember what I told you?"

"Aye, Dad," she said, crossing her arms and sulking a bit as Summer smiled at her. Lola leaned in and whispered, "You're going to trust him after the black pudding incident?"

She had to admit, Lola had a point.

"Are you sure it won't be on the water?" Summer asked him, doubtfully.

"Definitely not," he said. "Just *near* it..."

14

SCOTTISH HIGH

"This isn't exactly what I meant by low-key!" Summer screamed, clinging onto Hugh's broad back for dear life.

They were roaring across a dark hillside on a battered old quad bike. Summer had never been on one before. Nor, for that matter, had she ever really wanted to be.

But there she was, arms wrapped around Hugh, squeezing the life out of him, face buried in his back, too terrified to take another peek. Last time she'd done that, she saw that they were climbing up into the hills. The sea, swathed in moonlight, seemed fathoms below.

He appeared to be forging a path where no path had been before. The ground was rocky and uneven, and the quad bounced like its tires were trampolines, forcing her to squeeze him tighter so she wouldn't lose her grip. As they climbed, whips of bracken and heather slapped at her legs.

It might not have been on the water—or even near the water, as he'd said—but that didn't make it any less scary.

It didn't help that he seemed to be ignoring all her pleas for him to slow down, though it was possible that he just couldn't hear her over the roaring of the engine.

After twenty minutes of barrelling haphazardly through the half-darkness, he finally came to a juddering halt. When she dared to open her eyes and look around, she saw that they were right at the edge of a forest, the tall, dark trees lording over them.

He pried her reluctant fingers from his waist and stepped off the bike. She watched him, unwilling to follow.

"Where are we going?" She pointed at the sun, which was just settling behind the hills. "Shouldn't we get back before it gets dark? Or, you know, *darker*."

"Come on. You want the full experience, don't you? We won't be that long," he said.

"Promise?"

"Aye," he said from round the back of the quad bike, where he was busy doing something with the equipment he'd packed. "Be careful. The ground is boggy. Watch you don't end up on your arse."

Taking a deep breath, she slid off the seat, already sure she'd regret this.

Almost immediately, she did, because the moment she took a step toward the forest, she sunk into muck up to her knees.

"Ugh!" she groaned, then she froze, convinced any movement would make the soft ground swallow her like quicksand.

He walked over without saying a word, grabbed her arm, and pulled her out. The mud made a sucking sound as he lifted her back onto solid ground.

"This is... enjoyable," she said through gritted teeth. She looked down at her ruined shoes. "Still, at least I changed into hiking boots. Maybe it's just as well I brought all that luggage with me."

"Hm," Hugh said, not committing to an answer. He threw a pack onto his back, then set off into the forest. "This way. Watch your step."

She followed him into the woods, and was surprised by the spring in her step. She was, to her amazement, feeling quite positive about the outing, despite almost being sucked down into the Earth just a moment before.

An adventure on a faraway island! Beautiful scenery! Lush surroundings! She was grabbing life by the face, and refusing to let go!

This was way better than sitting around, moping over Brad.

Although, that said...

Mud had seeped into her boots and was now hardening, making her feet itch. The ground was goopy and uneven, and, to make matters worse, she was getting cold.

Suddenly, she felt an itch on her cheek. It came out of nowhere, and was instantly the most urgent, pressing problem she had.

Bringing a hand up, she scratched her cheek, squishing something there. When she looked at her fingers she saw a little black dot with tiny wings and, presumably, even tinier yet impossibly sharp teeth.

"Ugh," she moaned, wiping it on her pant leg. Then, just ahead of her, she noticed a small cloud of the things, all tumbling around in the air at head height.

She was too late to stop. She swatted at them and held her breath as she stumbled through the cloud. When she emerged, the bugs were crawling on her face and arms, and she yelped as she slapped and scratched them away.

"Argh! What the...? Is this place full of tiny mutant mosquito babies?"

Hugh turned back to her. "Eh? What's the problem now?"

She stopped mid-flap because she knew she looked ridiculous. "I'm getting eaten alive."

"Oh, aye. That's the midges." His brow arched and he shrugged. "They don't bother me."

"Well, lucky you!" Summer cried, still clawing at herself. "Because they seem to have got a real taste for me!"

"You must be very sweet," Hugh told her, then turned his back and continued on.

Was that a compliment? Probably not, considering his dismissive tone. She stopped and put her hands on her hips. "Do you have any bug spray in that pack of yours?"

"Bug spray? For midges? No, that'll only make them angry," he said. "You wouldn't like them when they're angry."

Summer scowled. "What do they do? Turn green and get bigger?"

"Shh," he said suddenly, raising a finger. He looked around, listening for something, then he pointed to a place where the thick forest gave way to blue sky, dotted with pale pink clouds.

Summer moved forward until she found herself on a white stone outcropping. As she did, she noticed they were above the sea, overlooking a stretch of silvery beach that seemed to glisten in the pastel colours of the dying sun.

"Oh," she gasped, drawing closer.

"Look," Hugh whispered, pointing out past the shore.

Summer followed his finger, and had to stuff a hand in her mouth to stop herself crying out in shocked delight.

A herd of red deer was playing at the water's edge. They frolicked in the surf, skipping across the sand, springing and skipping, and having the time of their lives.

Summer had been to the San Diego Zoo before with Brad. She'd loved looking at the animals, even if Brad had spent most of the time trying to put together a video of himself in which he either acted like or taunted every animal they visited.

But this? This was different. She felt like she was a real nature explorer observing these animals in the wild, undisturbed. It made her breath catch in her throat. For reasons she couldn't quite explain—would never be able to explain—tears rushed to her eyes.

"What are they doing?" she whispered, but he shushed her with a finger to his lips.

There had been no need to ask, she knew. Not really. It was clear what the deer were doing. They were enjoying the day.

And so, she had to admit, was she.

Despite all her doubts on the way here. Despite her rocky start with the man crouching in the brush beside her, she had been right to come here. Even if it ended right there and then, the trip had all been worth it.

She leaned closer, peering at the animals, trying to get a better look. None had antlers, so they were all female, she guessed. But there were a few smaller ones with spots on their backs. Babies. Fawns. They were so cute. She suppressed a giggle as she watched two playing together.

Oh, pictures!

This would be a perfect photo opportunity, too good to miss. She had to capture this for her blog. To remember this.

Fishing her phone from her pocket, she tilted this way and that, trying to capture the right composition, with the beautiful sand beach, the dark sea, and the cotton-candy-coloured sky in the background. She captured a few action photos of the deer, playing in the waves, splashing water about so the setting sun painted the spray in a rainbow of colours.

When she looked at the photo she took, she sighed with delight. She'd gotten the deer with the rainbow of water arcing over its head. It was *perfect*. If she sent it to *National Geographic,* she bet she'd win an award.

That was the beauty of nature—so much more stunning than anything man-made.

It was an honour, she thought, to see this. To be here. To witness nature up close like this. To be part of it.

Watching the babies frolicking gave her a warm, fuzzy feeling. She was basking in it when, from beside her, she heard a faint metallic *click*.

She turned to find Hugh staring down at the beach while quietly assembling a long, deadly looking rifle.

"Wait," she whispered, her jaw hanging open. "You're not—"

"Hush, now," Hugh muttered. "Quiet."

"What? No," she said, her voice rising. "They're playing. They're a family! You can't—"

"Keep your voice down, or you'll scare them off."

"Fine! Great!" she said even louder, jumping in front of him. "You're not going to—"

He stood up and, with very little effort, nudged her aside, then cocked the rifle on his shoulder. The deer, unaware, continued to skip and spring through the surf.

Summer couldn't take it. She wouldn't. No way.

She let out a scream and raced down the rocky incline, waving her arms as she jumped over the bushes and other obstacles in her way. When she reached the beach, the deer had already taken off, running in the opposite direction down the shore. She watched them disappear into the tree line, far down the coast, and threw both clenched fists in the air as the last of the babies disappeared into cover.

"Go on!" she screamed at them, jumping around like a madwoman. "Live free, you beautiful beasts!"

Triumphant, she turned to head back up the incline,

knowing it would be a lot harder to climb up than it had been to run down. Hugh would probably be angry and wouldn't help her, either. But it was worth it. Totally worth it.

Excitement buzzed through her, but there was another feeling, too. A sense of kinship with the animals, maybe. Right at that moment, crazy as it sounded, she actually felt she had become one with nature.

Then, as she clambered up the slope, she found herself face-to-face with an enormous red stag. The hot steam of its breath swirled from its wide, flared nostrils. It pawed at the ground with its front hooves, its enormous multi-pointed antlers lowered, ready to attack.

Summer gulped.

"OK," she whispered. "So, maybe that wasn't my *best* idea..."

15

SCOTTISH LOW

"Hello there, Mr. Deer, sir," Summer said in her sweetest voice, as if talking to a puppy. She held out her hands in a calming motion, and tried not to make any sudden movements. "Don't mind me. I was just saving all your friends from certain death on the beach. I mean you no harm."

She shifted her eyes to the side, in time to see a dark blur heading down the embankment.

Oh, no, not another one, she thought, taking a tentative step back. *They're going to surround me and play 'Let's Poke Holes in the Human.'*

With a powerful snort, the stag lowered its antlers, shook its head, and charged.

Before she could even think of running, something knocked her to the side. She fell and rolled back down onto the sand, all the air leaving her lungs in one big *whoosh.*

She righted herself, and her eyes darted around as she tried to gauge what had happened. They fell on the enormous stag, standing just a few paces away from her. It reared up on its hind legs, kicking its front hooves dangerously close to her head.

"Come on!" Hugh's voice called, grabbing her by the hand.

Somehow, mostly with Hugh's help, she managed to scramble to her feet, and they took off together, kicking up sand as they raced along the beach. He was fast, yanking her arm so hard she thought he might dislocate it. Her feet tripped and slipped on the sand, her lungs burning in her chest.

"Come on, shift your arse!" he shouted, pulling her along.

"*Trying*," was the only word she could squeeze out between tortured breaths.

She couldn't hear the pounding hoofbeats of the enormous animal behind her. All she could hear was the crash of the waves and the sound of her own heartbeat drumming in her ears. But in her head, she saw the sharp points of its antlers coming dangerously close to her back. She could almost feel it.

"This way!" he shouted, pulling her like a rag doll into the trees. They ran a little more, dodging through the brush, branches catching in her hair and pulling at her like they wanted to drag her back.

Finally, panting heavily, he finally pulled her down behind a giant bolder. She crashed up against his chest, landing awkwardly atop him. He threw her off him, then rolled over, wrapping an arm over her to shield her from the beast.

Breathless, shaking, she choked out, "F-feel free to shoot *that* one."

"Shh!" he warned.

A moment later, she heard the stag charging. Felt the ground shaking beneath its hooves.

Half a dozen feet away, it jumped over a fallen log, and thundered away into the forest.

Summer closed her eyes and let out a sob of relief.

When she opened her eyes again, Hugh was glowering down at her, his eyes more steely grey than brilliant blue.

"What the bloody hell did you think you were doing?" he demanded.

"Uh, running for my life," Summer said.

"Before that," Hugh snapped. "When you ran down the hill, chasing them all away! What was that about?"

She noticed that he still had the rifle slung across his back, and scowled her disapproval at him.

"You were going to shoot them!"

Hugh got to his feet, shaking his head. He swung the weapon down from his shoulder and waved it in front of her. "It's no' a hunting rifle. It's a dart gun. I was firing a tracking dart."

"A tracking dart?" She didn't know if that was any better. "For what?"

"For our conservation efforts. We mark all the animals on the island."

"Oh," she muttered, feeling foolish. "So you weren't going to kill them?"

He looked genuinely hurt by the very suggestion, but said nothing, just pulled the gun back up onto his shoulder. Still not saying a word, he took off and headed back toward the beach, his strides long and purposeful.

They were also impossible to keep up with. When she got to the beach, he was already halfway along it. Though her lungs were screaming for mercy, she broke into a jog and finally caught up with him.

"Why..." She had to stop and suck in a breath so she wouldn't pass out.

He stopped and stared at her. She held up a finger for him to wait, pointed at her chest, then leaned back, drawing in as much air as possible in a series of big, frantic gulps.

Finally, she recovered enough to complete her sentence.

"Why didn't you tell me?"

He shook his head and continued marching on. "You didn't give me a chance. You went running out there, flapping about like some wounded bloody seagull before I could explain."

She winced at the image. A wounded seagull? That seemed harsh. Then again, she could imagine how ridiculous she must have looked. She'd burped on him, spat on him, almost drowned him in the sea, and now this.

What must the man think of her?

They reached the incline beside where she had fallen. He barrelled right up it without stopping. She stared up at it, mentally preparing herself for the climb, and the possibility of the stag standing waiting at the top again when she got there.

"I'm sorry. I suppose I might have been a bit... rash," she called up to him.

Already at the top of the rocky outcropping, he turned. "Are you just saying that because you want my help to get up?"

"No!" she said.

She ran at the slope, got halfway up, then gravity got the better of her and she fell backwards, arms flailing, and rolled all the way back to the bottom.

"Yes," she said, through a mouthful of sand.

Hugh heaved a sigh and retraced his steps, took her hand, and dragged her up to the top of the slope with relative ease.

When she was finally on even ground, he extricated his hand from hers almost too quickly, then mumbled something under his breath about how they never should've come out here.

Once again, she had made a mess of what had, until that point, been a nice little excursion.

"Thank you," she said as he turned his back to her. "And

again, I'm sorry. That was a totally bone-headed thing for me to do."

When he looked over his shoulder at her, she smiled, extending the olive branch.

"Bone-headed?" He nodded. "Aye, you can say that again!"

Her smile fell. "Excuse me?"

"Absolutely idiotic, is what it was."

He marched down the path, leaving her standing there, steaming. What use was trying to be nice to him? He might've been a good guy, once—though she wasn't sure she believed what the Campbells had said—but now? Now, he was a stone-cold jerk!

She took a few steps and found herself stumbling over a branch. She quickly righted herself and said, "Listen. I was trying to be nice. To call a truce, but—"

He rounded on her so fast that she took a step back.

"Now, listen to me, lassie. It might be OK to make mistakes in your fairy-tale world of make-believe, but here? In this world? The world I live in?" He took another step forward, wagging a finger in her face, his voice becoming a growl. "The world you're in right now? Messing up could be a matter of life and death."

He spun away from her and stalked off, leaving Summer seething.

No wonder poor Lola shrank back from him the second he barked at her. No wonder everyone walked on eggshells around him. They were all afraid to make his grief worse. His wife had been dead for years, and yet, he refused to move on. So instead, he was allowed to have free rein over them, doing and saying whatever he liked, no matter how inconsiderate it was.

Well, Summer thought, *he's not going to do that with me.*

"Sorry, no," she spat out.

He stopped. "What did you say?"

"You heard me. I'm not like everyone else. I'm not going to just jump because Lord Lachart, or whatever, tells me I have to."

His brow knitted. "I'm not—" He shook his head. "Look. It's getting dark. We need to get back before—"

"Then go. Leave me here. I'd rather make friends with the stag who wanted to gore my eyes out than go with you. *That's* how pleasant your company is."

He let out a sour, mirthless laugh. "Fire on! Go right ahead, with my blessing!" He waved her off and turned. "Don't come crying to me when you're dead from your stupid mistakes."

He stalked off, his strides surer and faster than ever. Before long, he disappeared out of view between the trees.

"*Don't come crying to me when you're dead from your stupid mistakes!*" she mimicked in an overly exaggerated Scottish brogue that sounded nothing like him.

He's not going to leave me, she thought defiantly, noticing a nearby boulder. She sat down on it to wait for him to come back. *He can't. If he kills me, I'm not going to pay him for my stay.*

She stood there for a moment, shivering and watching the spot where she'd finally lost track of him.

The minutes stretched on, feeling like hours. She gnawed on her lip.

OK, so maybe he isn't *coming back.*

Above her, rather close by, a bird of some kind cried out, again and again. It sounded like a banshee. Each cry seemed to shout, *Beware! Beware! Beware!*

Finally, she could take it no longer. "Hugh!" she cried, running as fast as she could toward the edge of the woods.

When she broke free of the trees, she thought she'd see nothing but bogs and descending darkness. A fine mist was beginning to settle over the ground, like a blanket.

There, in the middle of it, she saw Hugh, standing absolutely motionless, facing away from her. She heaved a sigh of relief and went to join him.

She was about to thank him for waiting when she realised something.

The quad bike was no longer there.

Actually, it *was*. She could see the handlebars and the seat peeking out from the black, murky waters. But most of it had been submerged in the thick bog.

"Oh," she said, unable to think of anything else.

"Aye," he sighed. "Aye, that feels appropriate."

"Can we get it out?"

He shook his head solemnly.

"Then how do we get home?"

"We don't. Not tonight, anyway. It's getting too dark."

She hugged herself, shivering, until she thought of the last words he'd said to her. *Don't come crying to me when you're dead from your stupid mistakes!*

She tucked her hands behind her back, and traced a line on the ground with a tip of her boot. "That's some *mistake*, parking the bike there, huh?"

He didn't respond for a while, but when he did, his voice wasn't full of bluster, as it usually was. He nodded. "Aye," he admitted. "It was that, alright."

Well. At least he could admit it.

She grabbed her phone and checked it to see if there was any reception from this point on the island.

There wasn't. Of course, there wasn't.

"So… what do we do?" she asked him.

He hefted his pack onto his back. "We've got no choice. We set up camp," he told her. "We'll find our way back in the morning."

16

JERKY WITH THE JERK

The night became increasingly cold and damp, even before the sun had fully set. By the time they found a spot that Hugh declared dry enough to camp on, it was positively frigid.

Summer helped him pile up a few scattered branches and sat on a boulder as she watched him strike a bit of flint to start the fire. The wind, which seemed to come from every direction, kept killing whatever sparks he managed to create. Finally, though, he managed to get a small fire going. The heat was so welcome, she leaned into it, rubbing her hands and stamping her feet to let the warmth work its way through to her bones.

"Thank goodness you had that survival kit," she said to him as she helped him feed kindling into the fire. "You must get in situations like this a lot, huh? Where you have to live off the land?"

He frowned into the fire, the golden light casting serious shadows across his face. "I generally try to avoid that sort of thing. It's dangerous out here at night."

She swallowed and looked around as she hugged her knees to her chest. "Because of the stags?"

"Among other things."

She wanted to ask what those other things were, but he stood up and started to go through the pack. Maybe it was best that she didn't know; she was nervous enough as it was after the stag incident.

He took out a sleeping bundle and tossed it to her. She'd only been half-alert, thinking about killer deer, and it smacked her in the side of the face.

"Uh—thanks?" When he sat down on the ground, she added, "What about you?"

He stared into the fire. "I've only got one bag. You better take it."

"But maybe we could—"

"You take it, I said."

There was that hard, scary bark again, the kind that usually ended all conversations.

She felt silly as she untied the cords on the bag. She wasn't planning on inviting him to sleep *with* her. She just thought that maybe they could unzip it and lay it flat so neither of them would be sleeping with their heads in the mud.

But forget it, if that's the way you want to play it, she thought, unfurling the bag and laying it out flat. Like quad-biking, sleeping outdoors wasn't high on her list of must-dos, either, but the bag was plenty thick and warm, so at least she'd be cosy. She unlaced her boots, pulled them off, and climbed in.

She tried to get comfortable, but the ground was so hard, and those little bugs—what had he called them? Midges?—had tracked her down, and were trying to drive her crazy with their itching.

Grimacing and scratching, she turned onto her side and found Hugh staring at the fire, gnawing away on something.

On cue, her stomach growled. Her mouth watered. It felt like ages since that cauliflower curry soup.

"Um, what are you eating?" she asked, leaning forward on an elbow.

"Nothing for you, I'm afraid," he said, curtly.

She screwed up her face. *Ugh. Such a jerk!*

She collected herself before the words could slip out. After all, he *had* given her his sleeping bag, so she didn't want to seem ungrateful.

"Am I supposed to starve?"

He held up a long strip of dark meat. "Guess you will. Because this is all I have."

Beef jerky. She'd had it before, when she was younger. It wasn't vegetarian, of course. Not remotely. Still, she found her mouth watering even more.

Unable to take it any longer, she sat up. "Could I have a taste?"

He looked at her, mock-horrified. "No. I'd hate you to go against your principles."

"Well, actually," she said, glancing around sheepishly, as if she was worried there was someone else around who might hear her confessing. "Technically, I'm only a vegetarian *most* of the time. I can eat meat. Sometimes. Rarely. *Very* rarely. But sometimes."

Hugh narrowed his eyes at her. "Aye? After all that hooting and hollering about the black pudding?"

"I said I can eat *meat*," she said, then she shuddered at the thought of the blood sausage. "That wasn't meat."

Hugh shook his head, sighed, and tossed her a piece of his jerky.

She sat up and greedily tore off a bite, then chewed it slowly. Wow. It was so good. Definitely the best beef jerky she'd ever had.

Although, since it was also only the second beef jerky she'd ever had, this wasn't really saying much.

"Thank you," she muttered through a mouthful of the dried meat. "This is delicious."

"I take it that boyfriend of yours never got you jerky, eh? Sounds a bit questionable to me, a man who can't provide the finer things in life, like a good dried meat."

She shook her head, smiling sadly.

Hugh grunted. "Still, I'm sure he's the type who showers you with flowers and jewellery and chocolate and all that stuff."

She swallowed at the thought of her last birthday. The truth was, Brad had forgotten it, until she'd reminded him.

It was not the first time, either. He'd always laugh it off and say something like, "You know how I am, babe. I'm bad with dates."

But how hard was it to set a reminder? He literally had his phone in his hand twenty-four hours a day, seven days a week. If she mattered to him, he'd have made a point of remembering.

Then again, if she'd mattered to him, he probably wouldn't have dumped her on their wedding day and run off with her best friend, either.

"You never did those things for your wife?" she asked, neatly evading the question.

"Aye, I suppose I did," he said, almost wistfully. He stared into the flames. "A long time ago."

She could see the pain darkening his face, so she decided it was better not to pursue the topic any further. "Lola's great, isn't she?" she said, making a clumsy lane shift into a different conversation. "She's a really great kid."

Hugh blinked, surprised by the sudden conversational detour. "Eh, aye. Aye, and despite being saddled with me for a father, too. It's really quite impressive. I do everything wrong, and yet she's still a good person. She must get it from her mother."

Summer smiled. "I'm sure you're more responsible for it than you think."

He shrugged. "I don't know. I suppose it'd be easier if she'd been a boy. I know what to do with boys. What they need. Boys are easy. But with Lola, I'm always having to guess."

"I suppose that's only natural," she said. She was just waiting for him to close this topic of conversation down. She could tell by the deep creases that appeared on his forehead that it was difficult for him. She smiled kindly at him. "Shoe on the other foot, I don't think I'd have much luck raising a boy on my own, either."

He shook his head. "I'm sure you'd be grand. Women have a motherly instinct. I'm not sure men have it the same. Sarah, she..." He swallowed with some difficulty, and it looked like he was having trouble coming up with the words. "She always wanted a child. A lot of children, actually. Dozens. I wanted to make her happy. She died during childbirth. She never even got to hold Lola. Not once.

"Oh. God. That's..." Summer began, but she stopped there. There weren't words for how awful it was. None she could think of in that moment, at least.

"I love her to bits, of course. Lola, I mean," Hugh continued. "And I can't even imagine a day without her, but..."

He lowered his gaze to the fire. Wetness glowed in his eyes, but if they were tears, he blinked them away.

"It's OK," Summer whispered. "It's fine."

Hugh let out a tortured breath. "I'm just sorry that Lola

wants the things I can't seem to give her. I used to travel. Sarah and I, we both did. But after she died, I just... I settled here. Completely. And I've never left. Lola wants so badly to spread her wings and go places. I don't want her to. This is where we fit. Where we're safe. Our home. And she loves it here. She does, but..."

But the poor girl will never know what else is out there unless you let her go, Summer thought, but she didn't say it out loud. She didn't dare, for fear it would break him completely.

"I'm not sure I've fit in anywhere since my father died," she admitted.

She blinked in surprise at the words tumbling out of her mouth. She'd never told anyone that before. Brad wasn't exactly one for deep conversation. Or any conversation, for that matter, that wasn't about him.

What *did* she ever see in him?

"I live in Los Angeles," Summer continued. "Surrounded by the rich and the glamorous, but that's never really been me."

"No?" Hugh moved his pack to the side and stretched out across from her, resting his head on it.

"No, but it's a big world. And you'll never really know where you fit in unless you get out and explore some of it. Right?"

He grimaced, like she was confirming some unpleasant truth he already knew. "I suppose."

"Are you..." she ventured, not sure she wanted to be turned down again. "Are you sure you don't want to lie on this bag? It's probably more comfortable. Warmer, too."

To her surprise, he sat up and then crawled over to her. Together, they unzipped the bag and lay out, side by side. He let her have the side closer to the fire, but even so, it was still freezing.

She shivered, then gasped when he drew her closer, pulling

her gently in against him. There was nothing romantic in it, she thought, just his usual pragmatic practicality. That was it. That was all it was.

Wasn't it?

They lay there, her back pressed against him as they tried to get warm. It helped, having him so close, feeling the heat of his body next to hers. She told herself again that this definitely wasn't romantic. Not in the least. It wasn't a date, it was a survival situation.

And yet, she couldn't deny that she liked the woodsy, earthy smell of him, and the soft caress of his breath against her cheek.

His strong arms were around her, holding her closer, and she listened to the rhythm of his soft breathing. Despite the cold, and the thought of a psychotic, murderous giant stag that might come bearing down on them at any moment, she felt content.

Hopelessly, blissfully content.

"You know, Hugh," she said, her voice barely a whisper. "It's crazy, considering everything we've been through since I got here. But somehow... I don't know why... I can't explain it. I just feel safe here. Like, I don't know. Like... like home. You know?"

She held her breath in anticipation of his response. The silence dragged on, and it seemed like he was possibly contemplating what to say. Probably trying to decide between, 'You don't belong here,' or 'Don't talk shite.'

Or maybe he was going to tell her he knew exactly what she meant.

"Hugh?" she whispered. "Did you hear what I said?"

But then, over the crackling of the campfire, she heard the softest of snores, and she realised he had already fallen fast asleep.

17

UNWANTED VISITORS

S ummer wriggled in bed, enjoying those final few moments of not quite being fully awake. It was always a wonderful feeling, waking up in the arms of the man you loved.

Although... she couldn't remember it ever being this cold in L.A. before.

She ran her fingers down Brad's chest and found a button there. That was weird.

Since when did Brad wear anything in bed? He usually slept in the nude, and would stop to admire his reflection in the mirror every night before he got into bed.

And then again every morning, when he got back out of it.

And he usually smelled like a combination of suntan lotion and citrus, not woods, fresh air, and campfire.

Her eyes flew open as it came to her.

She wasn't in her bed at home.

She wasn't in a bed at all, for that matter.

She lay there motionless, taking in her position. The side of her head was resting on a firm chest. She had one leg thrown over two strong, muscular ones, and her breasts were squashed up against a ribcage.

She was curled around Hugh like she was a boa constrictor, trying to squeeze the life out of him. And maybe she had. His body was warm, and yet strangely motionless.

Her mind raced back to the night before. Had they...?

No. No, of course they hadn't! They'd huddled together for warmth, that was all. There was nothing more to it. Hugh didn't like her *in that way*.

In fact, she was pretty sure he didn't like her in any other way, either. He'd made that pretty clear over the course of her stay so far. Although, to be fair, she *had* almost killed him.

Maybe even twice.

And yet, here she was now, wrapped around him like a cheap coat.

She swallowed the bitter taste in her mouth from last night's jerky.

He had to be dead. He had to be. Given how much her existence seemed to annoy him, there was no way he'd let her curl up next to him and use him as a pillow.

She thought back to her pillows at home, and a horrible thought struck her.

Oh, God, am I drooling?

She licked her bottom lip.

Yes. Yes, she was very much drooling.

Maybe he wouldn't notice. Especially if he was dead. He definitely wouldn't notice then.

Letting out an uneasy breath, she raised her eyes up higher, higher, until she could see his face. He was lying there, eyes wide open and staring to the sky as if he'd been awake for hours. And yet, in all that time, he hadn't moved a muscle.

She sprung up and off him. "I'm sorry. Oh, gosh, I am so—"

Her face burned with embarrassment, but he didn't seem to notice.

"You were sleeping. I didn't want to wake you," he said, still not moving from his position.

She noticed him eyeing a damp spot on his shirt. She hurriedly wiped at her mouth before he could spot the string of drool.

"What do you mean? You were happy to wake me up yesterday morning at the crack of dawn."

"Aye. And you looked bloody knackered."

She adjusted her jacket over herself and raked her hair back from her face. "OK, well, I'm awake now. Are we going to head back?"

"You're in a rush?"

Summer squinted at him. Until now, he'd been the one hurrying her on at every opportunity. Now, he seemed content just to lie there on the cold, stony ground.

"No. It's just—" She scratched at her arms and neck, where the midges were having a field day. "I want to get back before these bugs devour me."

Hugh yawned, then sat up and began to throw their things together. "Aye, fair enough. We're going. I'll leave the quad here until I can get a couple of men to come with me to tow it out. Will you be okay to hike back? It'll be a few hours."

"Do I have a choice?"

Hugh looked around and shrugged. "No. Not really," he admitted.

"That's fine," she said, scraping her hair back into a ponytail. "Bring it on. I'm ready."

Hugh shot her a curious sort of look, then nodded, picked up the pack, and swung it onto his back.

"Alright then," he announced. "In that case, off we go."

THE HIKE BACK to the castle wasn't exactly pleasant, but it wasn't too strenuous, since it was mostly downhill. It helped, too, that Hugh didn't rush ahead like he was leading a race.

Though they didn't talk much, every once in a while, he'd stop to show her a place where you could see the best sunsets, or a tree that he'd fallen from as a child, or a field that came alive with purple splashes of lavender in the hottest summer months.

She quickly came to realise that, not only did he know the castle like the back of his hand, he knew the whole island in the same way. It was charming, the way he spoke of everything, and it was clear that he loved every inch of this place.

Each time he showed her something, he would look back at her for a response. She couldn't help thinking that he seemed a bit disappointed. No matter how much she fawned about the beauty of this place, he'd only grunt, as if that wasn't the reaction he had been hoping for.

"Over there is the cove where we'd go to catch fish for dinner, back when the castle was full of guests," he said, pointing down an incline to a secluded swath of beach. They were walking through a field of yellow grass that was almost as tall as Summer. She had to stand on her tiptoes to see what he was pointing to. "Been a long time since then," he muttered.

"Ah!" she said excitedly. She even applauded this time, because she'd already used every positive descriptive word she could think of. "Bravo!"

He looked back at her, his face a picture of confusion.

She smiled, gently cleared her throat, then stopped clapping. It was probably overkill.

"It's hard to believe that the castle, that this island, was once full of guests," she said. "I mean, it's lovely, don't get me wrong, but it's so... quiet."

"Wasn't always like this. Used to be hoaching with people. We had to turn them away. A lot of them were looking for that lily. But—" He stopped at a spot overlooking the valley and put one foot on a giant boulder there. "I do like the peace and quiet. So, as bad as it is that we don't have the money to fix up the place the way I'd like to, for selfish reasons I can't say I mind the remoteness. It might be good for Lola to meet people from outside, though."

"I guess so," Summer said.

"Oh, I have no doubt. Look how much she's learned in the past two days, just knowing you," he said.

Summer snorted. "She learned that Americans complain a lot," she said with a smile.

"Aye, well," he waved that away. "Don't worry. You don't complain nearly as much as some."

She smiled. "Why did you leave? Why did you go to Inverness, if you like it here so much?"

"Uni. That's what most kids who grow up here do. At the time, I fully intended to never come back. But then suddenly it was just me, and a bairn, and I couldn't handle it alone." He stopped and held out a hand to her. She stared at it, confused, until he motioned to the boulder. "Up you go."

Curious, she put her hand in his, trying to ignore how nice, how warm it was, and how reassuringly safe it felt having his fingers wrapped around hers. He helped her up to the top of the boulder, and she looked over the valley, gasping. There, past the rolling green hills studded with rocks, was the castle. The sea glimmered and shone like diamonds around it. The whole thing looked like a picture on a postcard.

"Gorgeous!" She fumbled for her phone, only to find it dead. "Damn. I have to come back here to take this picture."

"You have to take a photograph of everything you like?" he asked, as he helped her down.

"Of course. How else would you remember it?"

He tapped the side of his temple. "This works well for that. The important things you're apt to remember anyway, if they mean enough to you."

She had to admit, he was right. Truthfully, she hadn't tried to take that photograph so that she'd always remember it, it was to post online so that *he* could see where she'd been, so she could prove her life had gone on just fine without him.

Even without the photo, Summer knew she'd remember the moment just fine.

She stuffed the phone into her bag, and they walked the rest of the way in a surprisingly comfortable silence.

When they emerged from the high yellow grass, the beating of a helicopter's rotors could be heard in the distance. It seemed to grow louder and louder until it appeared on the horizon. Hugh stopped and watched it get closer, the frown on his face growing.

"New guests?" Summer asked hopefully.

Once again, he was back to the old Hugh—he grunted. When the helicopter was hovering over the castle and began descending, Hugh let out a muffled curse and broke into a run.

No way could she keep up with that. "Where are you—"

"I'll meet you back at the castle!" he called over his shoulder.

"Uh, OK. Fine!" she called after him, though she was miffed by his sudden disappearance.

Still, it *was* fine, she thought. She could find her way back from there. And, as far as she knew, there were no mutant stags lying in wait to gore her eyes out.

Probably.

But, would it have really hurt for him to wait ten minutes for her?

She trudged on, picking up the pace, determined not to fall too far behind him. Still, even at that speed, it took her the better part of twenty minutes to make it back to the castle.

When she finally reached it, she saw the helicopter parked out on the front lawn. There wasn't a pilot, or anyone else to be seen, though.

She heard muffled voices from one of the side rooms as she stepped inside, and though she was curious, she thought it best to head straight up to her room. Whatever was happening, it was none of her business.

Besides, she had her own problems.

Well, just one problem, currently, but it was a big one.

A few minutes later, she stood naked and alone in front of the steampunk shower from hell. She'd waded through mud, clambered through heather and bracken, slept on the ground, and had just trudged about five sweaty miles. She'd never gone this long without a shower, even at the best of times. Now, after everything she'd been through, she smelled so bad she could practically see the stink rising off her in wobbly cartoon lines.

You can do this, she told herself through gritted teeth. *You can get this done!*

She braced herself, said a silent prayer to any and all gods that happened to be listening, then threw the lever to ON.

A compressed jet of icy water practically sandblasted her skin. It stole almost all of her breath away, leaving her just enough with which to scream.

Every instinct—every pore of her body—told her to jump clear, to get out, to run from this nightmare contraption.

But, no. No way. Not today.

Still breathlessly screaming, she managed to shampoo her hair and wash her body in a record twenty-eight seconds.

Job done, she launched herself clear of the blasting water spray, skidded gracelessly across the bathroom floor, then slammed, face-first, into the door.

Grabbing for a towel, she wrapped herself up like a burrito, trapping what little body heat she had left inside.

Slowly, her breathing returned to normal.

She realised she was still screaming, and quickly stopped.

Her blood rushed through her veins, warming her. As it did, she felt a sense of near-euphoria. She'd survived the shower. Not only that, in some strange, perverse way, she'd actually enjoyed it!

And that, she thought, pretty much summed up her whole experience of the island so far. It had been mostly terrible. She should've hated every minute. And yet...

Smiling as she slipped into fresh jeans and a T-shirt, she had a momentary urge to do a write-up of last night and this morning for her blog. Her audience would love it, she was sure. They'd pore over every word.

But then, she thought about what Hugh had said. Some things weren't for anyone else. Maybe he was right. Maybe last night could be just for her.

For both of them.

As she finished finger-combing her hair, she heard the helicopter again. She looked up in time to see it rise over the battlements of the castle, and go sweeping off toward the mainland. Scuffing into her ballet flats, she went downstairs to see what was on her list of activities for the day.

And, she had to admit, to see Hugh again.

She stopped outside the dining room when she heard the sound of sobbing coming from within.

Summer peered in to see Lola sitting in one of the chairs, her face buried in her arms on the table. She looked tiny in the tall-backed chair—far smaller than she'd ever looked to Summer before.

Hugh and Duncan were there, one sitting on either side. Her father was leaning over her, whispering, "We'll figure it out, Lo. We will. I promise."

So, whoever the helicopter visitor had been, Hugh had been right to be worried.

Summer had never done well at being the only person who didn't know a secret. She cleared her throat to get their attention. "Uh, is everything okay?"

All eyes turned to her. Lola gasped. To Summer's surprise, the little girl rushed to her and threw her arms around her, burying her face in Summer's T-shirt.

"It can't happen!" Lola blubbered noisily.

Summer smoothed her hair back and looked up at the men. Hugh's expression was as astonished as Summer felt.

"No, of course not," she whispered. "Why don't you tell me what all this is about, and I'll—"

"It's none of your concern," Hugh barked.

Duncan nudged his son. "There's no point hiding it from her, either, boy," he said with a shake of his head. Then he turned to Summer, and when he spoke, all of that mischievous sparkle was gone. "The folks in the helicopter were representatives of a Chinese property development firm. They want to buy the castle and turn it into a private holiday retreat for the company's owner."

Summer's mouth fell open. "Oh. I see."

"The sale, unfortunately," Duncan said, solemnly, "will

include the entire island, which is legally part of the castle grounds."

Hugh dragged both hands down his face. Apparently, he'd decided that his father was right, and it didn't matter who knew anymore, because he added, "So it won't just be us losing our home. It'll be everyone."

"Oh, no," Summer said, now understanding why Lola was crying so hard. This was terrible. It was all she knew. Their home.

"Grandpa, you need to stop it," Lola wailed into Summer's shirt. "Somehow!"

"But what choice do we have?" Duncan said, going over to Lola and patting her back. He sounded uncharacteristically despondent. Was it really just yesterday morning that they'd been dancing happily about in the kitchen? "The castle is falling to pieces. The tourism industry has collapsed. We've been losing money right along, lass. We just can't afford not to sell. We can't."

"But there has to be some way," Summer said, and Lola looked up at her, eyes full of tears, but now edged with hope.

"Right! The Lachart Lily!"

"Now, Lola," Hugh warned, his voice hard.

"It's true! If we find it, everything will be OK! And I bet I can! I bet I can find it," she said, disentangling herself from Summer's embrace. Before anyone could make a move to stop her, she turned and went rushing out through the main door.

"Lola! Come back here!" Hugh cried, but she paid him no heed. Faraway, there was the sound of the castle's front door opening and closing.

Hugh growled something under his breath and took off after her, leaving Summer alone with Duncan.

"It's terrible," Summer said, shifting awkwardly from foot to foot and fiddling with her fingers. "I'm so sorry."

"Thank you, lass," Duncan said with a thin smile. "But, it's not all bad news. Come with me," he told her. "I have something I'd very much like to show you."

18

LOST CHILDHOOD

"What is it?" Summer said as she followed Duncan down a long hallway that hadn't been part of Lola's castle tour.

Like his son, Duncan didn't answer. Must've been a MacGregor family trait. Instead, he looked back at her, smiling a cryptic smile that left her none the wiser.

A particularly *annoying* MacGregor family trait.

Duncan creaked open a door, and they stepped into a small, dark room full of books and papers that were piled haphazardly all over the furniture. It took some time, but eventually, she noticed the large oak desk in the middle of the chaos.

"Oh," she said, glancing at one of the old books. "Is this your study?"

"It is the Laird of Lachart's study, aye," he said, going behind the mess that had once been a desk. "It was my father's before me. When I pass on, it'll be Hugh's." His face fell as a horrible truth dawned on him. "Or, it would've been," he muttered, then he shook his head, brightening again. "Anyway, this is what I wanted you to see."

He lifted a giant scrapbook from the top of a pile, triggering an avalanche of paperwork below it, which he didn't bother even trying to catch. He passed her the book, opening it up to a series of colour photographs that were faded and tattered around the edges.

She squinted at the first one—a picture of a man with a little girl, riding piggyback, along a long stretch of beach that looked like the one she and Hugh had passed earlier that day. The subjects of the photograph looked so happy, smiling open-mouthed, the girl's long auburn braid flapping as they ran.

She looked familiar, but Summer couldn't quite place where she'd seen her before.

"Who...?" she began, then she stopped when the answer clicked into place. She stared down, wide-eyed, her fingers trembled on the pages. "Oh, my God."

"Aye," Duncan said. "That's you, lass."

Her eyes welled with tears as she touched the photo of her father, tracing her fingers over his face. The only photos she'd seen of him before were staid, posed things, as lifeless as he now was.

But this? This showed him in a whole new light. So happy, so vivid, so very alive that she barely even recognized him.

"Yes," she wheezed, breathing like she'd taken a kick to the stomach from an angry mule. "I think—"

Her eyes fell further down the page, and she let out a gasp. There were even more photos of him.

Standing in front of the castle, beaming with delight. Walking shirtless, his tanned chest glistening in the sun, as he strolled the path among the same tall grasses she'd walked earlier that day. Excitedly pointing to some plant that only botanists like himself would be even remotely interested in.

Turning the page, she let out a yelp, and pointed at the

photograph of a tall, red and white striped tower. It was exactly as she remembered it. Exactly as she had pictured it for all these years.

"The Helter Skelter!" she blurted excitedly. "That's it! I remember this! I knew it was here!"

Duncan laughed. "Helter Skelter? It's the Bluff's Lighthouse, on the other side of the island."

"I totally remember it," she murmured, looking closer at the photograph. Her handsome father, with his reddish beard and thick curls, his slim, athletic frame, standing beside her, holding her hand.

And then, suddenly, she was back there, looking up at it from her child's point of view, being guided by the hand through the weeds around the lighthouse, listening to him explaining how misunderstood they all were. How special they were, and how strong. Just like she was.

"I remember," Summer whispered, tracing her fingers over the photos. "I remember this."

She flipped another page and the floodgates of her memory opened. All at once, she was running down the beach with him, or sitting on a jetty, throwing fishing lines into the calm, midnight sea, or writing their names in the sand with sticks they'd found floating by the shore. Pieces of the trip seemed to swim up from the depths of her mind with every photo she looked at.

"This is amazing," she murmured, unable to tear her eyes away. She felt like an explorer at the end of a long journey, finding the thing she'd been seeking all her life. She pointed to the castle. "I remember it, now. I used to sit on that rug in front of the big fireplace in the entryway. I was friends with another kid. He was older, maybe a teenager. I had *such* a crush on him!

I'd play games with him. Pick-up sticks. Jacks. Hide and seek. And—"

She froze.

Her eyes met Duncan's, and saw that his twinkle had returned, and his face was lit up by a mischievous grin. But there was also something else in his expression, like he was holding a secret.

"Who was he?" she asked. "Who was that boy?"

Duncan pointed to the book, then flipped to the very last page. Sure enough, there was that little five-year-old girl with the auburn braid, arms thrown around an older, lanky boy who looked like he was about to launch into a growth spurt, all skinny arms and legs, with a mop of cinnamon hair. They were laughing with gap-toothed smiles, as if they couldn't possibly be happier.

She shook her head, almost unable to believe it. And yet, despite the years that had passed since then, there was no mistaking who it was standing next to her in that photograph.

"Oh, my God," she whispered, her eyes fastened on the picture. "Are you saying that the boy I used to play with is...?"

Duncan laughed. "Aye! That lanky wee nyaff," he said with a grin, "is Hugh."

Summer clasped a hand over her mouth, hardly able to believe it. And yet, somehow, it made perfect sense. No wonder she'd wanted to come to this island. No wonder she felt like something had been calling her here all this time. She was meant to be here. But why?

Summer didn't have to think long before she had the answer.

"Duncan, you know what this means, don't you?"

He raised an eyebrow. "That you two can stop all your argy-bargy and friends? Well, I maybe wouldn't pin too many hopes on that, I'm afraid. Hugh already knows. I believe he *has* known."

"What do you mean?"

"I showed him this photo book before I showed it to you, and he didn't seem interested at all. He said, 'That was a long time ago.' Truth be told, I got the feeling he already knew exactly who you were before I'd showed him."

At first, she couldn't believe that was true. But as she stood there, it all gelled. That was why he'd been looking at her strangely, showing her things and trying to gauge her reaction. He was trying to jog her memory, to see if any of this struck a bell.

"Oh," she said, standing up and closing the book firmly. *Then why did he keep it a secret?* "I guess he's right. It was a long time ago. I barely remember any of it. But I do remember my father. So, thank you for that. It's lovely to see him so... alive."

Duncan bowed. "You're very welcome, lass."

Summer passed the book back to him. "But, Hugh said something earlier. He said you remember the important things, even without photographs. And I do. I remember my dad. I remember the memories we made here. They're all tied to the island."

"Aye, well, I'm very glad to—"

"I'm not finished!" Summer said, cutting him off. If she didn't say the next part now, she'd chicken out. She took a deep breath. "That's why you can't sell this castle. I won't let you. I refuse."

Duncan blinked, and his mouth formed a little circle of surprise. It lingered for a few moments, then became a kindly smile of apology.

He held up a stack of papers with red OVERDUE stamps on them.

"Oh, I'd love to agree to that, lass, but I don't think we've got much choice. Either we sell the place, or we go bankrupt and lose everything, anyway."

"Don't worry about that," Summer said. She drew herself up to her full height, pushed back her shoulders, and stuck out her chest. "I have a plan!"

19

BUZZKILT

Summer paced up and down alongside the dining table, trying to compose her thoughts. What had started as the seed of an idea had bloomed, and now her mind whirled with possibilities.

Once they saw it was the only way, she was sure they'd go for it. She just had to calmly communicate her ideas to the family, instead of babbling nonsensically like she usually did whenever she was excited or nervous about something.

And right now, she was both. Everywhere she went now, everywhere she looked, a fragment of a memory popped up. No wonder this table had looked so familiar. Now, she could easily remember her father, Callum Rose, jokingly groaning and grunting as he pulled the chair out, remarking that they "Should put wheels on these things." No wonder the scenery out the window piqued something in her. Yes, it was beautiful, but it was more than that. It had felt like home.

And it *was* a home for Duncan, Hugh, and Lola. And she was determined that it was going to stay that way.

When Hugh strode into the room, she couldn't help but see

bits and pieces of that skinny little boy she'd played with on the rug outside. His expressive eyebrows, the shape of his face, his eyes that were once a whole lot less weary, but still just as startlingly blue. Now that she thought about it, she'd always known he'd grow up to be handsome, even with his gawky, bird-like limbs and puny chest.

His eyes locked on hers, holding her gaze, and narrowed. He wasn't thinking the same thing, about how much more beautiful she'd gotten over the years. No, his expression clearly said, *How the hell can you possibly help matters here?*

And maybe he was right. Maybe she couldn't do anything.

But she had to try.

"Sit, sit, sit," she said when they were all assembled. "I'll explain my plan. I'll warn you, it might sound a little, you know, crazy... But, once you realise that the only other option is selling, I think you'll agree."

Lola clapped her hands. "I'll do it! I don't care! If it can save our castle, I'll do anything!"

"Will you tidy your room?" Hugh grunted.

Lola flinched. "*Almost* anything," she said, then she slapped a hand down on the table. "No, you know what? I'll even do that!"

Summer smiled at the little girl. She was grateful for the support, but she'd always known Lola would be all-in. It was a certain *other* person at the table who she knew would be more difficult to convince.

"OK, so here it is. Here goes. We use..." She paused for dramatic effect.

It worked for Lola, whose eyes bugged out, and on Duncan, who moved to the edge of the seat. But Hugh, sitting at the head of the table, remained completely impassive.

Ignoring him, she held her hands up and made enormous air quotes.

"The internet."

She didn't quite get the reaction she was looking for—even from Lola, whose freckled nose scrunched.

"How do you mean?" she asked.

"The internet?" Duncan repeated, saying the words slowly, like he was testing them out for the first time.

Hugh didn't miss a beat. "No," he said, already starting to get up from his chair.

She frowned at him. "Alright, Mr. Buzzkilt!" she said. She paused, just for a moment, hoping someone would appreciate the clever wordplay. If they did, they didn't let on. "Why not?"

"Because..." Hugh began, exaggerating the word as if what he was about to say was blindingly obvious.

It obviously wasn't *that* obvious, though, even to him, because he stopped there, adding nothing.

"Because you don't understand it?" Summer guessed. "Tough luck. That's not a good enough reason. I'm telling you, any business will tell you that the key to getting customers is by going on the web."

"What, like a spider?" Duncan asked, his bushy eyebrows almost meeting above his nose.

"Dad," Hugh ejected, silencing the old man. He turned back to Summer. "We are on the web. We got that Travelo-whatever thing set up. Cost us a bloody fortune, I might add."

Lola wrinkled her nose. "Aye, but you never update it, Dad," she said. "You told me you can't even remember the password."

Hugh waved her off.

"Oh, *that* internet?" Duncan said, finally joining them on the same page. "Oh, I'm not sure about that. I've heard the internet can be a dangerous place." He leaned in and shielded his mouth from Lola as he whispered, "For the wee ones."

Lola heard every word of it. "I'm not wee!" she protested.

"Aye, you are," Hugh said.

"You're tiny," Duncan agreed.

"OK, aye, I'm small, but I'm not a child!" Lola said. She corrected herself before either man had a chance to. "OK, technically I am, but I'm not an eejit!"

Hugh and Duncan said nothing. They couldn't really argue with that.

Summer quickly intervened. "You're right, Duncan."

Duncan looked surprised. "I am?" He pulled himself together, and nodded confidently. "Aye. I am!"

"The internet can be dangerous," Summer continued. "But my plan isn't. I promise. It's just going to bring a lot of good, positive publicity to the island."

Hugh didn't want to ask, she could tell. But he also couldn't help himself.

"How?"

"It's actually pretty simple," Summer said. "Travelers with lots of money to spend are constantly seeking out new and more interesting places to visit. And this place—Lachart Isle—it's exactly the sort of thing they're looking for. It's, like, Instagram Heaven, but people don't know about it. So, we just have to get the word out."

Hugh sat back and snorted. "Oh, is that all we have to do, is it? Tell people? God, why have we never thought of that before?" He shook his head and laughed bitterly. "Sorry to break it to you, lass, but someone already came up with the same plan decades ago. I believe they called it 'marketing.'"

She glared at him. "I'm not talking about a listing on Travelocity, or a few adverts in magazines. I'm talking about hosting a big, eye-catching event that will result in billions of social media views. I'm talking about making this place go viral." She shrugged. "After that, you'll have more visitors than you know what to do with."

"Viral?" Duncan muttered, looking worried. "I thought you said this plan of yours wasn't dangerous? I'm not wanting us all catching something."

Lola patted his arm. "Not that sort of viral, Grandpa."

"An eye-catching event?" Hugh asked, ignoring his father's concerns. From his tone, he clearly didn't like the sounds of it.

"That's right," Summer confirmed. "To attract the right kind of people. Social media influencers."

Hugh grimaced. "In what possible world are social media influencers 'the right kind of people'?"

"In the kind of world where you need visitors," Summer countered.

"Aye, but no' a shower of arses who spend their lives behind a camera, going, 'Look at me! Look at me!'"

"They'll also be saying, 'Look at this island. Come here. Spend your cash.'" Summer pointed out. She shot him a pleading look. "It'll work. Trust me."

Hugh folded his arms over his chest. "I don't want a load of awful outsiders swarming here."

Summer put her hands on her hips and stared him down. "Am I awful?"

"Sometimes," he muttered under his breath.

Duncan threw himself into the line of fire before things could escalate.

"All right, all right. So, let me get this straight. You think if we do this big thing, then all these social people will come here, and spend money?"

"I do," Summer told him.

Duncan looked around at the faded tapestries and thread-bare carpet.

"Is it maybe no' a bit... rustic for them sort of new-fangled folks?"

"Maybe," Summer answered honestly, looking around.

Audriandra would probably be looking for the spa, just like she had been, and would be even more disappointed than she was not to find one.

"But if we can work together and spruce this place up a little. Market it as quaint and charming, and an experience unlike the normal spa vacation in the tropics, I think people would be interested."

She was trying to ignore Hugh's eye daggers, but they made it through her defences when he asked, "So, these influencers, would one of them be your complicated boyfriend, by any chance?"

Summer took a step back as the thought of her ex hit her like a punch to the chest.

Oddly, she hadn't actually thought about Brad for most of the day. Not once, and certainly not in 'boyfriend' terms.

Lola's head swung to Summer, eyes wide in horror. "You have a boyfriend?"

"No, I wasn't planning to ask—"

"She does," Hugh said, arms crossed. "She told me that he—"

"For the last time," Summer snarled, getting annoyed. "We're not together anymore!"

Hugh froze, mid-sentence. They all stared at her as she cleared her throat, smoothed down her shirt, and collected herself.

"And no," she continued. "I wouldn't be asking him to come. I know of other influencers who have a good following."

Hugh nodded slowly. "Right. OK, then. That's... good," he said. He glanced at Duncan and Lola, who were both staring at him. "And, eh, sorry if I overstepped the mark," he added, quietly.

Summer hesitated, but then gave him a nod. "Apology accepted," she said.

The brief silence that followed was broken when Duncan clapped his hands and rubbed them together.

"Right, then! We have a plan! What do we do first?"

Hugh frowned. "Hold on, Dad. We're not jumping into anything without giving it some more thought. What if these buggers come here, all hate it, and write bad reviews?"

"Well, we'll be in no worse a bloody position than we are now!" Duncan countered.

"And we'll make sure they don't!" Summer said. "We'll have to involve the other islanders to help put on the event, but I can round up the guest list. If we get big enough names, then this place will be crawling with tourists before you know it."

She was sure Hugh grimaced a little at the idea, but she chose to ignore it.

"You really think people would come here?" Lola asked, her eyes dancing with excitement.

Summer nodded. "Absolutely."

"You really think you can get famous people?" the girl gasped.

"Robert Redford?" Hugh and Duncan both asked at the same time.

Summer frowned. "Seriously, what *is* it with you people and Robert Redford?"

"*Internet* famous people," Lola told them, with an air of authority like she was the world's leading expert on the subject. She looked up at Summer, all doe-eyed and hopeful. "Do you really think you can get them?"

"Yes. Yes, I'm sure I can," Summer said, though she sounded less confident about that.

The truth was, she didn't know any of the big influencers. Not really. Not personally. She couldn't just pick up the phone and invite them here directly.

But she did, unfortunately, know someone who could.

20

CALLING LA-LA LAND

With the plan agreed—reluctantly, on Hugh's part— Duncan took Summer back to his study, and rearranged the stacks of books and papers until he found an old-fashioned dial phone buried in one corner.

She'd turned it over, trying to find the buttons, before Duncan had given her a quick tutorial on how to use the big, chunky rotary dial on the front.

"Finger in the number, turn it all the way, let it go back," he explained, then he gave her a double thumbs-up, wished her luck, and retreated out of the room, leaving her to make the call.

Summer opened her phone to get the number, then slowly and carefully began to dial the long number, complete with US country code.

For a long time, there was silence. She'd started to think she'd done it wrong, when she finally heard it ringing.

It rang just once, before it was answered. No real surprise there, of course. Audriandra always had her phone close to hand.

Summer cringed when she heard the familiar, high-pitched strains of her best friend's voice.

She shook her head. *Former* best friend. *Former.*

"Hey, who's this?"

Audriandra sounded as chipper as ever. Of course she did. She was getting married in just a few months. Her perfect life would be complete.

"Yeah. Hi, Aud. It's me. It's Summer."

"O.M.G. No way! Summer?!" Audriandra squealed. "Like, wow, girl! Where have you been?"

Summer opened her mouth to reply, but was quickly cut off.

"Oh, and FYI? It's Audriandra. I'm, like, *so sick* of people shortening it, you know? I'm trying to get them to stop, but it is, like, *such* a struggle! They just don't get it. I mean, how hard is it just to say the whole thing? Am I right? But I'm trying. I'm fighting the fight. It's crazy, I'm kind of like, I don't know, I don't want to say 'Malcolm X,' or something, but I feel kind of like Malcolm X."

Summer rolled her eyes. This was Audriandra all over. It had seemed endearing back in L.A. but, here and now, Summer couldn't quite remember why.

She had brought the name thing on herself, too. She was born Audrey Foxley, but when she was sixteen, she'd had her first name legally changed to Audriandra. Her wealthy entrepreneur parents encouraged it, in the same way they encouraged her many nannies and tutors to give their princess anything she asked for. Anything to make her stand out a little more.

And it'd worked. She'd used all that excess to her advantage. Now, she had millions of followers hanging on her every word, eagerly waiting to see what earrings she'd wear or what blush she'd use. Men had always wanted her—the only difference now was that they wanted her in every country around the world—while a global network of teenage girls all wanted to be her.

There was a time, when Summer was single and Audriandra had been between boyfriends, that they'd been number one on each other's speed dial. But after the wedding-that-wasn't, Summer had blocked her number. She'd only restored it a week later, when Brad had sent her a message: *You didn't block her, did you? Real mature.*

She'd unblocked her right away, feeling guilty.

She, after everything they had done, had been the one to feel guilty.

"Yeah, it sounds rough," Summer said. "Good luck with that."

She had learned long ago that, with Audriandra, it was better to just agree. If you didn't, she'd wind up making an unflattering TikTok video about you. She was big on dancing in a crop-top, all the while calling people out for perceived injustices. The video she'd done on the lady in Starbucks who'd put full-fat milk in her latte had forced the poor woman to move to another state.

And, if the rumours were to be believed, made her teenage children cut all contact with her.

"It's *so* great to *hear* from *you*!" Audriandra gushed, exaggerating every few words, as she usually did. Once again, perhaps with the benefit of distance and time, it all seemed so fake.

But then, of course, it always had been. Audriandra had always been as plastic as could be, and yet, no one cared. If anything, it only made them love her more.

"I *totally* knew you'd call once you got the *invitation*!" she drawled down the line. "You *are* coming, aren't you? Tell me you're coming, girl! It's going to be off the chart awesome!"

From her gushing enthusiasm, it seemed that Audriandra

had forgotten that she'd stolen Summer's husband-to-be right out from under her. Either that, or—more likely—she just didn't care.

She didn't care that she'd humiliated her alleged 'BFF.' She didn't care that the whole world had laughed at Summer's heartbreak, or that Summer had spent that afternoon single-handedly devouring a four-tier wedding cake, while using the veil of her dress as the world's most expensive handkerchief.

She didn't care. Period.

"Yeah, I got the invitation," Summer said.

She went to the window of Duncan's study, only stopping when the cable of the phone went tight. His window faced the same way as the one in her room, and she looked out at the courtyard and the overgrown gardens.

She tried to imagine the rich and fabulous congregating out there. It was, she hated to admit, a stretch.

"What did you think of it?" Audriandra pressed.

Summer frowned. "Of the invitation?"

"Duh! Yes!"

Summer thought back to the email. She'd been more focused on the content than the design. "Yeah. It was nice," she said.

"Ew! Nice?!" Audriandra cried, like Summer had just said something cruel and insulting.

"No, I mean... very nice. Really pretty. Beautiful."

Down the line, she heard her former best friend relaxing a little.

"Did you like the two doves?" Audriandra asked, her enthusiasm quickly surging again. "One has my smile. The other has a tattoo. Did you see? Like the one Brad has? So freaking cute! I saw it, and I was like, *O.M.G. I could just die!*"

Summer allowed herself a moment to enjoy that thought.

She hadn't noticed the doves, though she found herself wondering how she could have missed a dove with Audriandra's big, beaming smile. It wasn't often, after all, that you saw a dove with teeth.

And she did know of Brad's tattoo. On his chest. It was of some Chinese symbols that he was told meant something like, *Live Life to the Fullest.* Summer had never had the heart to tell him that she'd used her translation app on her phone while he was sleeping, and it'd come up as, 'Fried turkey sandwich.'

"Yeah, it was so amazing!" Summer lied. "But anyway, that's not what I'm calling about."

"Oh?" Audriandra sounded surprised. "But, like, do you want to talk about it some more, anyway? I had to pay extra to get the artist to do it right away. He's so talented. But totally worth it."

Of course, she wanted to keep talking about her own subject of choice, regardless of the reason for Summer's call. Audriandra was the centre of her own world, so she expected to be the centre of everyone else's, too.

"Yes, well," Summer began, only to be immediately cut off again.

"Please tell me you're not still sore about that little thing with Brad. I did try to tell you, Summer, that you two weren't right for one another."

"What? No, you didn't!"

Audriandra hesitated. "Didn't I? Shoot. I know I totally meant to say something. I guess I forgot. You know how it is."

Summer gritted her teeth, resisting the urge to get drawn into an argument.

"Yes," she seethed. "Yes, I know how it is. But *anyway*, that's not what I'm calling about, either. I wanted to..." She took a deep breath. "...ask you a favour."

"At five in the morning?"

Summer winced. The time difference. She'd forgotten the time difference! It was 11AM in Scotland. It hadn't occurred to her that it would still be so early back in L.A.

"Um, whoops! Sorry, is that what time it is there?"

"It's fine," Audriandra said. "I've started doing the whole early morning thing, you know? Everyone's doing it. I sleep, like, forty-five minutes a night, max. It's awesome. Gives me *so* much more time to do the important stuff, you know? I totally blast through cardio by six, and last week, I started reading a book. Like, you know, an actual *book*. Crazy, right?"

"Wild," Summer agreed.

"I mean, I have crashed my car, like, four times in nine days, but it's *totally* worth it," Audriandra continued. "Can you imagine if I, like *slept*? Like full-on *slept*? No way I could do all the stuff I need to do. I mean, even today, I've got meetings with my publicist, I need to go shout at the cake decorators, and then I'm doing a photo shoot for my new perfume."

"You have a perfume?" Summer cheeped.

"Oh, yes! Didn't I say? It smells like vanilla and patchouli, and well, me!"

"Sounds… nice," Summer said, then she hastily corrected herself. "Incredible, I mean. It sounds incredible!"

"O.M.G. I know, right? Anyway, Sums, you know I love you, but I'm just, like, so, so, so busy with everything, and my wedding planner doesn't seem to be getting with the program. She wanted me to wear white, can you even imagine? Like, when are we, the nineties?"

She laughed, a snorting, braying sort of laugh that set Summer's teeth on edge.

"I wore white."

"Oh, I know, but you made it look *amazing*! How could I compete with that?"

Summer thought back to how her dress had looked by the end, covered with cake and snot.

Fortunately, she didn't have time to dwell too much on the memory before Audriandra butted back in.

"So, listen, if it's a quick favour—like, zip-zip quick—then maybe I can swing it, but I really don't have a lot of time on my hands right now. Even with the whole not sleeping thing."

"Right. OK. I was wondering if I could get some of your other social media influencer friends to come to a castle in Scotland?" Summer said, just blurting it right out. "I'm here right now. There's a huge social media event going on."

"What? A castle? You're at a castle? Seriously? An actual castle, like, from the old days?" She let out a squeal. "That's kind of romantic! Is the King of Scotland there?"

"Uh..."

"Is he cute? Is he hairy? I bet he's hairy." She gasped. "Wait! Is he single?"

Summer tried to get a word in edgewise about how Kings of Scotland hadn't really been a thing, for, oh, the past four hundred years. But Audriandra had launched into a rant about how she was way prettier than Meghan Markle, and how she didn't understand what that royal guy saw in her.

"I've always wanted to be a princess," she added. "It's totally on my bucket list, for sure."

Summer's mouth hung open. "You do remember you're marrying Brad in a few months, don't you?"

"Well, duh. But exceptions can be made! If a Scottish King proposed to me? I think Brad would totally give me his blessing. Our followers would go *cray-cray*."

Summer blinked, so confused by the turn this conversation had taken that she momentarily forgot what her reason for calling was.

It came back to her a second later, and she quickly pressed on.

"Anyway, Scotland! I know it's not right around the corner, and you're very busy, so obviously *you* couldn't come. But you know everyone who's everyone, so I was hoping—"

"Oh, Sums!" Audriandra gushed, the condescension dripping from her voice. "When you have a private jet, the whole world is just around the corner. Consider me there."

"What? No, you don't have to—"

"Shh. Hush. You don't have to thank me, Sums," Audriandra said.

"I wasn't going to... I wasn't asking you to come!"

She heard the smirk all the way from Los Angeles. "Suuure, you weren't! It's fine, I'll totally be there. But I have one question. Are you going to introduce me to this obscenely wealthy and handsome prince of yours?"

"Well, actually—"

Audriandra sighed. "Sums, let me be straight with you, mmkay? We've known each other long enough to be totally straight with each other, and you know I'm way too busy to play around. When I go places, I have to consider whether it's good material for my channel. Every time I get invited somewhere, I have to ask myself, I.I.A.? "

Summer frowned. "I.I.A.?"

"Is it awesome?" Audriandra explained. "So, is it?"

"It is! I promise you! It's this amazing island with this old castle and the scenery is—"

"Yeah, yeah, sure. Castle, hills, blah, blah, I get it. Does it have a handsome prince who looks good on camera?"

"It has a laird."

"A what?"

"It's kind of what they call princes in Scotland," she said

quickly, completely sidestepping the truth. "*And* he owns this entire private island off the coast."

"Alright! Now you're talking my language."

Summer could hear her flipping through pages, probably in her planner.

"Here's what I can do. I'm like, *ohmygod, totally* booked up for the rest of the year. It's insane. But I'm on my way to Europe tomorrow with a couple of social media pals for a big publicity event. I guess I can stop by for a few hours."

"Tomorrow?!" Summer gasped.

"It's that, or nothing, Sums."

"No! Tomorrow's great!" Summer looked out at the tangle of plants and weeds, and grimaced. "Tomorrow's perfect."

"Awesome. Just email me the deets, and I'll be there."

"Email? Well, actually, service is kind of—"

"All right, whatever, I don't care. I'll give you my assistant, Philip's, number. Give him the deets and an address to send my luggage on ahead, all right? He's so efficient."

"OK, sure." Summer swallowed, the question that had been crowding her thoughts suddenly bursting from her mouth. "You won't be bringing Brad, will you?"

A pause.

A long one, too.

She'd wanted a quick 'No, of course not.' But as the seconds drew out, she hated herself for even asking the question.

And yet, she had to know.

"Well, I don't know. It would be fun for us all to get together, wouldn't it? Like old times."

Summer cringed. Oh, sure, the three of them together would be a regular *hoot*.

"I mean, just us girls would be fun, too!" she suggested.

"Listen, I've got to go, Sums, Philip's calling me. He's drawn me my mud bath, and I have to get in while the mud's still warm. I mean, can you imagine if it goes cold? Ew!"

Summer thought back to the knee-deep mud she'd almost drowned in the night before.

"Yeah," she said. "Ew."

The line went dead as Audriandra hung up the phone. Summer stared at the handset for a while, then gently replaced it on the cradle.

So, that was that.

Audriandra herself was coming to Lachart Isle.

She leaned on Duncan's desk, trying to imagine what that might look like.

Audriandra on the ferry.

Audriandra climbing down the rusty ladder into Hugh's small boat.

God. And Hugh thought Summer had a lot of luggage. He hadn't seen *anything* yet.

There was no going back now. Audriandra had agreed to it, and if anything could be said about her, it was that she was driven. Once she said she was going to do something, she never backed out.

Unlike her fiancé.

Summer's mind reeled at the thought of them both. What if Brad came? What if she had to see them together, holding hands, kissing for the cameras?

She felt her stomach lurch, and she doubled over, gagging.

"So, is it a go?" a voice said behind her.

She straightened up immediately, and spun to find Duncan, Lola, and Hugh standing in the doorway, looking anxious. Actually, they looked more concerned about her than anxious. Probably because she looked like death. She felt like it, too.

How much of the conversation had they heard?

She nodded, forced a smile, and gave them a thumbs-up.

"Yes!" Lola shouted, and she and Duncan exchanged an excited high-five.

"But there is one slight problem," Summer said, holding up a finger.

Hugh grunted. He didn't look as excited as the others. In fact, he still seemed downright dubious. But he was here, which might have meant he, too, had realised there was no other way.

"And what's that?"

Summer smiled sheepishly.

"She's coming tomorrow."

"Tomorrow?!" Hugh spluttered.

Summer nodded. "Yes. Which means we have twenty-four hours to get everything ready for her arrival."

21

CLEAN SWEEP

Two hours later, thanks to Duncan's organisational skills, the island's entire population had descended on the castle and were working together to brighten the place up.

Getting everyone to come and help had been surprisingly easy. As soon as Duncan went to the village and explained what was happening, everyone dropped what they were doing and followed him back to the castle, where Summer and Lola gave everyone their list of chores.

And long lists they were, too.

Most of the island residents were older, but they worked with the energy and urgency of people half their age. And, by late morning, Summer began to see some improvement.

The overgrown gardens had been trimmed, some of the castle walls had been painted, and a few of the less palatable items—animal heads, mostly—had been tucked away in one of the less-used areas of the house.

They'd also fixed up a few of the nicer hotel rooms upstairs for the guests to stay overnight, if they'd like. They weren't anything like the Four Seasons, but the rooms were clean, and definitely held a quaint sort of charm.

As Summer ticked her way through a To-Do list, Lola came running down the stairs, out of breath, carrying a big cardboard box.

"I found all this bunting. I think it was used for Christmas, or something, but I bet we can use it now. It'll be really pretty in the foyer and the ballroom. What do you think, Summer?"

Summer pulled out a few of the long strings of flags, and nodded. "I think it'll work nicely! Great idea."

Lola practically vibrated with glee at the compliment. She dropped the cardboard box on the ground and started to hurry off. "I'll go get the ladder!"

Before the girl could get away, Summer grabbed her by the collar of her tweed jacket.

"Whoa there, little miss! I'm not having you climbing up ladders. You might fall off."

"But I might not fall off," Lola countered.

"True. And you probably won't. But just in case, *I'll* hang the flags. There's lots of other things for you to do. See how your grandfather's doing with the menu."

"Oh, he's doing fine with that on his own. He's got it all figured out."

"Are you sure? It's all edible? No *possibly-turned* shepherd's pie?"

"Blurgh. No! But that cauliflower curry soup is definitely on the menu."

Summer nodded, satisfied. Summer had been a vegetarian for years, but had only become one because Audriandra was. Summer had mistakenly thought that being a veggie would give her the same figure, the same glowing skin, the same everything.

It had not.

"Perfect!" Summer said. "Well, there's plenty of other things for you to do, like..."

She looked around, but before she could give Lola a job, the girl pulled a bundle of construction paper from the box.

"I could carry on making the stuff we need for the activities we're planning," she suggested.

Summer leaned over Lola's shoulder to take a look. "What are you planning?"

Lola showed her what she'd already done, and held up a bundle of posters that featured a very professionally-drawn picture of the Lachart Lily, obviously copied from the painting in the kitchen. Over it, it said, "REWARD: Two Jam Scones."

Summer giggled. "Oh, so you're trying to convince these influencers to be treasure hunters, is that it?"

Lola shrugged. "Might as well have them do the dirty work for us while they're here. I'm going to pin them up all over."

"Good luck with that," Summer said as Lola bounded away, looking for places to pin the posters.

Summer didn't want to dash Lola's hopes. Considering Lola had grown up here, kept away from the world at large, the little girl had reason to be excited.

In another few hours, this place would be a little more fabulous because Audriandra would be here, along with who knew how many of her friends. They'd certainly liven the place up.

But as for digging around in the dirt for a flower? That was not their scene. Despite Audriandra's love of mud baths, the woman did not like getting her hands dirty. She'd never go out on a nature expedition. Never.

Summer grabbed the cardboard crate and went through the bunting, untangling it all. There were some artificial flower garlands in there, too, which she straightened out. Those would look good winding up the outside of the staircase, and across the railing at the bottom of the upper mezzanine.

She wrapped the garland in place, then found a ladder in an old store room, and set about pinning up the bunting flags.

This involved clambering up to the top of the shaky stepladder, and stretching up to her full height to pin the hanging strings in place.

She was glad she'd stopped Lola from attempting this. There was no way the little girl would have been able to reach from even the very top step of the ladder. Knowing her, as determined as she was, she'd have piled other things on top, and climbed up those until she could reach the wooden railing.

Disaster would surely have followed soon after.

Summer's fingers fumbled as she plucked one of the tiny tacks from the packet. She watched it fall to the ground below, and heard a tiny, tinny sound as it bounced on the wood floor.

Oh no. Someone might step on that. Someone could get hurt.

That, though, was the least of her problems.

Looking down, it had suddenly occurred to her that she was very high up. Ridiculously high.

Stupidly high.

Her legs began to tremble. The ladder shook beneath her feet, which in turn wobbled her from side to side. She gripped the bunting like it was a lifeline, even though there was no chance that it would hold her weight if she fell. She'd only put three tacks in it so far, and one of them had only gone in halfway.

The room began to spin, as a wave of dizziness washed over her.

"Ooh, this isn't good," she whispered, screwing her eyes shut. She abandoned the bunting, and instead grabbed the top of the ladder, holding onto it for dear life.

She breathed in, slowly, deeply, until the panic started to pass. Only then, did she open her eyes.

Only then, did she see Lola skipping back into the room, headed directly for where she'd dropped the tack.

"Lola, watch out!" she cried, afraid of the girl getting hurt.

The second she cried out, her dizziness became full-blown vertigo. Everything swivelled around her, somehow moving fast and slow at the same time, like time no longer made sense. Her stomach lurched. Her legs shook. She felt herself slipping, her feet leaving the rung of the ladder, and then she was toppling backwards, arms flailing, mouth opening to scream.

The fall was twenty feet onto a hard wooden floor. Maybe even farther.

She screwed her eyes shut, and braced herself. This was *really* going to hurt.

"Easy, now," a voice said, and then two strong, warm hands caught her around waist, breaking her fall, then setting her gently down on her feet.

Breathless with shock, she looked behind her and found Hugh there, his arms now wrapped around her, holding her up.

"You OK?" he asked, his voice gruff, but with a hint of concern to it.

Summer found herself speechless, and off-balance in an entirely different way. She looked up at him, inhaling his woodsy smell, and all her terror of the last few moments left her, along with most of the thoughts in her head.

His eyes locked on hers, and she felt even dizzier. "Summer?" he said, frowning a little, his brilliant blue eyes searching her face.

She couldn't remember if she'd ever heard him say her name before. Certainly not when he wasn't angry or annoyed with her.

His deep Scottish brogue made it sound completely new to her ears, like she was hearing it spoken aloud for the very first time.

"Are you all right?" he asked her again.

Truthfully, no. She didn't feel all right. Her body was tingling, warm and yet shivery cold at the same time. Her face burned red hot, like she was running a fever.

"Summer?"

Wow, he made the word sound good. He made it sound—

"Tack!" she cried, one of those thoughts that had left her head now forcing its way back in. "There's a tack! Lola, careful you don't—"

"Found it!" Lola announced, holding the pin up above her head like it was some sort of ancient magical sword. "Just what I need, too!"

Summer breathed a sigh of relief as the little girl headed off to find other places to pin her posters.

She became aware—first dimly, then pressingly—that Hugh hadn't moved his hands from her waist.

There was a lot to do before Audriandra's arrival. An impossible amount to do, in fact. She should shoo him away, hurry him on, so they could both get back to work.

And yet, she found that she couldn't. That she didn't want him to let her go.

"Are you sure you're all right?" Hugh asked her. "You look like you've seen a ghost."

"Fine! I'm fine. Fine, totally fine," Summer babbled. She pointed upwards. "I, uh, I fell off a ladder."

I fell off a ladder? She cursed herself below her breath. Why had she said that?

"Eh, aye. I know. I saw it," Hugh told her. "Quite impressive it was, too, with all that arm flapping you were doing. For a second, I almost thought you might actually fly back up."

Summer laughed a little too loudly, realised she sounded like a madwoman, and quickly composed herself.

"I can't fly," she said.

The little voice in her brain screamed at her again, and it took all her willpower not to slap herself on the forehead.

"I mean, *obviously* I can't fly. I didn't need to... You didn't actually think..." She smiled and grimaced at the same time, cleared her throat, then shrugged, trying to appear relaxed. "But, yeah. Fine. Totally fine."

"You seem stressed," Hugh told her.

"Duh, well, *yeah!* Of course, I'm stressed. We're trying to save the castle here! We should all be stressed. We've got so much to do! Fixing this place up is going to be hard work!"

"Aye, well, like I said before, a little hard work never hurt anyone." He scratched his head, like he wasn't quite sure how to say the next part. "I have to say, though. I, eh... I heard some of your conversation on the phone, and I got the impression that you weren't over the moon about these influencer friends of yours turning up."

Summer kept her smile in place, but inwardly winced.

Could he really see through her like that? Was she really that transparent?

She pulled free from his grip, and announced, "Better finish pinning these flags!"

Then, she hurried up the ladder again to get away from him, ignoring the way her legs shook, or the thundering of her panicked heart.

She was halfway up when she heard a rung creaking below. Looking down, she saw Hugh just a couple of feet behind her, arms braced to catch her if she fell.

"Safety net," he said, then he nodded upwards to where the bunting hung loosely from the ceiling.

"Thanks," she said. She climbed on, her nerves fading now that she knew she had Hugh to stop her falling.

That also meant, though, that she hadn't escaped the conversation he had started.

"I'm very happy they're coming," she said.

Hugh grunted. "My arse you are. You didn't look happy."

She shot a look back down at him. "Oh, and you're suddenly the expert on happiness?"

"No," Hugh admitted. "But I know it when I see it. And you on that phone, that wasn't it."

Summer stared at him for a while, then heaved out a sigh. "Fine. If you must know, remember the complicated ex-boyfriend?"

He nodded. "Aye. The one you said wasn't coming?"

"Yes. Well, turns out he might be."

He nodded. "Ah," he said, and there was a creak as he made his way down a rung, putting a few more inches of space between them.

"Trust me, I don't want him here!" Summer insisted. "The big-name influencer I did invite is my best friend, Audriandra. She's engaged to my former fiancé, Brad, who left me at the altar for her."

"I think you might need to go get yourself a dictionary from the castle library," Hugh remarked, "and check the definition of 'best friend,' because I'm pretty sure that's no' it."

Summer smiled grimly. "Yeah," she conceded. "I guess I partly came here to escape them."

"I don't blame you," Hugh said.

"But, we want to save this place. *I* want to save this place. I know it's your home, and I have no right to feel, well, anything, really, but..." She looked around, being careful not to dwell too much on the ground all those feet below. "It means a lot to me."

Hugh looked up at her in silence for a long time, those blue eyes of his sweeping her face like spotlights.

"You're serious?" he said. "About the wedding thing? Being dumped at the altar, I mean?"

"Oh, yes!" Summer spat, unable to hide the bitterness. "Don't believe me? Google it. You'll find hundreds of videos online, all making fun of me. I'm a meme."

"I don't know what that is," Hugh told her.

For some reason she couldn't explain, that made her feel better. She'd always assumed her humiliation had gone global, that everyone, in every corner of the world had seen her standing sobbing at the altar, while Brad and Audriandra skipped away together.

And yet, it hadn't made it this far. It hadn't made it here.

She poked the last pin into the wooden rail, securing the bunting. "All right. I'm done. I'm coming back down, so—"

She yelped as her foot missed a rung, and for the second time in almost as many minutes, she fell into Hugh's arms.

This time, she stopped suddenly as her back hit the densely packed mass that was his chest.

She found her footing and stood there, pressed between his warm body and the cold metal of the ladder, her face angled to look back and up into his.

His breath fanned across her face. She could feel the heat from him, smell his raw, woody musk.

Summer found herself staring into the crystal clear pools of his eyes, and realised, after a moment, that he was staring back. She was safe now, with no danger of falling any further, and yet she suddenly felt dizzy again, the edges of her vision blurring until she could see nothing but his face.

"I should tell you something," he murmured. He was

studying her lips now, she was sure of it, like he wanted to kiss them.

Did he want to kiss them?

Her heart thrummed in her chest at the thought of it, and at the realisation that she wanted nothing more than for it to happen.

"Yes?" she whispered, hardly able to get the word out.

From somewhere nearby came the sound of Duncan announcing he was putting the kettle on to make tea, and telling everyone within earshot to, "Be quick and get your orders in, or forever hold your peace!"

Hugh blinked, whatever trance he had been in suddenly broken. His arms stiffened around hers, and he looked away.

"I just wanted to say that I appreciate everything you're doing for the castle. I suppose... I suppose I had the wrong idea about you. You're not the person I thought you were."

"I'm not?" Summer asked, still a little breathless.

"No. You're, eh, you're a good friend," he told her.

That must've taken him a lot to admit, Summer knew, and yet she couldn't help but feel a wrench of disappointment.

Friends. That's how he saw them.

Better that than mortal enemies, of course, but still.

Friends.

"Why didn't you tell me that you knew who I was?" she asked. "Why didn't you say that you remembered me?"

The question came out harsher than she'd intended. Hugh disentangled her from his arms and shrugged. "I didn't think it mattered. You didn't remember it. And we—"

"We remember the things that matter," she parroted, recalling his words. "But I do remember. It just took me a little while. It was a long time ago, and I was a lot younger than you."

"Aye. I was twelve. You were only... What? Six?"

She nodded. "That's when my father died, so maybe five."

"But you were still the only other child on the island. So my dad had me look after you."

"That must've been a pain for you," Summer said, hoping he'd tell her that it hadn't been. That he'd loved every minute of it, just like she had.

"Aye, it was a bit," Hugh said, crushing her hopes. But, then, he sighed and shrugged. "Actually, I didn't mind it too much. I mean, aye, you were a pain in the arse even then—"

"Hey!" Summer laughed and slapped him on the arm, then let her hand linger there for a few moments.

"I'll admit that having you around made for... an interesting few weeks," he told her. "I remember actually being sad to see you go."

"I think that's probably the nicest thing you've ever said to me," Summer told him, and she realised that she was twirling a lock of her hair around a finger.

Hugh scratched his chin, pretending to be deep in thought. "Aye," he said. "Aye, it probably is. Maybe best not to get used to it."

Summer laughed. "I wouldn't dream of it," she said.

"Here! What's going on?" a voice demanded from the bottom of the ladder. Lola stood there, holding what was left of her posters and eyeing them suspiciously. "Hold on!" she gasped. "Have you been snogging?"

Hugh jumped back like he'd been electrocuted. He seemed to hang there in mid-air for a second, then landed with surprising grace and agility beside his daughter at the foot of the ladder.

"What? Pfft. No!" snorted Summer, still perched on her rung. "As if!"

"Snogging? Where did you hear about a thing like that?" Hugh demanded.

"From everywhere," Lola told him, her eyes still narrowed with suspicion.

"Oh. Right. Aye," Hugh blustered. "Well, no, there was none of that... funny business going on. I was helping with the..."

He motioned to the bunting, but seemed to have temporarily forgotten the word. Summer, annoyingly, had forgotten it, too.

"Little flags," she said.

"Aye! That. The wee flags," Hugh said. He was fidgeting uncomfortably under the heat of his daughter's glare, like she was the parent and he was the child in trouble.

It was, Summer thought, ridiculously cute. He'd always seem so strong and in control, and now here he was, dancing on the spot like he had midges in his underwear.

Lola regarded them both in solemn silence, then shrugged. "Aw. That's a shame," she said, then she drew in a breath so big it practically inflated her. "So, listen, anyway... When we have this party tomorrow, Dad. I was thinking that maybe I could wear makeup?"

Hugh stared at her in horror. "Over my dead body!"

"But Dad!"

"Not at your age, young lady. Not until you're older. Much, much older."

"*How* much older?"

Hugh picked a number that he felt more comfortable with. "Forty."

"Forty?!" Lola spluttered.

"Mid-forties," he said.

Then, before Lola could argue, he muttered some feeble excuse, turned away from them both, and went jogging off back to work.

Lola stamped a foot in frustration, watching him go.

The ladder creaked as Summer clambered down the final few rungs. She put a hand on Lola's shoulder, and smiled down at her. "Don't worry," she whispered, then she winked. "We'll talk him round."

22

SPECIAL TREATMENT

That night, when all the villagers had returned home, Summer wandered the halls of the castle, checking off a list of the final few things that would need to be finished up the following morning. It had been a long, crazy day, and every part of her body now ached.

After working, the whole island had gotten together for a meal around the dining room table, and there hadn't been an empty seat in the place. She'd gotten to meet dozens of new faces—families who'd lived there for ages. They all knew each other, like one big, happy family, and though everyone was so welcoming to her, it only made Summer more nervous.

She couldn't imagine all these people picking up and moving away if the island was sold to the developer. She wouldn't imagine it. She refused. Her plan was going to work.

It *had* to.

She reached the last item on the checklist—clearing the cobwebs from above the reception desk, which she'd get Hugh to help with—and was just tucking the clipboard under her arm when she caught a whiff of something sour and unpleasant.

It took her just a few moments to conclude that the smell was herself.

It really had been a very long day, and she'd worked harder than she had in... well, perhaps ever.

She winced when she thought of the shower waiting there in her bathroom upstairs. She badly needed to get clean, but she was still sore from the last sand-blasting the contraption had given her.

Still, she couldn't exactly smell like this when Audriandra arrived. Her ex-bestie always smelled good. She even had her own perfume line now! If Summer reeked of stale sweat when she and the other influencers turned up, Summer would never live it down.

"Shower," she said, heading for the stairs. "Shower, right now."

By now, she knew her way around the castle pretty well, and she found herself detouring past Lola's room on the way back to her own. As she crept past the door, she heard Hugh reading more of *Charlotte's Web*. Summer had read the book herself years ago, and by the sounds of things, it didn't sound like Hugh had gotten very far through the story.

"I think that rat is going to be trouble," Lola observed, interrupting him mid-sentence.

Summer heard Hugh give a sigh. "Do you?"

"Aye. I just get a feeling. Don't you?"

"The only feeling I'm getting right now is growing impatience," Hugh said.

"Sorry," Lola said. "Continue."

Summer smiled. No wonder they weren't far into the book. Clearly, Lola liked her bedtime story to be an interactive experience, and kept asking questions.

She reminded Summer a lot of herself at that age. She'd

fired question after question at her father, and he'd always patiently answer them. That's why he'd taken Summer, and not her sister, Indigo, on the trip here all those years ago. She'd had 'an inquisitive mind,' he'd told her. He'd even made her a little badge with 'Research Assistant' written on it.

From inside the room, Hugh said, "Thank you. I'll do that."

He started up again, but only a moment later, he was interrupted again.

"Dad?" Lola asked, and her voice was so hesitant and nervous sounding that Summer instinctively held her breath.

"Lola," Hugh said.

"Do you think tomorrow is going to work?"

A pause. "I don't know," Hugh admitted. "I hope so."

"Summer's really smart. And she told me that one of her best friends—the one who's coming tomorrow—has her own perfume line and millions of followers on social media. Isn't that brilliant?"

"Well, I mean, I suppose. It's no' my cup of tea, but if you're into that sort of thing..."

"I've never met anyone famous before, Dad! That's why I wanted to get dressed up and put on some makeup. Just for the party tomorrow night, that's all. And then I won't wear any again until I'm fifty."

"Fifty?"

"Maybe even sixty!" Lola stressed, and Summer bit her lip to stop herself giggling at how serious the girl sounded.

Hugh gave a non-committal grunt. "Well... We'll see."

"No, you always say that, then never talk about it again!" Lola said, seeing straight through the deflection. "Summer said she'd help me! She knows everything about makeup and fashion. Can I, Dad? Can I?"

Hugh let out a sigh. "Fine."

"Aw, but *Dad!* It's just for…"

Her voice trailed off.

For a moment, there was only silence from the other side of the door.

"Wait," Lola finally said, her voice trembling like she was trying to hold herself together. "Did you say I could?"

"Aye," Hugh confirmed. "I mean, personally, I think it looks trashy, but I suppose, if it really means that much to you…"

"It does!" The bed creaked, and from her place in the hallway, Summer could see Lola's shadow lean forward on the bed and give Hugh a hug. "Thankyouthankyouthankyou!" the little girl cried, then she leaned back and gasped as an idea occurred to her. "Can I wear high heels?"

"Don't push it," Hugh laughed. "Now, back into bed, you. Come on."

There was some rustling of covers as Lola clambered back under them.

"I can't wait to tell Summer," Lola said, settling in. "She's so nice, isn't she?"

Summer held her breath, listening for Hugh's reply. When it came, it wasn't exactly full of gushing praise.

"She has her moments, I suppose."

"I'm not a baby anymore. You know that, don't you, Dad?"

"Unfortunately, yes," Hugh said. "Why do you ask?"

"So, you can tell me the truth. I can handle it," Lola said. "Were you kissing her?"

"What?! What sort of question's that?"

"*Were* you, though?"

"No. I was not!"

"Did you want to kiss her?"

"No."

Summer heard Lola let out a gasp. "*You did so!*" the girl cried. "You're rubbish at lying, you look all shifty! You want to kiss her! Are you in love? Are you going to get married?"

"That's quite enough of this conversation!" Hugh said, becoming stern. "I think she's nice. She's going out of her way to help us, and I appreciate that, but that's all it is." He tapped the book. "Now, haud yer wheesht, and let's get back to this book, so you can get to sleep."

"OK, fine," Lola said. She lowered her voice to a whisper. "But you *so* wanted to kiss her!"

Summer listened to them going back to the story, then smiled. At least she hadn't imagined things. Lola had seen it, too. He *had* wanted to kiss her.

Her heart fluttered at the idea of it, like it did every time she thought back to being close to him, his muscular arms wrapped around her.

Still shivering, she about-faced and headed back to her room. She still had that shower to survive, and then a few hours of sleep to grab, if she was going to tackle the miles-long last-minute chore list in the morning.

When she reached her room, she saw Duncan standing by the top of the stairs.

"Good evening, lass," he said, tipping an imaginary hat to her.

"Hi, Duncan," she said with a wave. "I thought you would've gone to bed by now."

"Ah, no. Just having a wee last look around the old place, seeing what needs to be done for your friends."

She laughed and held up her list. "Me, too."

Duncan took it from her and studied it. "*Help ma Boab!* We'll need to be up at the crack of dawn to handle all this."

As he read through the list, Summer heard the clanking of the central heating somewhere beneath her feet. She'd gotten quite used to the sound of it now, but it gave rise to a sudden thought.

"Wait! You built the heating system in this place, right?

"Aye, I sure did!" Duncan declared. "With these own fair hands of mine." He held up both hands, then raised the one on the right a little higher. "Mostly this one."

"Do you know anything about the shower? I can't seem to do anything but get it to blast me with cold water," Summer said. "Like, *icy* cold water. Lots of it." She winced, recalling the morning's high-pressure cleansing. "So, so much."

"Well, of course I do, lass! I built those, too! All my own design!" He went to her door. "Come with me, and I'll show you how to tame the muckle great beastie!"

He led her into her room and skipped straight to the bathroom, practically dancing through the door.

"It's actually very easy," he declared, then his hands flew across the controls like a conductor leading an orchestra. "All you need to do is turn that one there, twist this, give that a flick up, then flick it again, turn that one high, shift that one into low, and then, with a simple jiggle of this knob..."

He finished up, then stepped back, just before a steady spray of water shot out of the shower head above where he'd been standing.

"And there we go!" he announced. "That wee dial there adjusts the temperature, but I think you'll find it's just spot-on."

Summer reached in and felt the water. He was right. It was delightfully warm. Perfectly so.

"Wow. It's really *that* straightforward, huh?" she asked, and either he missed the sarcasm, or he chose to ignore it, because he responded with a grin and a nod of his head.

"You shouldn't need to mess around with anything now. A wee jiggle of yon knob there, and you'll always be good to go," he told her.

"Thank you!" she replied, already excited by the thought of running hot water.

"Not a problem, lass," Duncan said, retreating out of the room. "So, have you enjoyed your excursions on the island while you've been here?"

Summer followed him, nodding. "Yes. Amazingly. I didn't think I would. They're far out of my comfort zone. But I figure, since I booked the deluxe package, I had to get my money's worth."

Duncan stared back at her in surprise. "Deluxe package, eh?" he asked, and she thought she saw the beginnings of a smile playing across his lips.

"Yes. That's right." She stared at him, a little confused. "Why? What's so funny?"

He tucked his hands behind his back and shook his head. "Oh, nothing."

Summer wasn't letting him off the hook that easily. "I'm onto you, Mister! There's something you're hiding. Did he deliberately pick out the worst trips for me out of spite, or something?"

"Oh, no," Hugh said, now positively beaming from ear to ear. "It's nothing like that."

"Then, what?"

"Well, let's just that that we've been running this place as a hotel my whole life," Duncan told her. "And, in all that time, Lachart Castle has never offered a deluxe package of any description."

"What do you mean? That can't be right," Summer said, frowning. "But he took me on those excursions."

"Aye, he did," Duncan said, then he winked and headed for

the door, leaving her standing there in shock. "Now, I wonder why on Earth that could be...?"

23

CHANGE OF PLANS

The shower was good.

No. That wasn't doing it justice. The shower was *amazing*. Summer hadn't kept a list of her all-time favourite shower experiences, but if she had, this one would've slid in somewhere near the top spot.

And yet, she hadn't been able to fully relax, her mind whirring as the bathroom filled with steam around her. The steady stream of hot water cleansed her body, but it did nothing to wash her worries away.

They still had so much to do to get the castle ready, and she hadn't yet fully nailed down the perfect plan of activities and events that would keep the influencers happy.

And then, of course, there was the issue of her appearance. It didn't seem to bother anyone at the castle, but Audriandra and her friends had much higher standards, which Summer struggled to achieve at the best of times.

Now, without her makeup, straightening iron, setting mist, and all the other balms and potions she used to make herself look halfway presentable, she was in big trouble.

She wanted to look like a million dollars, as if time away from Brad had made her better in every way. Like being here on the island was really working for her.

Summer tried not to think about why that was so important to her. Was she trying to make Brad jealous? Was she still, even now, hoping to win him back?

She shut off the shower by jiggling the knob in the opposite direction, then stepped out and grabbed a towel. Her teeth chattered in the sudden cold of the bathroom—although, it might equally have been nerves.

Audriandra hadn't specifically said that Brad was coming, but there was a heavy sort of feeling in Summer's chest, and she knew—she just *knew*—he was going to appear.

She remembered one of the first Instagram posts of Audriandra's she'd seen after the aborted wedding. The picture showed Audriandra and Brad squeezed together in a dressing room at a Rodeo Drive boutique, and the text below it had read:

'The love of my life! Totally inseparable. So glad there are no more obstacles between us!'

The thought of that 'inseparable' part made Summer's stomach twist itself into a knot. She wasn't particularly pleased about the 'no more obstacles' part, either.

Was that all she'd been? An obstacle to be overcome?

She tried to push those thoughts away as she slipped into her pink silk pyjamas, and wrenched her still wet hair into a bun on the top of her head.

OK, Summer, what's still to be done?

The answer, she knew, was, 'A lot.'

Fine. She could do a lot. They'd already *done* a lot.

They just had to do roughly the same amount again—perhaps a little more—and everything would be fine.

She let out an anxious *cheep*.

Yeah. That's all!

She grabbed a piece of paper and began drawing up the schedule for the influencers' trip.

"Arrival, between two and four pm," she said, writing the words down. She knew that much, since Audriandra had Phillip call the castle with her flight information. "Then..."

She paused and squeezed her eyes closed. Then, what?

"Cocktail reception, out in the courtyard," she decided.

She wrote that down, then added, '*Finish fixing up courtyard,*' to the to-do list.

"Great. Perfect. Excellent start!" she declared, congratulating herself. "It's all coming together. Now, what?"

Nothing. Blank slate. She chewed on the end of her pen as she contemplated the options. What usually followed a cocktail reception?

"First dance, dinner, bouquet toss, cake," she muttered, listing off the schedule she'd drawn up for her last big event.

And look how well that one went...

She set down the paper and pen, and began pacing back and forth, the old floorboards squeaking and creaking beneath her feet.

Audriandra had told her about big publicity events before. She'd never invited her along to any, obviously, but she'd gushed about them plenty afterwards. Summer rifled through her memory banks, trying to recall what usually happened at them.

Basically, she thought, it came down to a few key elements – photo ops, entertainment, food and drink, and schmoozing.

She could handle that, she thought. When the guests arrived, they'd have cocktails in the grounds, and grab photos of the castle, the gardens, and the shore, plus anything else that took their fancy.

After that, a tour of the castle, maybe?

Summer gasped. No! A *ghost* tour. Duncan could really push the history of the place, and hopefully the heating system would supply a soundtrack of creepy clanks and groans.

After that, socializing and drinks in the ballroom—whisky tasting, maybe—with some music and dancing, and then a grand, lavish dinner in the dining room, all gathered around the big table, sharing stories and snapping hashtag-foodstagram pictures.

Argh! A hashtag! The event needed a hashtag to help keep everything on brand, and help spread the word.

She stood by the window, looking out in the direction of the sea. It was dark now, though, and she saw only her own reflection gazing back at her.

"Hashtag-Lachart," she said, then both versions of her screwed up their noses.

Nah. That was no good.

She tried again.

"Hashtag-Lachart-Isle. Island? Hashtag-Lachart-Island?" She shook her head. "Hashtag-Visit-Lachart-Isle?"

No. No, no, no, no!

These were all terrible. Far too literal. They said nothing about the place at all.

She flopped down onto the bed, and thought about her experiences of the past few days. What had she learned here? How did this place make her feel?

How had it changed her?

She lay there for a moment, chewing at the inside of her lip.

"Hashtag-Life-Love-Lachart," she said, and she knew that was the one. That was perfect.

Jumping up, she went to the desk and wrote down #LoveLifeLachart, then did a little jig of celebration.

This was all taking shape, and the hashtag sealed the deal.

Some of the world's top influencers were coming here tomorrow. They'd have a lovely time, and would use that hashtag to share their experience with the whole wide...

And then, a little nagging voice at the back of her head piped up. It had been mumbling quietly for a while now, she realised, but had gradually become too insistent to ignore.

"Oh," she whispered. "No!"

Her arms, which had been helping her gyrate just a moment before, collapsed to her sides. Her feet, which had been dancing on the spot, suddenly froze in place, as icy tendrils of panic bloomed through her veins.

Oh, please, no!

This was a disaster! This was a nightmare!

There came a soft, questioning sort of knock at her bedroom door, like someone was checking if she was still awake. Summer raced to the door and threw it open to find Hugh standing here, hand still raised as if in mid-knock.

"Oh. Hello. You're awake," he began, then he saw the look on her face and frowned. "What's happened? What's wrong?"

The answer exploded out of her in a high-pitched squeal. "There's no internet!"

Hugh's frown only deepened. "What?"

Summer flailed her hands around like she was back swatting midges again.

"There's no internet on the island!" she cried.

"I told you the reception from the mainland is spotty," Hugh told her.

"Spotty? It's not *spotty!*" Summer shrieked. "It's worked for maybe an hour the whole time I was here! That's not spotty, that's barely even a single spot!"

"It is a problem?" Hugh asked.

Summer just stared at him for several seconds, her eyes and mouth forming three little circles of shock.

"Of course, it's a problem!" she yelped. "What are a bunch of social media influencers supposed to do with no internet? Maybe they could just *fax* their videos to TikTok?!"

"We don't have a fax machine," Hugh told her.

"I was being sarcastic!" Summer shot back.

She turned around, marched to her bed, then fell onto it, face down. Hugh stood outside the door, like a vampire who hadn't yet been invited in, and watched as she spent almost twenty seconds screaming into her pillow.

When she was finally screamed out, she turned her head so she was facing away from the door, and groaned.

What had she been thinking? Had she really thought she could pull this off? That she could stage a world-class event with one day's notice, make it a roaring success, and save the island?

It was going to be a disaster—yet another humiliation to add to the growing pile. Brad would come, of course. He'd see what a mess she'd made of everything, and be grateful that he'd chosen Audriandra over her.

And he was right to, of course. Audriandra wouldn't have made a mess of things like this. Audriandra would have pulled it off without a hitch.

"Are you OK?" asked Hugh, still hovering outside the door.

"My life is over," Summer mumbled, her face partially squashed against her pillow.

"I'm sure it's not that bad," Hugh said.

Summer rolled over, swung her legs onto the floor and bounced to her feet. "Not that bad?" she said. "We're bringing a bunch of the world's leading social media influencers to an island without any internet! Do you know what'll happen to them if they're cut off from the web for a whole day?"

"They'll become better people?" Hugh guessed.

"No. No, the opposite," Summer told him. "They'll go feral. They'll become monsters. I know this place has thick walls, but there's every chance they might tear it to the ground!"

"Blimey," Hugh said.

Summer raised her hands, as if in surrender. "I know what you're thinking."

Hugh smirked. "I really doubt that."

"No, I do! And you're right. You're right. This is all my fault! I jump into things without thinking them through. And I never see what's right in front of my face."

"And what might that be?" Hugh asked.

"That I'm a failure! That I can't do anything right! I mean, I can't even get through my own wedding day without turning into a global running joke. I mean, seriously, this is the thing I'm going to be remembered for!"

She pointed at her face, then scrunched it up like she was ugly crying.

"That! That's my legacy. A million memes of that."

"Hey, now," Hugh said, but she kept going. There was no stopping her now.

"How *dare* I think I could save this place? How dare I get Lola's hopes up, or Duncan's, or... or yours!"

"That's enough of that!" Hugh barked, and the sharpness of his tone dragged her out of her pity party. "You're not a failure, Summer. And if all everyone knows you as is a big crying face on the internet... Well, then that's their loss."

She managed a smile at that. He sounded so sincere and so caring, that some of her worries melted away.

And then, a moment later, they all came rushing back, and she sat down heavily on the end of her bed.

"It's no good," she said, throwing her arms in a shrug. "It's a disaster. We just need to admit defeat."

"Aye. Well, about that..." Hugh said.

His gaze flicked up and down, taking her in, and Summer suddenly felt self-conscious about sitting there in her pyjamas.

"Get dressed and meet me out front in two minutes," he said. "There's something I should probably have told you..."

24

CONNECTED

Summer was so curious as to what Hugh had in mind that she threw on her robe and slippers and arrived out at the front of the castle in under a minute.

When she got there, she realised how silly she must've looked in her nightclothes, her wet hair piled on her head, but curiosity had gotten the better of her, and she didn't particularly care.

Hugh was wearing a dark barn jacket and jeans and looked much more appropriately dressed for the occasion. He gave her attire a curious look, but said nothing about it.

"Right, what did you want to show me?" she asked, shivering slightly in the cold.

"Follow me to the garden," Hugh told her, setting off down the steps.

"The garden?"

She hadn't been out there, but she'd seen it from afar—a tangle of overgrown weeds poking out from behind a broken white picket fence. She knew the Campbells had been out there, diligently trimming and weeding all day, so she was hoping it looked a bit better.

Even so, and no matter how green the couples' fingers might have been, she was reasonably confident they wouldn't have grown an internet connection.

"Well, come on, then," Hugh urged, stopping at the bottom step. "Get a shifty on!"

He led her along a stone pathway she'd glimpsed through one of the windows during her first tour of the castle. It had been choked with bushes and weeds then. Now, it was clear, the Campbells having worked their magic.

Hugh stopped at a gate with a trellis arching overhead, and opened it. The moonlight illuminated some of the flowering bushes, and the smell of roses was intoxicating.

It would've been the perfect place for a romantic stroll, but with Summer damp and shivering, and Hugh marching ahead like he was racing into battle, it didn't feel romantic in the least.

When they reached the corner of the fence, Summer looked over and saw the moon dancing over the calm, dark sea. The sight of it reflected in the water caught her breath, and distracted her so much that she almost didn't notice the hulking metal monstrosity of a thing lurking on a concrete platform right in the corner of the garden.

Hugh tapped on the rectangular metal block. It was roughly three feet high by four wide, with various bits and pieces attached to the top and sides.

"This should do the job," he told her.

Summer squinted at the thing, trying to make out what it was. It was only when she spotted the round metal dish on top, and a large screen protected by a clear plastic cover that it clicked.

"Wait! Wait a minute!" she gasped. "Is this...? Is this a satellite broadband receiver?!"

"Aye," Hugh told her.

She gawped at him in disbelief, not sure whether to hug him or attack him.

"But you said there was no internet!"

"No, I said the internet from the mainland is spotty," he explained. "But, when I turn this on, it's very reliable. It's expensive to run, though, so I only really put it on when we have guests."

Summer *really* considered attacking him at that point.

"But, I'm a guest!" she yelped. "I was on the deluxe package! Doesn't that come with internet?!"

Hugh shook his head. "You needed to get away from all that rubbish," he said.

"Says who?!" Summer demanded.

"Well, you did," Hugh reminded her. "When you booked. You said you wanted a 'digital detox.' And, after I looked up what that meant, that's what I tried to give you."

Summer ejected a series of shocked sentences, without ever making it past the first few words of any of them.

"Yes, but— I didn't— Why did—?"

"You think you need all that stuff," Hugh said, gesturing to the satellite equipment. "You think you need to keep connected, trying to get likes, or comments, or whatever the hell it is you do. But, you don't. You don't need any of it."

"I do, actually. I have my blog to run. People are relying on me."

"For what? Pictures of your dinner? A story about that time you saw a little horse? Oh, aye, however will they cope without that?"

Summer's eyes narrowed. How did he know about the little horse?

"Have you been reading it?" she asked. "Have you been reading my blog?"

Hugh hesitated, then shook his head. "No, it was just a lucky guess," he said.

Lola was right. He really was a terrible liar.

"But my point is, have you missed it? Any of it?" he asked her. "Really?

She shifted uncomfortably on the spot, her fluffy slippers *squelching* on the damp grass. She pulled her robe more tightly and hugged herself to keep out the worst of the cold.

"I want the connection details," she told him, ignoring the question. "I need them."

"You don't," he told her. "You think you need them, but you don't."

"I do! It's the big event tomorrow. We need them to get online, and I have things I need to do."

He looked back at her for a long time, the moon picking out the creases of his face. Summer held out a hand, palm upwards.

"The connection details," she said. "If we want this plan to work—if we want to save the castle—then I need them."

For a moment, it looked like he was going to refuse, but then he reached into his pocket and took out a creased, battered old business card with various usernames and passcodes printed on it.

He held it out to her, and she snatched it from him greedily.

"Thank you," she said, already turning away. "I'll go post on my blog. See if I can get us some more publicity."

"If you must," Hugh muttered.

Summer turned and looked back at him. "You do want this to work, don't you? You do want to save the castle? The island?"

"Of course I want to save it," Hugh told her, but she felt that there was something he wasn't adding. Something he was holding back.

When it was clear that he wasn't about to come out with it, she nodded.

"Good. Then I'd better get to it. I'll see you in the morning."

"Aye," he grunted. "Night."

She stalked back to the castle without glancing behind to see if he was following her, the card clutched tightly in her hand.

By the time she reached her room, her slippers were soaked through. She kicked them into the corner, grabbed her phone, and quickly thumbed the screen until she found the internet settings.

It was going to be great to finally be back online. There was so much she would've missed. So much great content. So many interesting posts.

She stopped then, the phone in one hand, the card in the other.

What sort of 'great content'? she wondered.

What had she really missed?

Videos of Audriandra gloating, while Brad fawned over her? Another hilarious meme of Summer's sobbing, scrunched-up face?

Did she really care what Brad had put up on Instagram in the last few days?

Another picture of a skateboard. Whoopee!

Since the wedding-that-wasn't, every time she'd opened her phone, she'd felt worse. Despite all those billions of potential connections, she'd felt so utterly alone.

And then Lachart Isle had happened. Hugh MacGregor had happened. And all of a sudden, she didn't feel alone anymore.

She thought of how she'd felt on that beach with Hugh, or

sleeping on the ground beside him, or wrapped in his arms on that ladder, his body against hers.

No contest.

She set the phone and the card with the connection details down, turned out the light, then climbed into bed and tried to sleep.

But sleep took a long time to come. Not because she was worried about what might be happening on Brad's Instagram, but because tomorrow was going to be a day of reckoning.

And, though she tried not to dwell on it, because she couldn't wait to see Hugh again.

25

THE BIG DAY

The following morning, as soon as the sun began to rise, the castle became a hive of activity.

Summer had slept in fits and starts, too excited—or perhaps too terrified—to get more than an hour or two of rest at a time.

Even when the worry about the internet connection had been removed, another had jumped right in there to take its place. What if Brad, Audriandra, and the others completely trashed the castle to all their followers?

Summer had pitched the event as the only way to save the castle, but there was every chance that it would do the precise opposite. If the influencers had a bad time, the island's reputation would be ruined.

Everything had to be perfect. And, right now, it was anything but.

There were still too many weeds, the castle was too leaky and old, and there weren't any luggage carts. She felt the first stirrings of a full-blown panic attack.

What had she been thinking? Twenty-four hours wasn't

nearly enough to get the place ready. Twenty-four days would've been pushing it.

She tried her best to smile at the few islanders she passed as she went to the front of the house, making her final inspections. They were all working so hard, tackling the rest of Summer's list, hoping she'd save their homes.

But what if she couldn't? What if this was the kiss of death for life here on Lachart Isle?

What if, just like most other things she touched, she ruined everything?

"Deep breaths, Summer. Deep breaths," she whispered, sucking air down into her lungs in slow, steady gulps.

She turned a corner and skidded to a stop when she saw the front door of the castle.

There, just visible through the double doors, twenty or more pieces of designer luggage crowded the foyer.

They were a bright, shocking shade of pink. Summer recognized them at once.

They were Audriandra's!

Oh, God! She's here! She's early! Summer thought, racing towards the entrance.

What if she'd found Hugh? There was no way he'd know how to talk to her. No chance! If Hugh thought that Summer had been hard work, then his whole understanding of the concept would be redefined after two minutes in Audriandra's company!

She ran faster, closing quickly on the doors, telling herself she was hurrying for Hugh's benefit, so she could save him from her former best friend.

But that wasn't it, she knew. Deep down, she knew she wanted to get there so she could get between them. Audriandra had already stolen Brad from her.

And yet, the thought of her getting her hooks into Hugh somehow bothered Summer more.

She went charging through the front door, slid on the wooden floor, and almost crashed straight through Audriandra's bags like they were skittles.

"Is she here?!" Summer hissed.

Duncan looked up from the reception desk, where he was making a note on a pad.

"Is who here, lass?"

Summer was too stressed out to even say Audriandra's name, so she just gestured frantically at the assembled luggage and stared so hard at Duncan that her eyes almost popped out of her head.

"Oh, you mean your friend?" Duncan said. He smiled and shook his head. "Not yet, no. A boat came over from the mainland with her bags." He eyed the cases as he stepped out from behind the counter. "By the looks of things, she's planning on moving here permanently. I'm sure I saw a kitchen sink poking out of one of those."

Summer laughed, not so much at the joke, more with relief. Audriandra wasn't here. She wasn't on the island.

At least, not yet.

A couple of villagers came along to take the bags up to the room that had been set aside for Audriandra. It was, ironically, the honeymoon suite, though Summer tried not to dwell too much on that thought.

Instead, she went through to the kitchen with Duncan, and they finished up the schedule sitting at the table.

"The first guests should start arriving at about two, with the majority coming at four," she explained, checking her messages. She was online now, and had a whole bunch of DMs and mentions rolling in, some even using the hashtag she'd sent to Philip during one of her more sleepless hours last night.

"And what happens after that?" Duncan asked, peering at her clipboard.

"After they're checked into their rooms—most aren't staying overnight, but they'll want a place to freshen up—we'll have welcome cocktails in the courtyard. Then, they can wander around the island and enjoy—we have some ATVs to take them to the south beach cove, and someone volunteered to lead a tour up the mountain. You know, Ben Lachart?"

Duncan smiled kindly. "I'm aware of it, aye."

"Ha! Right. Yes. Of course," Summer said. "So, they could do that, or, they can just stay around the castle. Of course, we'll keep them out of the parts of the building that might collapse and kill them."

"Probably for the best, aye," Duncan agreed.

"Then we'll have dinner in the dining room. I checked out the menu, and it looks great. Well done on putting that together."

"Och, it was nothing. Besides, Hugh helped with most of it."

Summer lifted her eyes from the paper and looked around. She'd been looking for a chance to ask the question, and now pounced on it.

"Speaking of Hugh, where is he?"

Duncan shrugged. "He said he had somewhere to take Lola."

"Oh. Right," Summer said, though she had a nagging feeling that he might be avoiding her. "Where are they off to?"

As if in answer to the question, the kitchen door swung open and Lola skipped in, followed closely by Hugh. Their faces were both ruddy from exertion and sunburn, and they carried the scent of fresh air and the sea on their clothes.

Lola squeezed onto the stool next to Summer and smiled up at her. "So, what's going on?"

"We're just planning today's festivities," Summer explained, showing her the list.

"It's going to be brilliant!" Lola cheered, once she'd read it. "Don't you think, Dad?"

Hugh had the refrigerator doors open, so Summer couldn't see his face, but he mumbled, "Aye," as if he'd just been sentenced to death.

When he appeared, he was holding a basket of eggs, a block of cheese, and a loaf of bread. He laid everything out and began working away at it, not looking at anyone.

But perhaps, Summer thought, *especially* not looking at her.

There was a definite chip on his shoulder. A big one. So big that people in L.A. could probably see it.

Fine, Mr. Buzzkilt, Summer thought. *Be that way.*

His silence was creating a tension in the room, and Summer wasn't the only one who could feel it.

Lola rolled her eyes so that only Summer could see, and silently mouthed, "*Ignore him.*"

Summer wanted to. Oh, how she wanted to. But she kept looking over at him, at his lips, and she found herself wondering what it would be like to kiss him.

No! Stop that, Summer! Look somewhere else!

Her eyes went to his hands. Those hands, which had once wrapped so neatly around her waist, holding her, protecting her, pulling her—

No! No, that's worse!

"Ooh, there's going to be *refreshments* in the courtyard," Lola gushed, reading off the list. "*Refreshments!*" She said the word again, stressing it like it was some strange, exotic term. She giggled. "That sounds fancy!"

Hugh finished drying some of the utensils and set them out, then threw a dishcloth over his shoulder. "And what time are all these freeloaders getting here?"

Summer tutted. He really was being a buzzkill. Despite what he'd said last night, she got the feeling that he wanted all this to fail. But why? He wanted to save the castle, so the only possible reason for wanting everything to go wrong was so that Summer would be made to look bad.

Was that it? Had she really annoyed him that much, just when she'd thought he was starting to warm towards her?

"They're called *influencers*," Summer corrected, flipping her hair over her shoulder. "And they're going to start coming at two."

He checked his watch and grumbled something under his breath. "How many?"

She blinked. "Sorry?"

"How many of these buggers are we expecting?" He spoke the words more slowly, accentuating every word, as if he was speaking to someone who didn't understand the language.

He still hadn't looked at her. Not once.

"Oh, uh, I'm not really sure," she admitted with a shrug. "Four or five big ones, at least."

"How big are we talking?" asked Duncan. "Six feet? Seven?" He gasped theatrically. "They're no' giants, are they? They'll no' get through the doors!"

Lola giggled, and dug an elbow into him to stop him making any more terrible jokes.

"Grandpa!" she said. "Not *tall* big, *famous* big. That's right, isn't it, Summer?"

Summer smiled down at her. "That's right," she said, then she suddenly got the feeling she was being watched.

Sure enough, when she looked over at Hugh, he was staring at her, a butter knife clutched in one hand.

"Let me get this straight," he said. "You really have no idea how many people are coming?"

Summer shifted in her seat. "Well, I mean... Not *exactly*, but I'm sure it won't be more than—"

"How could you not know? Didn't you think to ask?" Hugh growled at her. "What if there are hundreds? We don't have the food or the room."

"It won't be," she said dismissively. "This was too last-minute. It definitely won't be hundreds. *Definitely*."

She folded one hand over the other on the table, then adjusted her position, folded them the other way, and quietly cleared her throat.

"Probably."

"You don't know that!" Hugh cried.

"Yes, I do!" Summer spat. "These people are in huge demand, they're massively busy, and they jet all over the world. We'll be lucky if we get four or five of them. If we get a hundred, then it'll be tough, but we'll cope!"

"Oh, aye? And how will we cope, exactly?" Hugh demanded. "Will we stack them up in the McMillan's cow shed, one atop the other?"

"Oh, Dad, wheesht! It's not going to be a problem. It's going to be brilliant. Summer can totally handle it!" Lola glared at her father until he sighed and returned to making breakfast, then looked up at Summer again. "Who are they, these people? What are they like?"

"Well, I guess they're a bit like me," Summer said. She opened her phone and flicked to Audriandra's Instagram page. "Only better."

"Better?!" Lola laughed, like this was impossible. "No way! They can't be!"

"Oh, no, she does look better, right enough," Duncan muttered, peering over the rim of his glasses at the phone in Summer's hand. He very quickly coughed and shook his head. "If you like that sort of thing, I mean! Far too skinny for my liking. Give me a lassie like you, any day, Summer!"

From the way his eyes widened, he realised right away what he'd implied.

"Not that you're... I'm not saying you're fat, or... No. No, no, I'm no' saying that at all!" Duncan babbled, then he jumped to his feet, cupped a hand to his ear, and frowned. "I think... Did you hear someone shouting me there?"

Summer, Lola, and Hugh, all shook their heads.

"No, Dad," Hugh said, looking like he was enjoying the old man's discomfort. "Didn't hear a thing."

"No. I'm sure... There was definitely something..." Duncan said.

He looked across their faces. His hands dropped to his sides.

Then, a moment later, he turned and ran out of the room, his old bones creaking as he went.

"So, anyway," Summer said, drawing out both words. She angled her phone so Lola could see. "That's one of them. She's a definite."

Lola, despite herself, couldn't help but stare at the picture of beauty on the screen. She looked like a model, or a big star at a movie premiere.

"She's coming here? Now I really do need makeup," Lola whispered, clearly star-struck. "She has millions of people following her! And look at that boy she's with! He's so hand-some, and—"

Suddenly, Hugh's hand swept down and grabbed the phone.

"That's enough of that. I don't want you looking at any of that garbage, Lola."

"Aw, Dad!"

"It's harmless," Summer protested, holding out her hand for her phone, which he wasn't yet making any move to return.

"Harmless? It's feeding junk to young minds, is what it is!"

"Well, at least it isn't feeding meat to a vegetarian," Summer fired back. "That was just mean!"

He shook his head, nostrils flaring. She waited for his snippy comeback, but then realised the room had fallen silent. She looked over at Lola, who was smirking as if she knew a secret.

"What?" she demanded, and she was surprised when Hugh said the same thing, having spotted his daughter's reaction at the same time Summer had.

Lola giggled. "Is this what they call a lover's tiff?"

Summer's face flamed. "What?"

Hugh gnashed his teeth so loud she could hear it. He slammed her phone down in front of her. "See what this stuff can do? Giving her ideas like that!" He pointed at Lola. "You're never having a phone, ever, young lady. You understand? Not even when you're forty."

Lola was still grinning. For all Hugh's bluff and bluster, Summer knew the girl had him wrapped around her little finger. The day she decided she wanted a phone, she'd get one.

Still flushed, Summer looked over at Hugh. They made eye contact for one brief, humiliating second, and then Hugh turned his back on her, and returned to preparing Lola's breakfast, and Summer took her cue to leave.

26

MISBEHAVING

"Psst. Lola! Up here!"

Lola turned at the bottom of the staircase, and looked up to find Summer beckoning to her with a finger. The little girl grinned, excited, then raced up the steps two at a time.

"What is it?" she whispered, following Summer towards the open door of her bedroom. "Is it a secret mission?"

"Very!" Summer laughed.

She stepped aside to let the girl through. Then, before she could even close the door behind them, she heard Lola let out a *squee* of delight.

Thousands of dollars' worth of top-of-the-range designer makeup had been laid out on the dressing table. Powders, blushers, mascaras, and lipsticks of all different shades and colours stood there, like an army getting ready to face the enemy in battle.

Lola slowly reached a hand out for one of the lipsticks, like it was calling to her, but then she stopped and drew her arm back, like she was afraid it might turn out to be some sort of mirage.

"Where did you get it all?" she asked in awe.

"Well, you know that woman I showed you on my phone?" Summer asked. "Her name's Audriandra."

"Audrey-what-a?" Lola asked, struggling over the word.

Summer smiled. "Aud-ree-ann-dra," she said, slowing it down. "She's my... friend. Her bags arrived earlier."

"Oh!" Lola looked from Summer to the mass of makeup. "Isn't she going to be upset you went through her things?"

Yes, Summer thought. *Yes, she will.*

Out loud, though, she laughed, waved a hand, and said, "No! We've always shared everything. Makeup, clothes..."

Husbands-to-be, she added, silently.

"Besides, she's so famous she gets sent all this stuff for free. She won't miss a few pieces."

Lola picked up a compact filled with blushes, then sat on the bed, and turned the compact over in her hands like it was some rare, magical artefact. "It's all so lovely. I don't even know what half of it is for!"

"Do you want me to show you?" Summer asked.

Lola's eyes widened, and she bobbed her head. "Oh, yes, please!." She shuffled around on the bed, like she couldn't get comfortable. "Just... Dad says it looks trashy."

Summer sat down beside the girl. "Well, I mean, he has a point—too much can look that way. But we won't do that to you. We'll make it very natural. He'll hardly even notice." She leaned in closer and dropped her voice to a whisper. "But, we'll know. Won't we? Us girls."

Lola smiled, but there was a strange, sombre sort of sadness to it, too. "My Dad doesn't know much about girl stuff. Hair, and makeup, and clothes, and stuff." She tugged on the tweed pants she was wearing. "These trousers are his," she said. "From when he was my age."

Summer's heart broke for her. It had been difficult for Summer growing up without her father around, but she couldn't imagine what it must've been like for Lola without her mother.

"Well, I can't help you with the clothes since I don't have anything your size," she said, taking Lola's hand in hers. "But I could do your nails for you? Help with the makeup, maybe do your hair? Would you like that?"

Lola didn't answer. Not out loud, at least. Instead, she threw her arms around Summer, and hugged her tightly, like she daren't let go.

"Well, OK, then," Summer said. "Miss MacGregor, it's time we gave you a makeover!"

It took Summer the better part of an hour to complete the transformation. It was an hour she knew she didn't have spare, but that didn't matter. Right then, nothing else mattered but giving Lola the makeover she so clearly craved.

When she'd finished styling the girl's hair, dusting her cheeks with blusher, and painting her nails, she stood back, nodded her approval, then announced with a flourish, "Introducing the all-new Lady Lola MacGregor!"

She turned the mirror so Lola could see, and smiled, delighted, as the girl sat there, wide-eyed with wonder.

"Is that even me?" Lola whispered.

Summer laughed. "Of course it's you. And it's very natural."

Lola reached up and gingerly prodded at her hair, like she was worried it might be alive. A smile spread slowly across her face as she turned her head left and right, admiring herself like a movie star. Summer giggled as the little girl got more and more theatrical with her poses, pursing her lips, and shooting sultry looks at herself in the mirror.

There was a knock on the door that caught them both by surprise. It opened without warning, and Hugh poked his head in. "Sorry to intrude, have you seen...?"

His eyes fell on Lola sitting in the chair, and the rest of the sentence died in his throat.

Nobody spoke. Summer thought that Lola was holding her breath, then realised that she was, too.

Maybe Hugh wouldn't notice. Or, maybe he'd see it, but think it looked good.

"What they hell did you do to her?" he demanded.

OK, so much for that idea...

"It's just a little makeup," Summer said. "Nothing trashy. Just some light, natural—"

"No." He stalked over to the tissue box, plucked one out, and handed it to Lola. "Take it off."

"But, Dad, you said I could!" she reminded him.

"Aye, well, I changed my mind!" Hugh barked, so suddenly that it made Summer jump.

Lola was made of sterner stuff, though. Or maybe she knew better than to be afraid of him.

Instead, she just stared up at him, eyes wide, her bottom lip trembling slightly. "Do you not think I look good, Dad?" she asked. "Do you think I look ugly?"

"What? No!" Hugh said, his voice softening. "No, of course not! Never!"

He dropped to his knees in front of her, like he was begging for her forgiveness. His eyes searched her face. He brought up a hand as if to stroke her cheek, but then pulled back from it, like he was afraid he might mess things up.

"I'd never think that. You could never be ugly, Lola," he told her. "It's just... I don't know how to do all this stuff. I don't know how to help you with any of it."

"You don't have to!" Lola said, brightening. "We've got Summer now!"

Hugh opened his mouth to reply, then closed it again, and took a moment to compose himself before answering.

"Summer's no' going to be around forever, Lo," he said, so softly it was like he was afraid he might scare his daughter away. "What happens then? What happens when she leaves? How do I do..." His eyes darted to her hair, and to her carefully painted nails. "...any of this? How am I supposed to help with any of it?"

"What if I didn't go?"

Summer glanced around in surprise, like she wasn't sure who'd spoken. She blinked when she realised it had been her.

Lola and Hugh both turned their heads in unison, both looking just as shocked as she felt.

Lola drew in a long, enormous breath, like she was preparing to let out a scream of pure excitement. Hugh jumped in before she could blow all their eardrums out.

"What do you mean?" he asked.

"Uh, well..."

Summer started to backpedal, still unable to believe that those words had come out of her mouth. She couldn't stay here. Of course she couldn't. Her life was thousands of miles away, back in L.A.

That was where her family was. Her mom. Her sister. That was where she belonged.

"I mean, what if I stayed longer?" she said. "For a while. You know? Maybe until the fall."

Lola's excited squeal didn't get a chance to come to anything. She deflated, disappointed, but then realised that a whole summer with Summer was still much better than one without her.

The girl nodded enthusiastically, then glared at her dad with a look that said, 'Don't you *dare* mess this up!'

Hugh stroked his chin. "I mean, we do have space," he said. "Unless this plan of yours works so well that we end up fully booked..."

"But she was here first!" Lola cried.

"Yes! Exactly!" Summer said, straightening up. "Thank you, Lola. I was here first. I get first dibs!"

Summer found herself liking this plan more and more. She could stay here on the island for two or three months. It would be much easier now that she had internet access.

And, if she was lucky, she'd be able to completely avoid all mention of Brad and Audriandra's wedding.

"Right, well, we'll see," Hugh said, committing to nothing. He got up and headed for the door, then called his daughter over to him. "Right, Lola, come with me. There's no way you're going to this party looking like that."

"Oh, Dad!" Lola pleaded.

"Let her keep it on!" Summer said. "Don't be such a Mr. Miserykilt."

"I want to keep it on!" Lola insisted. She laced her hands under her chin. "Pleeeease, Dad?"

"Oh, look at that face!" Summer cried. "How can you say no to that?"

"Yeah, you tell him, Summer!" Lola cheered.

Hugh glowered back at them both, then held his hands up, calling for silence.

"Hold on, hold on, cool your beans!" he called. He beckoned Lola with a crook of a finger. "Come with me. Now," he said, then he shot a look at Summer. "Both of you, and you'll see what I mean."

He strode out of the room and down the hallway, not looking back. The girls exchanged curious glances and followed him down the hall, until they arrived at a part of the castle that Summer had never been to.

No, wait. Hold on. Actually, she had been there. She remembered the way the corridor ended at the spiral staircase she'd stumbled upon a few nights ago.

They climbed it, Hugh first, Lola second, and Summer bringing up the rear. It creaked and swayed a bit under their weight, leading Summer to wonder if it could support all of them at once.

From Lola's wonderstruck expression, Summer had a feeling she'd never been to this part of the castle, either.

Curiouser and curiouser.

"Where are we going, Dad?"

Hugh didn't answer, reverting once again to his usual cryptic self.

At the top of the spiral staircase, they came to a small, plain wooden door. Hugh hesitated outside it for a moment, like he was pulling himself together, then he pushed onwards into the room beyond.

The room was completely round, and Summer got the impression that they were in one of the castle's turrets.

An enormous old wardrobe stood against one curved wall. It was a wide, ancient-looking thing, that made Summer think of talking lions, and ice-cold witches, and magical lands far, far away.

Beside the wardrobe had been placed an old freestanding mirror, its frame made in matching oak, a crack running across the bottom corner of the glass.

"Right, then," Hugh muttered, and Summer wasn't sure if he was speaking to them, or to himself.

He opened both wardrobe doors, and stood there for a moment, staring inside, like he was frozen in time.

"What is it, Dad?" Lola whispered. "What is this?"

Without a word, Hugh stepped aside to reveal that the wardrobe was packed with brightly coloured clothes in rich, expensive fabrics. There were fancy hats of all shapes and sizes, and a rack holding accessories like beaded purses, and long, elegant gloves.

"Some of these," Hugh announced, "belonged to your grandmother, when she was your age. Your Grandpa and I thought we should hang onto them." He looked down at his daughter, who now stared into the wardrobe just like he had, utterly transfixed. "We thought maybe you'd want them someday."

"Oh, Hugh," Summer said, her voice cracking, both at the gesture, and at the magical look on Lola's face. "They're beautiful."

Hugh grunted. To her surprise, Summer realised she was starting to understand how to speak *Grunt*, after all, because she knew that one meant he was pleased.

"Maybe, if you don't mind," he said, turning to look at her. "You could help Lola find something for the party?"

Lola gasped and looked up at him. "I can get dressed up?"

Hugh put a hand on her shoulder and smiled. "No point getting your hair and makeup done, then turning up in my old tweeds," he told her.

She threw herself at him, grabbing around his waist and burying her face into his sweater. He started to stroke the back of her head, then stopped when her muffled voice warned:

"Hey! Watch the hair!"

"Sorry!" he said. He met Summer's eye, and they both had to fight the urge to laugh.

The moment was only broken when a bell began to *clang* from somewhere downstairs. Far below, they heard shouting— Duncan's voice, urgently calling for them.

Frowning, Hugh went to one of the narrow windows of the room and looked through the dusty old glass. Isla Campbell stood in the garden, gesturing wildly out to sea.

Hugh followed the direction she was pointing, and Summer saw his jaw drop.

"What is it?" she asked, hurrying to join him. "What's...?"

She didn't need to ask. The cause of all the panic was clear.

Yachts, jet skis, and other small boats were cutting through the still waters, churning up foam in their wake as they closed in on the island.

Hugh grimaced. "The freeloaders are coming," he said.

Summer nudged him with an elbow. "Influencers," she said.

Beside her, Hugh sighed. "Aye," he muttered. "That's what I said."

27

THE ARRIVAL

There was no time for the dress-up fun that Lola—and Summer, secretly—had been hoping for. The influencers were on their way, and it was taking all of Summer's self-control not to run around the castle shouting, 'Battle stations!' at the top of her lungs.

Hugh set off to check on preparations, while Summer and Lola quickly decided on what the girl should wear. Almost at once, they settled on a sky-blue, empire-waist dress that had been one of the first garments they'd spotted, then they hurried down the spiral staircase and along the corridor to Lola's room.

"You get ready, here," Summer instructed. "I'll be back soon."

Lola looked as if she were about to burst with excitement as she unhooked the child-sized dress from the hanger and laid it on the bed.

"OK! But Summer, wait—"

Summer stopped in the doorway. "Yes?"

The little girl gnawed on her lower lip. "Did you really mean it that you might stay?"

Summer considered the question for a moment, then

nodded. It wasn't such a crazy idea. And the more she thought about it, the more sense it made. "I'd like to."

Lola clapped her hands and jumped up and down. "I'd love it. And maybe not just for the summer, either. Maybe you'll like it so much, you could stay forever!"

"Forever? Lola, I'm not sure that's... Forever's a long time."

The girl looked sheepish. "Aye, but... It's nice being the lady of the castle, but I wouldn't mind having another one around," she said. "Will you think about it?"

Forever?! Summer thought. She couldn't stay here indefinitely, could she? What about all those things she'd miss in L.A.? All those things she'd hate to leave behind, like...

Summer's mind went blank.

Huh, she thought. *Maybe it's not so crazy an idea, after all.*

"I'll think about it. I promise," she said. "But, we can talk about it more later. I have to go out there and meet everyone. The event is about to begin!"

Lola reached for her dress. "Did you see them, Summer? All them boats? It's way more than four or five people. It looked like a hundred!"

"Yes! How exciting," Summer said. She forced a smile despite the twisting in her gut, and the cold sweat breaking out on her forehead.

There really were an *awful* lot of boats.

She turned and raced back to her room to change, feeling dizzy and nauseated.

A hundred people? That was a low estimate. Especially if all the influencers had all brought their entourages. Some of the entourages might even have brought entourages of their own, knowing Audriandra's circle of friends.

Credit where it was due, though, Audriandra had clearly done a good job when it came to pitching this event to her friends. Maybe *too* good. Audriandra's word carried a lot of clout, but for all those rich and powerful people to have dropped everything and come racing halfway across the globe? She must've promised them an event to remember.

And now, all Summer had to do was fulfil that promise.

She grabbed a fashionable, floor-length sundress from her closet and threw it over her head, then gathered her hair up into a low chignon with tendrils curling loosely around her face, with help from some of the equipment she had 'borrowed' from Audriandra's luggage.

Slipping into her sandals, she ran for the doors, in time to see Hugh and some of the other islanders heading toward the steps that led to the pier.

Summer had requested that they all wear kilts, to help give the event an authentic Scottish flavour. They had all followed her orders, but now she was starting to have some doubts as to whether it was the best idea. Dressed like that, and determinedly marching the way they were, they looked like they were headed into battle, not going to greet some social media superstars.

Down at the bottom of the steps, the narrow dock seemed to be in danger of collapsing or being pulled apart by the weight of all the people gathering there, and the number of boats moored to it.

Hugh waited at the top of the steps while the other menfolk of the island hurried down to greet the Influencers, take their luggage, hand them the internet connection details, and then direct them up the steps.

This was a vital role, Summer had stressed during the planning meeting, because—while the influencers were all successful, some of them weren't exactly intelligent. Left to their own devices, a few might fail to spot the hillside staircase, and eventually just wander aimlessly into the sea.

The gathered islanders had all laughed at that, but when Summer hadn't joined in, they'd eventually realised that she was being serious.

Summer joined Hugh at the top of the stairs, watching the first of the influencers making their way up. As they waited, Summer wrung her hands anxiously, her heart thumping somewhere in her mouth.

Hugh, on the other hand, just stood there, scowling.

"Your expression isn't exactly welcoming," she remarked, as they watched the masses of beautiful people gliding up the steps towards them in their brightly coloured, extravagant outfits.

There must have been thirty or forty on the staircase now, with more piling out of the boats and climbing off the jet skis. Several were already taking photographs of the staircase and the sea view, which Summer was choosing to take as a positive sign.

"Funny, that," Hugh muttered.

A woman dressed head-to-toe in pink reached the top of the stairs first, and came teetering towards them on five-inch heels. She had a pink sequin purse slung over her shoulder, with a small, confused-looking dog poking out of the top. Summer didn't know her, though she immediately made her think that a *Barbie* doll had somehow been brought to life.

"What in the name of God is she meant to be?" Hugh mumbled.

"Like, *Ermygod!*" the Barbie clone cried, looking Hugh up and down. "I so love the skirts you guys wear. It's, like, so now, you know? So *totally* of the moment. Hashtag-Trans-Women-Are-Women. Am I right?"

"What the hell's she talking about?" asked Hugh.

He shot Summer a sideways look, but when he saw her, his eyes widened and his mouth fell open a little.

Summer caught his expression and frowned. "What's wrong?" she whispered.

"Eh, nothing," Hugh said. "Doesn't matter."

The Barbie clone had gone teetering off, and was now posing for selfies that took in the sea view. In her place, half a dozen other young, equally extravagant-looking women, had appeared at the top of the stairs.

"They look like bloody Lemmings," Hugh remarked. "I bet if one walks over the edge there, they all follow."

Summer nudged him with an elbow.

"Just *try* to be welcoming. It's only one day," she instructed. She took a deep breath, muttered, "Right, here goes!" then paced forwards, her arms held out wide, a big smile plastered across her face. "Welcome, everyone! Welcome! We're so glad to have you here!"

"Aye. Thrilled to bits," she heard Hugh grumble, but she ignored him.

The reaction from the influencers was not quite what she'd been hoping for. She'd expected them all to gather around her, instantly recognizing her as the person in charge around here.

Instead, around half of them completely ignored her, while the other half looked down their noses at her, like they resented her opening her mouth.

There were a few familiar faces piling up the stairs now. A TikTok star named Chelsea—who Summer had been briefly introduced to by Audriandra back in L.A., before being sent to get them drinks from the bar—practically elbowed her way through the crowd when she saw one of the villagers, Mick, coming towards them with a tray of Champagne flutes.

Mick had been given the job of dishing out the drinks partly on the basis that he had once been a Barman at Campbell's pub, but mostly because he was one of only two or three men on the island who could be trusted not to drink all the Champagne himself.

The other influencers spotted his approach, and turned on him like a horde of zombies, with Chelsea leading the pack. Mick stopped, alarmed by the sudden stampede. He shut his eyes and braced himself as the influencers descended like a swarm of alcoholic locusts, snatching the glasses from his tray and quickly draining them dry.

"Ugh. That's, like, the worst Champagne I've ever tasted!" Chelsea declared. A smile curved the corners of her mouth. "It's so kitsch and ironic! I love it!"

She returned the glass to the tray. Beside her, a floppy-haired skater boy in a white tank top and trousers so baggy he was in danger of being blown into the sea, grimaced as he knocked back his own drink.

"Where can I get more?" Chelsea demanded of Mick. "I want to get completely wasted!"

Skater Boy glanced up at the castle, then let out a low groan. "We're going to have to get wasted for this. This place sucks."

Mick looked down at all the empty glasses being returned to his tray, then shot Summer a pleading look.

"Get more! Go get more!" she urged.

Mick did not look confident. "I'll, eh, I'll see what I can do," he said, then he quickly beat a retreat back up the hill and through the castle doors.

Hugh leaned in closer to Summer. "So much for four or five people, eh?"

"This is good!" Summer told him, trying very hard to sound convincing. "This is way better than I thought!"

"Interesting," Hugh muttered. "Because it's worse than I thought. And we're barely two minutes into it."

Before Summer could reply, Skater Boy piped up with another loud criticism.

"That's not a proper castle," he declared. "It's a total dump. Look at it, it's ancient."

"Aye, that's the point, you floppy-haired eejit!" Hugh ejected, spinning to face the loudmouthed skater.

Summer quickly inserted herself between both men, switching seamlessly into peacemaker mode.

"Oh, Laird McGregor!" she said, trilling out a laugh. "You really are so funny sometimes! What he *meant* to say, of course, was that the castle may look a little run down, but that's because it's steeped in history. I was a little unsure about it when I first arrived, too, but I promise you, by the time you leave, you'll have fallen in love with it, just like I have."

Chelsea took her boyfriend by the arm and giggled. "Yeah, give it a chance. This place is so bad it's great! And they might have more of that terrible Champagne in there!"

They set off towards Lachart Castle, and the rest of the influencers followed, sensing the very real possibility of more alcohol.

Hugh's expression darkened when several camera flashes went off in his face, as some of the visitors took photographs of him, or posed for selfies with him standing in the background.

"Can I, like, take a picture up your kilt?" asked the Barbie clone, appearing suddenly behind him.

Hugh stared back at her for a moment, then shook his head. "No," he said. "No, you cannot."

Barbie pouted, then stroked the head of her tiny dog so hard that its eyes bulged.

"Oh, pwease?" she said, putting on a baby voice. "Not even for Mrs. Poochcooch?"

Hugh continued to stare at the young woman for several more seconds, aside from a brief glance at the animal in her handbag.

"Mrs. Poochcooch?" he asked, raising an eyebrow.

"Yeah. You know? It's, like, *Mrs. DogVagina*," Barbie said, as if this were the most normal thing in the world. "Only better, because it rhymes."

Hugh sighed. It was a heavy, weary thing, like the weight of the world had just landed on his shoulders.

"God help us all," he whispered.

"Hey, look!" said Summer, pointing to the enormous building beside them. "A castle!"

Barbie turned, gave a little gasp of surprise, then went wobbling up the hill on her precariously high heels.

Hugh and Summer both stood in silence for a while, watching her go.

"Your friends are weird," Hugh eventually remarked.

"They're not my friends," Summer corrected. "And they're not weird, they're just... different."

Hugh's raised eyebrow had remained fixed in that position for the last while. Now, the other climbed up his forehead in solidarity.

"*Mrs. DogVagina?*"

Summer opened her mouth as if to say something, hesitated, then nodded. "Yeah," she said. "Yeah, you're right. That is weird. Still, everything's going well so far!"

"Is it?" asked Hugh, unconvinced.

"Yes! And thank you for busting out the kilt," Summer told him. "You look... good. Great! You look great."

Hugh shrugged. "Aye, well," he muttered. He sighed again,

though this one sounded completely different from the one of just a few moments before. "You, too. Look good." He frowned, like he was replaying the words, then shook his head. "You look good, too, I mean."

Summer smiled at him. "I figured it out," she said. She self-consciously smoothed down the front of her dress. "And, um, thanks."

She was about to say more, when the fine hairs on the back of her neck tickled, like a cool breeze was blowing through them.

Her heart *thumped* as she became aware of the slow, horse-like *clip-clop* of heels on the stone steps behind her.

Even before Summer turned, she knew who she would find there. She could sense her presence, like the way the air became heavy and oppressive before the breaking of a storm.

Finally summoning her courage, Summer turned in time to see a meticulously sculpted head of platinum-blonde hair rising into view at the top of the staircase.

Audriandra had arrived!

28

THE OTHER ARRIVAL

S ummer froze at the sight of her former best friend, standing there in all her magnificent, sparkling glory.

She was wearing a tight red tube dress that showed a significant amount of her flawless, tanned skin. Her shoes matched the colour of the dress, and gave her six or seven inches of additional height thanks to the pointed heels that, despite the rough terrain, she strode confidently in.

Her hair was piled atop her head like she hadn't done a thing with it. It looked incredible, though, and Summer knew from experience that it took two-to-three hours of work to get it looking *precisely* that accidental.

The sky was a little overcast, and nowhere near as sunny as she'd be used to back in L.A., yet she wore a pair of dark sunglasses that wouldn't have looked out of place on a movie star.

Every islander down on the dock was looking up the stairs after her, and those standing around the castle swung their heads to look at her as she approached the two-person welcoming committee of Summer and Hugh, walking in big, confident strides, like she was a catwalk model at Paris Fashion Week.

Which, as it happened, she had been three times before.

"Philip!" she called as she walked, lifting a perfectly manicured red fingernail. "Can you hear me? Don't forget to put the caviar on ice for the return trip. The good stuff this time, Philip. Let's not have a repeat of earlier."

Hugh leaned in closer to Summer. "Who's she talking to?" he whispered.

Summer murmured something about phones, which Hugh understood, and Bluetooth, which he didn't, then went back to gawping at Audriandra.

Watching her approach, she felt that familiar swirl of all those old feelings come rushing back. Inadequacy, mostly. For most of her life, Summer had been made to feel invisible in Audriandra's presence.

And now, when she spotted the diamond ring glinting on Audriandra's finger, Summer could feel herself disappearing all over again.

The ring was enormous. Ludicrously so. It was so big it probably had its own zip code. Every time she raised her left hand, the ring was probably visible from space.

Where did that come from? she wondered.

When Brad had got down on one knee to propose to Audriandra at what was supposed to have been Brad and Summer's wedding, he hadn't a ring with him. And, to his credit, he hadn't been *quite* cruel enough to demand that Summer hand back the one he'd given to her.

That ring didn't compare to this one, though. Summer's engagement ring had been small and unassuming, much like Summer herself.

She supposed that Audriandra's ring fit her personality as well—big, brash, and blinding.

Not to mention ludicrously expensive.

Summer held her breath, eyes darting from her ex-BFF to the top of the staircase behind her. From here, the view stretched out to sea, where a shaft of sunlight had punched a hole through a layer of grey cloud, and was dappling the water below.

And that, to her relief, was *all* she could see. Nobody was coming up the stairs at Audriandra's back.

She was, it seemed, alone.

Audriandra tapped a finger to her ear, then picked up the pace, like she was in a hurry to reach Summer. Her mouth folded itself into a big, beaming smile, as if a button had been pushed on the back of her head.

She threw her arms wide, and did a little skipping sort of dance that probably would've made Summer fall flat on her face if she attempted it, even without the heels.

"*Darling!*" Audriandra oozed. She assaulted Summer with a series of air kisses, complete with *mwah, mwah* sound effects. "How I've missed you!"

"Uh, you too," Summer said. "And, you know, *wow!* Look at you! You look amazing!"

Audriandra did look at herself. It was quite a lingering look, too, that started at her feet, then moved up her long, slender legs, and lingered, just for a moment, at her impressive cleavage.

"Yes," she agreed. "You're right. I do!"

Summer smiled, hoping that maybe—just this once—the compliment would be returned.

It was not.

"So, uh, thank you for coming so quickly," Summer said. "And for bringing all your friends, too!"

Audriandra snorted. "Oh, these aren't all my friends. This is, like, a fraction. I just made an Instagram story to say I was going, and asked if anyone wanted to tag along, and... Voila!"

While she'd been talking, she was also admiring the man standing silently beside them, dressed in the full Highland kilt.

"And who is this?" she purred. "Is this the king?"

Hugh snorted out a laugh. "The king?"

"Of the castle?" Audriandra said. She looked past him, then grimaced, baring the perfectly polished pearls that were her teeth. "Ew. We have some issues here, don't we? The whole building's been overpowered by the outside. Don't you think, Sums?"

Summer followed Audriandra's gaze. "Um..."

"It's fine. It's fine. Not much you can do about it, I guess. It's fine. It's... nice. No. It is. It really is," Audriandra said, sounding like she was arguing with herself. She thrust a hand out to Hugh, palm down, like she was presenting it for him to kiss. "Audriandra IOUK. I'm sure you've heard of me."

"Aye, I have," Hugh said. He took the hand, shook it firmly, then returned it to her. "Summer's told me all about you."

"Only good things, I'm sure," Audriandra said, and from her tone it was clear that she actually believed that. That she didn't think Summer could possibly have *anything* negative to say about her. "So, are you the king?"

"No," Hugh told her.

"Oh. So you're the handsome Prince Charming?" Audriandra said, her tongue flicking tantalizingly across her plump, glossy lips.

"It's actually 'Laird,'" Summer corrected. "Not prince."

Irritation flitted briefly across Audriandra's face. She laughed, but it was a dry, impatient sort of thing. "Yes, well *Laird*

Charming doesn't work, does it, Sums? No, that just sounds stupid!"

Flustered, Summer just gawped awkwardly back at her taller, skinnier, infinitely more successful former friend. She had absolutely no idea how to reply to that, so was relieved when salvation came in the form of Duncan and Lola, who were striding down the slope from the castle, hand in hand.

Lola's eyes were like saucers, as she stared at all the vibrant, colourfully dressed people snapping off photos of the front of the castle. They were a world away from the drab tweed and bulky sweaters she had grown up around.

Lola was swinging her grandfather's arm, as if his legs were pistons, and pumping them might make them work faster.

The old man was decked out in full kilt regalia, complete with a tartan sash slung across his chest and one shoulder. Beside him, Lola looked every inch a princess in her vintage blue dress.

Clearly, they hadn't been able to find matching shoes in her size, because every time the hem of the dress raised up when she skipped, Summer caught a glimpse of the Wellies she was wearing underneath.

It was a bold combination, and yet she somehow managed to pull it off.

"Well, hello there!" Duncan called, approaching the group standing near the head of the stairs. He tipped an imaginary hat to Audriandra, and smiled warmly. "I'm Duncan MacGregor, owner of Lachart Castle. This here is Lady Lola MacGregor."

Audriandra's face screwed up as she looked at them both in turn. "She's your wife?" the socialite gasped.

Duncan laughed. "Good one!" he cried.

Audriandra continued to stare at them both, her face fixed in a mask of horror.

"Oh. She's serious," Duncan said, side-eyeing Summer. "No, miss. No. Lola here is my granddaughter. My *favourite* grand-daughter, I might add."

"And only," Lola added.

"And that, yes," Duncan confirmed. He winked at her, and she stuck out her tongue, then he turned his attention back to the woman in the barely-there red dress. "And you are...?"

"Beautiful," Lola whispered.

Audriandra batted her eyelashes, accepting the compliment. "Naturally! And, can I just say, I l-o-v-e *love* that dress! You've got to tell me who you're wearing."

Lola looked down at her outfit, then back up at Audriandra. "What do you mean?"

"That dress! Whose is it? Is it one of Gucci's?"

"No," Lola said, firmly shaking her. "It's one of my granny's."

"Oh. Right," the socialite said, her perfectly smooth forehead creasing a fraction as she frowned. "Well... good for her."

"This is Audriandra," Summer said, desperately trying to smooth over the growing cracks in the conversation. "She's also from Los Angeles, and runs a successful social media empire."

"*Highly* successful," Audriandra said.

"Sorry, a *highly* successful social media empire," Summer corrected.

Duncan had just smiled and nodded through that, barely understanding a word of it.

"Well, very nice to meet you, Audrey," he said.

"Audriandra," the woman in the red dress corrected.

Duncan hesitated, but kept smiling. "Andrea."

"No, *Audriandra*."

There was plenty more nodding from Duncan, though the smile faded a bit.

"What an interesting name," he said, no longer bothering to

even try to pronounce it. "Very... cosmopolitan." His gaze flitted past the group, just for a moment. "And who, might I ask, is your gentleman friend?"

Summer frowned. 'Gentleman friend'? What was Duncan talking about?

She heard the *slap-slap* of approaching flip-flops, and felt her heart drop into her stomach, even as her stomach tried to force its way up into her mouth. She almost choked on the resulting tangle of organs.

Oh, God. Oh, no!

"Whoa! Like, those steps would be *so rad* to skate down!"

Summer felt the whole island start to spin around her. Beads of sweat appeared on her forehead. She stumbled sideways, off-balance, and was only saved from a humiliating fall when Hugh caught her by the elbow, and righted her without a word.

And suddenly, there he was, striding so confidently towards them that he looked like he owned the place.

He was dressed for a day on Santa Monica beach, with a Hawaiian shirt open to show most of his smooth, tanned chest, and a pair of thigh-length shorts that displayed his skinny, but well-toned legs.

The sunglasses he wore were very similar to Audriandra's and, just like them, could well have been a matching pair.

The look was miles away from the grungy skater that Summer had fallen in love with. She was used to seeing him in baggy T-shirts and board shorts that came down below his knees. Now, even his socks had a designer name on them.

A few weeks with Audriandra, it seemed, had moulded him into something he wasn't.

He was her fiancé, yes, but he had become something else, too, Summer realised.

An accessory.

"Wow. Summer! Is that you?!" Brad cried, pushing the sunglasses up onto his head.

He leaned in, took her hand, and gave her a kiss on the cheek. A real one, this time, not one of Audriandra's air kisses.

The touch of his lips was like electricity on her skin, and she was sure that, when his lingering lips finally left her cheek, a perfect impression would be left there in the form of goosebumps.

Audriandra had changed his look, but she hadn't changed his smell. That citrus aroma was the old Brad—*her* Brad—before he'd been stolen from her.

"I didn't know you were going to be here!" Brad said.

Beside him, Audriandra rolled her eyes. "Yes, you did," she said, like she was talking to a child. "I told you on the plane."

"You did?" Brad frowned and scratched his curly, bleach-blond locks. "Huh. Wow. Totally must've zoned out. But, *wow*, Summer. You look amazing! Doesn't she look amazing, Auds?"

"It's *Audriandra*." Summer's former best friend flashed a smile that lasted for approximately three-fifths of a second, then shot her an appraising look. "And, you've obviously put in *so much effort*, Sums!" she said, and it sounded every inch the insult Summer knew it was intended to be. "You've tried *so* hard! And what you've done with your hair, it's..." Audriandra inhaled, stared at Summer's head for what felt like a long time, then finished with, "...very admirable."

Summer felt herself fading away again, turning invisible before everyone's eyes.

And then Hugh's hand was on her elbow again, holding her there, anchoring her in place.

"Well, I think you look amazing," Brad told her, and his stare was so honest and intense that she let out a breathless little giggle.

"Right, well, unless you two are going to run off and get married—and we all know how that turned out last time," Audriandra said, interrupting their shared moment. "Let's get going with... whatever we're here to do, shall we? Some of us have places to be." She gestured disparagingly at the castle. "Even if that place is this... What was it you called it? A hovel?"

"A castle," Hugh said, and his voice was a deep, resonating growl. "It's a castle."

"Right. That was it," Audriandra said, smiling sweetly. "Tell me it at least has running water. Tell me I can at least take a bath."

"You can take a running jump off the pier, as far as I'm concerned," Hugh muttered, too quietly for anyone but Summer to make it out.

"I'm sorry?" the woman in the red dress asked.

Before Hugh could repeat himself, only louder, Summer elbowed him aside.

"Of course it has running water!" she laughed.

"And your room's really nice!" Lola added, lending Summer her support. "It's the nicest one in the whole place!"

Audriandra let out a little laugh. "Oh, that I *have* to see," she said.

"I can show you, if you like?" Lola gushed, the sarcasm whooshing over her head. "I can, can't I, Dad?"

Hugh looked from his daughter to Summer, who opened her eyes wide, forced a smile, and nodded encouragingly.

"Fine," Hugh said, exhaling slowly through his nose. "Just be quick, alright? And don't you go making a nuisance of yourself."

"I'm sure she won't," Brad said.

Hugh met the other man's eye. "That bit wasn't aimed at her," he replied, shifting his gaze from Brad to Audriandra, then back again.

Lola released her grandfather's hand, then set off up the hill towards the castle. "Come on, this way! Come with me, I'll show you!"

Audriandra followed the girl without so much as a backwards glance. Brad hung back long enough to put a hand on Summer's bare shoulder. Once again, his touch was electric.

"You really do look amazing," he told her.

"Thanks." Summer swallowed. "Do you sew?"

Brad frowned. "Do I sew?"

Summer had to fight to stop herself slapping a hand against her forehead.

"I mean, so do you," she mumbled, her cheeks burning red.

"Brad! Hurry up!"

Audriandra's tone left no room for argument. With a final smile, Brad turned and hurried up the slope after her and Lola, leaving Summer to pull herself together.

She was still watching them when Hugh's voice spoke in her ear.

"I get what you see in him," he said. "I mean, the way he wears those sandals..."

"They're not sandals," Summer said. "They're flip-flops."

"Oh, well pardon me," Hugh said, putting a hand on his chest like he was shocked. "Because a grown man in flip-flops is *much* better."

Duncan quietly cleared his throat, reminding them both he was there.

"I'll just, eh..." He glanced around, and then pointed in an apparently random direction. "...go that way."

And he did, springing away like a mountain goat, and hurrying off to mingle with the other visitors.

Once he'd left, Summer turned back to Hugh.

"Could you please just try to be on your best behaviour? If

you want this to work, you have to play nice! Otherwise, you might as well kiss the island goodbye."

"What do you mean?" Hugh asked. "I am playing nice. This is me being nice."

"Then be *nicer*," Summer sing-songed through a toothy grin.

She waved at a few influencers who were taking photographs in front of a rusted old wagon, overgrown with weeds, *oohing* and *aahing* like it was the most interesting thing in the world.

A few were posing in front of some moss-covered standing stones in the wide strip of grass in front of the castle.

"It's no' that easy to be nice when they're smiling away and taking photos of my dead mother's gravestone," Hugh pointed out.

Summer winced. "Oh. Is that what they are? I thought those were just for decoration."

Hugh shook his head. "If they were just for decoration, we wouldn't have gone to all the trouble of chiselling 'Rest in Peace' into them."

"I am *so* sorry! I'll sort it," Summer said. She rushed ahead, clapping her hands to get everyone's attention. "Everyone! We're about to have refreshments in the courtyard, and then several of our islanders will be offering ATV tours of the grounds, and ghost tours of the castle. So, if you'd like to follow me..."

She headed for the doors, beckoning for the influencers to follow her. It didn't take much effort on her part, as the word 'refreshments' had already done much of the heavy lifting for her.

They swarmed in behind her, and she heard them chattering away as she led them into the main hall, and through the corridors.

Shrieks of laughter and disbelief rang out through the castle hallways.

"Oh my God, look at the décor!" one influencer shrieked. And not, Summer thought, in a good way.

She heard the sound of phone cameras snapping pictures, and felt her cheeks burning again as she led them through to the courtyard.

It was all going wrong. She could feel it. Her plan was unravelling before her eyes.

Or, more accurately, behind her back.

She stopped at a set of wooden doors that had been fixed open, and directed the group through to the castle courtyard.

There were a few gasps and murmurs from the influencers, and when Summer followed them through, she soon saw why.

The islanders had somehow worked a miracle. The courtyard wasn't just neat and tidy, it looked like something out of a fairy-tale, with strings of twinkling Christmas lights crisscrossing the seating area, and fine mesh nets hanging over every picnic bench so they looked like the play tents of a prince or princess.

Or—and the thought twisted Summer's stomach again—like the veils of a wedding dress.

"Midge nets," mumbled Mick, appearing beside her with a tray of weird and wonderful alcoholic drinks. "Hugh thought it best that your friends don't all get eaten alive."

Summer blinked. "Hugh?"

"Aye. He did this," Mick said, nodding to the twinkling lights. "Up half the night, Duncan tells me."

Summer watched the colourful lights fading on and off. They looked lovely now. Once it got dark, they would transform the place into something truly magical.

"He never said," she remarked, but by then Mick was being

swarmed by thirsty visitors, all grabbing for the glasses on his tray.

"Don't you worry, lads and lassies," he boomed. "There's plenty more where this came from!"

She watched the guests taking their cocktails and wandering around the courtyard. Some took photos of the drinks. Others snapped selfies sipping them. A few were already typing away on their screens, and Summer's heart skipped a beat when she heard the first *whoosh* of a post being published.

Another followed. And another. And another.

Yikes! This is it!

Hand shaking, she took out her phone, opened up Instagram, and typed in her 'Love, Life, Lachart' hashtag.

With so many people using the internet at the same time, it took a moment for the results to load.

She'd expected a handful, and almost fell over when she saw a full page of matching results.

No. More than that. She swiped with her thumb, and found herself scrolling through dozens of photos and comments. It was blowing up—photos of scenery, the castle, the grounds, the drink, the kilts, and... yes... Hugh's grandmother's gravestone.

That one was unfortunate.

It was the comments that excited her most, though. People were jumping on the posts, demanding to know where the photos were taken, and how they could come see the place for themselves.

"It's working!" Summer cheeped. "It's actually working!"

"What's working?"

Summer spun around to find Audriandra looming over her. Somehow, in just the past few minutes, she'd managed to get changed into a completely different outfit. This one was mostly silver, and with her extravagantly long legs and slender frame, she looked vaguely alien.

Not the sort of slimy, violent alien that would eat your face off. More a sort of hypnotically beautiful one, who would steal your husband-to-be right out from under your nose.

"Uh, this! The event! It's going well," Summer said, trying to keep the surprise from her voice.

"Oh. Right," Audriandra wrinkled her nose and looked around. "Is it? That's... nice." She turned and looked back over her shoulder through the open doorway. "Come on then. Don't keep me waiting," she urged.

Summer braced herself for seeing Brad again. She'd hoped they'd stay out of her way for longer. She wasn't sure she was ready to face him again just yet.

As it turned out, she needn't have worried. It wasn't Brad who stepped through the door, but Hugh.

"Uh, what are you doing?" Summer asked him.

"You told me to be nice," Hugh said. He shrugged. "This is me being nice."

"Well, yes, but..."

"You want this to work," Hugh said, throwing her own words back at her. "Don't you?"

"Well, *yes*, but..." she said again.

But then, before she could continue, Audriandra hooked her arm through Hugh's and started to pull him away.

"Come on, then, Prince Charming," she purred. "Let's get me a drink."

Summer stood there, frozen to the spot, as they walked off, looking every inch the couple. Audriandra was in full flow, chatting away, laughing at her own jokes and lightly touching Hugh on the arm.

At one point, Hugh smiled—he actually smiled! Until then,

she hadn't even been sure that he had teeth, and yet, there he was now, grinning away like he'd just won the lottery.

And, with Audriandra on his arm, maybe he had.

She felt her phone buzzing, and looked down to see a fresh round of Instagram posts appearing. These ones were not like the previous few, though. One showed a dead bird lying in the grass. Another showed a patch of damp on a wall, and some cobwebs that must've gone overlooked during the castle clean-up.

No, no, no!

This wasn't good.

She looked over to where Audriandra had slipped an arm around Hugh's waist. That wasn't good, either.

She felt herself switching back into panic mode, sensing impending disaster. And not just a regular-grade disaster, either —the biggest, most spectacular disaster of her life!

Summer thought back to her wedding, and the million memes of her crying face it had spawned.

OK, maybe the *second* most spectacular disaster, but it would be a close-run thing.

Her heart plummeted, and she spun away, desperate for a cocktail—or many cocktails, ideally—with which to drown her sorrows. She rushed off to look for Mick, then walked straight into the slim, tanned figure who had been standing right behind her.

"Oh, sorr—"

She stopped, sucked in a breath of sweet citrus air, and was almost knocked over by a smile as dazzling as it was familiar.

Brad.

29

CHANGE OF HEART

S ummer anticipated the incoming kiss to the cheek, moved to avoid it, and their heads collided with a faint, hollow *knock*.

"Sorry, sorry," she babbled. "My fault."

Brad smiled at her as he rubbed his forehead, but made no other move to kiss her.

And why should he? she thought. *One greeting kiss had been quite devastating enough.*

"It's fine. Don't worry about it," he said, placing a hand on her bare shoulder.

There was that electricity again, but there was something else, too. Something she realised she had been craving. The familiarity of his touch. Even after everything that had happened, his skin against hers felt so natural.

Too natural.

She subtly squirmed away from his hand. Friendly was fine. She could deal with that. Step over that line, though, and there was no saying where she'd end up.

"How was your trip here?" she asked, mechanically.

"Oh, you know," Brad said. He snatched a cocktail from the passing tray, and drained it in one gulp. "It's always a good time with the Bradster!"

Summer winced. She'd managed to forget about his annoying habit of referring to himself in the third person. It was even worse when he called himself 'the Bradster.' As nicknames went, it was equal parts uninspired and irritating.

At one point, she'd convinced herself that his whole routine was entertaining. She'd told herself she positively adored how goofy and idiotic he could be.

And then, when the novelty of it all had worn off a little, she'd told herself he wasn't really like this. 'The Bradster' was just performing for the camera, and for all his dedicated followers.

Now, she wasn't sure if it was an act, or if all that stuff *was* the real Brad. Either way, she finally realised just how annoying it was.

"Yep. Always a good time," she agreed.

Except when you ditched me on our wedding day, you self-centred idiot man-child, she added inside her head.

He gazed around the courtyard, and looked largely baffled by what he saw. "So, this place is, like… a castle."

"It is, yes," Summer confirmed, because it was sometimes difficult to tell if Brad was making a statement or asking a question.

"Right. Right," he said. He nodded slowly.

It had been a question, then.

"How the hell did you wind up here?" he asked. "Did you get on the wrong plane or something? Because I did that once. Was supposed to be flying to Georgia—you know, the state?—and ended up in, like, Russia. It was wild."

Summer remembered that story. And she should, because he'd told her it around a dozen times before.

"No. I came here on purpose," she said. "I wanted to get away."

"And you came *here*?!" Brad looked around and shivered, like he was suddenly feeling the cold. "I told you, you should've just gone to Hawaii."

"But I didn't want to go to Hawaii."

It was entirely possible that someone as vapid as Brad could fly solo on the honeymoon he was supposed to spend with the forever-love of his life, but Summer hadn't felt up to that particular task.

"I wanted to come here. My father used to visit this place before he died. This castle was one of the last places we visited together."

Brad shot the building a scathing look. "It's not exactly much of a castle, though, is it? It's, like, a pile of rubble with a roof."

"No. It's rustic and charming," Summer replied, feeling her hackles rising. "There's so much history in this castle. And the flora and fauna on this island are incredible, too."

She stopped when he laughed at her, smiling condescendingly at her as if she were a toddler on the brink of her first big tantrum.

There was no point trying to sell him on all the good points of Lachart Castle, anyway. He was the son of two Hollywood actors, after all, raised in Beverly Hills. He lived for glamor. Not this.

"I always loved that about you, Sum. How you'd always find the best, even in, like, the worst situations."

She raised an eyebrow. He'd never said anything like that to her when they were dating.

"This is far from a bad situation. I'm happy here."

He pulled a face that showed his surprise. "Happy? Here?" His lips moved as he silently repeated those words again, like he was trying to find a way to make them make sense.

Summer stood her ground, waiting for him to finish. The truth was that maybe she *was* happy here. Over the last couple of days, she'd stopped dwelling on the past, and had started to imagine that maybe she might actually be able to live again.

"Oh, wait! I get it!" Brad said, snapping his fingers. "I know what's going on."

"What do you mean?" Summer asked.

"It's stock market syndrome."

Summer frowned. "It's what?"

"You know, when, like, people fall in love with their kidnappers, or whatever?"

"Do you mean Stockholm syndrome?"

"Right! Like *Beauty and the Beast*."

Summer didn't think that was *quite* what that story was about, but chose not to get into a debate about it.

"I don't understand," she said.

Brad put an arm around her shoulder. She wasn't quick enough to dodge it this time, and was suddenly surrounded by the citrus smell of his cologne.

"Think about it, babe. You always convinced yourself you loved stuff like this. Boring nature trips. That time you made us go to that place with the trees, or whatever."

"Redwood Forest," Summer said. She'd wanted to go see it because she shared some of her father's love for botany. "And you didn't come. Like you didn't come when I wanted to drive out into the desert outside Palm Springs to check out the terrain."

"Because who wants to see that?!" Brad snorted.

"I did! I do! I love places like that! Places like..." Her breath caught at the back of her throat, as the realisation hit her. "Like this. I love places like this."

"But there's no views in it, babe," Brad oozed. "With great followers comes great responsibility. We talked about this. I can't make a video about some stupid trees, or rocks, or whatever. My followers want sunshine! Glamor! Excess!"

Summer pulled away from him. "Oh, well, clearly Audriandra must have you wrapped around her little finger to drag you all the way over here."

Brad clasped his fingers together, interlocking them all except the two index fingers, which he held in front of his mouth, his face becoming solemn and serious.

"Cards on the table, truth be told, she didn't want me here," he said. "She didn't want me to come. Like, at all."

Summer glanced over to where her former best friend was gliding through the throngs filling the courtyard, a still-smiling Hugh striding along beside her.

"What?" Summer muttered, turning back to Brad. "Why?"

"Because she knows the truth, babe," Brad said. He was staring so intently at Summer now that her legs were becoming weak.

He really did have very nice eyes. She'd always loved that about him.

She was almost too afraid to ask the question, but she had to. She had to know.

"What truth?"

"That we're meant to be together."

Summer blinked.

Summer stared.

Summer threw a thumb back over her shoulder.

"You and Audriandra?"

Brad smirked and shook his head, his gaze still lingering on her.

"You and me, babe," he whispered.

She watched, helpless, as he reached out, took one of her hands in his, and gently massaged it.

"Me and Auds, to start with, it was awesome. I mean, she's beautiful, you know? And so full of life. And the sex? I mean... Wow. Some of the things she can do! I can't even describe them."

"Please don't," Summer said.

Brad stared vaguely into the middle distance for a few seconds with a faint smile on his face, then shook his head and continued.

"But it wasn't real. Her and me, it's just... There's this book I read that kind of sums it up perfectly."

"You read a book?"

"Hey! I've got more levels than people give me credit for!" Brad protested. "This book, it's like... It just nails it, you know? This whole situation."

"What's it called?" Summer asked.

"*The Three Little Pigs*," Brad said. "Have you heard of it?"

Summer stared back at him in a somewhat stunned silence for a few seconds, wondering if he was making a joke. From his expression, though, she quickly concluded that he wasn't.

"The one with the big bad wolf?" she asked. "Huffing and puffing and..."

"Blowing the house down! Yes! You've read it? Awesome!" Brad said. He squeezed her hand a little tighter. "So, here's the thing. Over the last week, I've realised that me and Auds? We're, like, we're straw and sticks. You know? One big gust, and we're gone. But you and me? We're bricks. We're solid."

Summer looked down at her hand in his, trying to untangle the metaphor.

"So... am I the pig in this scenario?" she asked.

"Yes!" Brad grinned. "I mean, no. I mean, *we're* the pig. I'm, like, several pigs, actually. I'm the bricks pig, *and* I'm the straw and sticks pigs. You're just the bricks pig."

Summer sighed quietly. First Hugh, now Brad. What was it with men comparing her to farm animals?

"Auds is... I mean, she's great. She's rich, she's beautiful, she's famous, and she's just, like, *perfect*, you know?"

"Oh, I know," Summer said, and she wasn't quite able to keep the bitterness from her voice.

"And you're not like that!" Brad gushed, in a way that made the comment sound like a compliment.

"So... I'm a pig. She's perfect, and all that stuff, and I'm a pig?"

Brad smiled at her, showing the dimples in his cheeks that had first attracted her to him.

"That's not what I'm saying, and you know it, Sum," he laughed, still massaging the palm of her hand. "I'm saying that I love you."

Summer made a sound that she'd never heard herself make before. It was some blend of gasp, sob, and cough, with just a hint of hysterical laughter thrown in for good measure.

"You love me?" she asked, and the trembling of her voice betrayed her. "But... Audriandra."

"She isn't you," Brad said.

Was his cologne getting stronger? Were the electric tingles of his touch becoming more powerful?

"You and me, babe, we're meant to be together. I see that now. I was scared, that's why I did what I did. I was an idiot. But I'm here now. I'm back. We can go home. Together."

It was everything she had been hoping to hear since her

wedding day. The admission that he'd made a terrible mistake. An apology for betraying and humiliating her like that.

Technically, she hadn't actually *had* the apology part yet, but this was as close as she was likely to get, she knew.

And that was fine. She didn't need him to *actually* say he was sorry. She could see how bad he felt...

Oh, God.

He was doing it again.

Drawing her in, like she was caught in a tractor beam. She could feel everything else falling away. How many times in the days following the wedding-that-wasn't had she imagined this moment? How many tears had she shed curled up in bed, dreaming of him giving her this speech?

"So, what do you say?" he asked.

"To what? I'm not even sure what you're asking?"

"I'm asking you to come with me. Come away from this..." He gestured to the castle. "...third-world hellhole, and come back to L.A."

"It isn't a hellhole!" Summer protested, though her defence of the place sounded less robust than before. "I like it. And I'm helping here."

"You can help in L.A. You can, like, I don't know, wash the homeless, or something. There's a ton of those guys, and they all stink."

Summer winced. "That's not quite the same as this."

"Because this is a castle? Babe, my channel's blowing up right now. I'll buy you *five* castles!" Brad declared, then he quickly walked it back. "Three castles. Castles are crazy expensive."

Summer shot an anxious look back over her shoulder, but Audriandra and Hugh were still mingling, Hugh holding her bag for her while Audriandra posed for photos.

"Does Audriandra know about this?" Summer whispered.

"I didn't tell her I was planning this, but I think she suspects something," Brad admitted. "But I don't care. I love you, Sum. Don't you love me?"

Summer searched his face, his wide eyes staring back at her, full of hope.

"I do," she admitted.

They'd spent five years together. Half a decade. He'd been the first real love of her life, and despite all that had happened at the end of their relationship, she knew she'd always have feelings for him.

"Awesome! Then let's do it. Let's get back together. Let's get married. We'll do it your way. Anywhere you want. Just, you know, not here, obviously, because it's cold, and it sucks."

Summer couldn't feel the cold. If anything, she suddenly felt too hot, like all her blood was rushing to her head, making her sweat.

If he'd come here with this proposal two days ago, she'd already be running down the steps with him and jumping on the first available seaworthy vessel.

But that was then, and a lot had changed in the last forty-eight hours.

She had changed.

But how much? Was her dream of building a life without him just a fallback, because the other option had been taken away? They'd always said they belonged together. Had they been right? Was it her destiny to run off with him now? Could she resist, even if she wanted to?

Before she could unravel any of those thoughts, Duncan appeared at the entrance to the courtyard, and banged once on an old ornamental brass gong.

"Ladies and gentlemen!" he began, then he glanced back

over his shoulder to where Lola was giving him an encouraging nod. "And... those of other genders."

Behind him, Lola whispered something. Duncan frowned, then turned and whispered to her.

"How can someone have *no* gender?" he asked. "What are they, rocks?"

"Just get on with it!" Lola urged.

Duncan turned to the hundred-strong crowd and pressed on as best he could.

"And those who, for reasons not entirely clear, apparently have no gender, I would like to invite you to join me in the castle ballroom." A broad smile lit up his face. "Where we're going to *really* get this party started!"

There were whoops and cheers, and the odd bit of cruel-sounding laughter from the influencers. They'd already guzzled up all the complimentary alcohol out here, though, and the thought of more freebies drew them to Duncan like iron filings to a magnet.

As the first of the influencers swept past, Brad hooked an arm and held it out to Summer. "So," he said, fixing her with that intense stare again. "Shall we?"

30

THE PROPOSAL

A few minutes later, Summer found herself standing in the doorway of the castle ballroom, holding onto Brad's arm. She was staring at, but not really seeing, the grand, lovingly decorated room spread out before them.

There was a war raging inside her head, and snippets of old conversation, past hurts, and raw emotions all clashed together.

"Sum? Babe? Did you hear me?"

"What?" Summer asked, snapping out of her trance.

Brad smiled at her, showing his neatly arranged, whiter-than-white teeth. "I said, are you ready for this?"

Summer took in the room properly for the first time. She hadn't been in here since arriving at the castle, and yet she recognized it from her time here long ago. She remembered a big party with a lot of Scottish music and laughter. She remembered her and Hugh holding each other by both hands and spinning in circles until they were dizzy, accompanied by the whoops, cheers, and clapping of the supportive crowd.

The people filling the space now were supporting nobody but themselves. The influencers had descended on the place like locusts, and were already grabbing whatever free food and drink they could get their carefully manicured hands on.

"Ready for what?" she asked, having zoned out through whatever he'd been saying to her just a moment before.

Brad patted her on the hand. "You'll be great. It'll all be awesome!" he said, then he led them into the room.

Summer's foot stretched out, but found nothing waiting for her besides empty space. Brad had noticed the two stone steps that led down into the ballroom, but Summer hadn't got the memo, and her stupid fancy shoes meant there was nothing she could do about it.

She slipped, tumbled, flailed, and tried to hold on to the man beside her. Brad, however, either wasn't fast enough to catch her, or didn't bother trying. She tumbled down both steps, then landed unceremoniously on her butt on the ballroom floor.

Thankfully, the music—a rousing Celtic fiddle tune that was being mostly ignored by the socialites—didn't scratch to a stop. Laughter rang out from all corners of the room, though, and Summer's cheeks burned hot as she scrambled awkwardly to her feet.

"Summer! Are you OK?"

It was the sort of thing she'd been expecting Brad to say, but the concern had come from Lola, who had dashed over when she'd seen Summer fall.

"Fine! I'm fine!"

"Don't worry, she does this sort of thing all the time," Brad laughed. "It's adorable!"

Summer turned and glowered at him. As he stood there laughing, she realised what an idiot she was for even *thinking* about taking him back. As he had just so elegantly demonstrated, Brad was never there when she really needed him, and he never would be.

Before she could say as much, though, Lola grabbed her by the hand.

"I need to talk to you!" the little girl whispered, and her face was so serious and solemn that Summer felt a flutter of panic in her chest.

"What's wrong? Is it Duncan?" Summer asked. She swallowed. "Is it... is it Hugh?"

"Just come on," Lola urged, pulling her through the crowd.

Summer followed, all thoughts of Brad immediately forgotten.

"Lola, you're scaring me now," Summer said. "Is everything OK?"

"No. No, it's awful!" Lola said, and when the little girl looked back over her shoulder at her, Summer could see tears building in her eyes.

She led Summer to a corner, where Duncan paced back and forth, chewing on his fingernails. To Summer's surprise, Hugh was there, too, his face lined with concern.

Her first thought was that she was pleased to see they were both apparently fine.

Her second thought, though she'd never admit it, was relief that Hugh wasn't currently off somewhere with Audriandra, getting to know Summer's ex-BFF more intimately.

"Found her!" Lola announced.

Duncan stopped pacing, went wide eyed for a moment, then offered Summer a shaky smile.

"What's going on?" Summer asked.

"Oh, lass!" Duncan whispered. "It's a disaster!"

"What is? Have we run out of food? Is the internet down?"

"The internet's fine," Hugh muttered. "Though, I'm tempted to go and switch the bloody thing off."

"Lola figured out how to check yon hashtag thing of yours. They're being brutal," Duncan explained. "Your friends."

"They're not my friends," Summer quickly stated. "And what do you mean?"

"Have you looked at what they're saying about us?" Hugh asked.

"Not for a while, no," Summer admitted.

"Well, you might want to take a wee peek," he suggested.

With a shaking hand, Summer took out her phone and opened up Instagram.

The first video she saw was of the Barbie clone with the tiny dog. She was rolling her eyes so hard they were almost entirely white.

"So, guys, listen up," she said. "If this was all my trip to Europe was going to be, I'd be jumping off a bridge right now. If this island even *had* a bridge, which is doesn't. I don't think. And, if it does, I guarantee it'll be the worst bridge you ever saw."

Summer winced, then flicked to the next video. The preview image showed the skater boy from earlier frowning and giving two thumbs down.

She skipped that one, and moved on to the next.

A chisel-jawed young black guy with a blocky haircut and pink eyeshadow was flipping a middle finger at Duncan, who stood with his back to him, smiling anxiously at the throngs of influencers.

"Seriously, this place sucks," the finger-flipper said. "Everything's even older than this dude, and he's, like, a thousand years old."

"I'm eighty-seven," Duncan muttered, shooting the phone a dirty look.

The hashtags on the post jumped out at her. Along with her #LoveLifeLachart, a new one had appeared.

#HateLifeLachart

She clicked on it, and was immediately presented with hundreds of images and videos, all mercilessly mocking the castle, the island, and the residents of both.

"I don't... This isn't..." she whispered, her head spinning.

Her legs wobbled, and she stumbled, only for Hugh to catch her by the arm, stopping her falling to the floor for the second time in as many minutes.

From somewhere across the ballroom, she heard a burst of high-pitched laughter. Much as she would've liked to believe it was someone having fun, she now knew the truth. They were laughing *at* the castle. Laughing at everything she and the islanders had worked so hard to pull off in the last twenty-four hours.

She met the eyes of the man holding her up. Their brilliant blue had dulled to a sort of steely grey.

"Oh, Hugh. I'm so sorry," she whispered.

To her surprise, he smiled at her. It wasn't like the smiles he'd been directing at Audriandra, but Summer quickly realised why.

This one was genuine.

"Ach, don't worry about it. It's not the end of the world," Hugh said, and he sounded surprisingly upbeat, all things considered. "I mean, if we had to tolerate more people like this coming here, I'd probably have burned the place to the ground, eventually."

"Aye," agreed Duncan, appearing beside her. "If Lachart Castle is going to die, then it'll do on its own terms, not pandering to stuck-up, self-important eejits like these."

Summer expected to feel a tiny bit insulted at that. She had been a 'stuck-up, self-important eejit,' too, until recently. The influencers weren't her friends, but they were her *people*. They were who she had always aspired to be.

And yet, she felt nothing. Duncan was right. They were everything he said, and worse.

They weren't her people. Not by a long way. Her people, she realised, were the ones standing around her right now.

"But *Dad*!" Lola cried. "If we lose the castle, Summer won't stay with us!"

Hugh frowned. "What's that, Lo? What do you mean?"

"She said she was going to stay with us forever," Lola told him, the tears returning to her eyes. "And it would have been so lovely to have a big sister around the house! Or... or..."

She gulped down a big breath, like she need to prepare herself for the rest of the sentence.

"Or a mum!"

Summer's eyes went wide. "A what?"

"Oh, Lola," Hugh whispered, putting a hand on his daughter's shoulder.

Ching-ching-ching!

Before anyone could say any more, the clinking of silverware against China quieted the crowd. The guests all turned their heads toward the front of the room, but Summer crouched in front of Lola, smiling gently at the little girl with tears running down her cheeks.

"Hey, all. Listen up, everyone. Can I have your attention, please?"

The sound of Brad's voice made Summer's insides twist themselves into a tight knot. Taking Lola's hand, she stood up and looked over to see him standing on an antique table with a flute of champagne in one hand, and a silver spoon in the other.

"Oh, God. What now?" she whispered under her breath as she squeezed Lola's hand.

Lola wiped her tears on the sleeve of her dress, and stood on her tip-toes to see around the bodies of the adults. "Who's that? What's happening? What's he saying?"

"Nothing," Summer said. "Nothing, he's not saying…"

Suddenly, it hit her, and her blood ran cold. She remembered the last time Brad had made a big announcement like this.

The night of their engagement.

No. Surely he wasn't going to…?

No, of course he wasn't. He would never.

But that was the problem with Brad. She'd learned to expect the unexpected from him.

And to expect the worst.

"Thank you, thank you!" Brad boomed, his voice echoing around the cavernous room. "First of all, I want to extend my sincerest apologies to anyone who Audriandra dragged out to this dump." He grinned and lifted his glass. "Guess we could all drink to that one, right? This place is a total dump!"

The crowd roared. "Hear, hear!" someone shouted amidst the laughter, and people drank. Around Summer and nearby, Hugh, Duncan, and the rest of the islanders stood stony-faced and unmoving.

"Don't worry, don't worry, guys. After all this is over, you can come to Europe and party on one of my yachts! That's a promise!" Brad said, to a chorus of more cheers.

Lines were drawn in Summer's mind. Her earlier confusion over what to do now seemed laughable. Everything was clear now—this wasn't just an influencer event, this was a battle for the heart and soul of Lachart Isle.

And she knew, as clear as crystal, which side she was on.

She gave Lola's hand another squeeze, then let it go. "I'll be right back, OK?" she whispered.

Then, she kicked off her shoes, and began marching bare-foot across the dancefloor, elbowing influencers out of her way.

"There she is!" Brad called, when he caught sight of her cutting through the crowd. "Yeah, get up here, Summer, this involves you!"

"Brad," she hissed, as the audience parted around her. "Stop."

She could feel every eye in the place on her now as she made her way across the floor. She could feel them all staring. Judging. Waiting to see what was going to happen next.

It was just like the aftermath of her wedding, all over again.

"This here is the beautiful Summer Rose, my other half for five whole years of my life."

She wanted to call out to him, to make him stop talking, but embarrassment had stolen her voice away, and it was all she could do to squeak out another, "Stop."

Up on the table, Brad waved his half-empty glass around. "I'm sure every one of you has seen the video. I mean, like, we *all* saw the video, right?"

He pulled a crying face that mimicked the one Summer had seen on so many memes, and the crowd laughed along with him.

"But, see, the thing is," Brad continued, slipping seamlessly back into serious mode. "I have big news. As of right now, our wedding is back on! Presenting the future Mrs. Summer Swash!"

A collective gasp rose up from the audience, but no cheering or applause followed it. Instead, the room descended into total, absolute silence.

No, not quite. Not exactly.

From behind her, Summer heard faint sobbing. She turned, and saw Hugh trying to comfort Lola, who was frantically wiping away tears on the sleeve of her pretty blue dress.

"Lola," she whispered. "Hugh, no, I'm..."

"How *dare* you?" a voice screeched from across the hall.

The crowd parted again, the influencers shuffling aside with their phones in their hands, capturing every moment for posterity.

There, in the growing gap, Summer saw Audriandra striding towards her and Brad, her face twisted in ugly hate.

It was, Summer thought, the first time she'd seen her look anything but beautiful.

"You're choosing *her* over *me*?" Audriandra demanded. "I mean, have you lost your mind? Look at her!"

Summer ignored the remark. She didn't care. Audriandra could say what she liked. Brad could, too. Neither one of them had any power over her anymore.

She turned back to look for Lola, but saw only an empty space where she had been. Duncan and Hugh were both looking around in surprise, like they hadn't seen her go.

And then, at the back of the ballroom, a door slammed, and Hugh took off running.

"Lola, wait! Come back!"

Summer stood there, frozen to the spot, lost, alone, and with no idea what to do next.

It was her wedding day all over again.

And now, just like then, a hundred cameras were beaming her humiliation all across the globe.

31

RETURN POLICY

The ballroom erupted into chaos. Of course it did. How could it not? There were a hundred social media hounds in the room, and moments like these were what they lived for.

Summer stood in the middle of it all, her senses dulled, her ears ringing. Everything moved at a crawl around her, like a record at too slow a speed. The cheering and screaming blurred until it was nothing but a buzz, background noise to the beating of her heart.

She saw it all in front of her like it was a scene from a movie —Audriandra, screaming her head off, face red and hair practically standing on end, like the witch in a fairy-tale.

Brad, standing there, practically impenetrable, with the same smirk he'd had on his face when he'd ditched Summer at the altar. He didn't even blink when Audriandra grabbed a flute of champagne and threw it in his face.

The crowd went wild, all of them scuttling to get closer, pressing in. This was an influencer's dream. Whoever had the best angle would win.

For Summer, it felt like a nightmare.

"Well? Do you!?"

Summer blinked as she realised Audriandra was staring at her now, and her dulled senses suddenly came back to life.

"Um... Sorry, what?"

"Do you realise what you've done? You underhanded, scheming... *creature!* I knew from the moment I decided to let him come that you were going to try to dig your claws into him!" she accused, jabbing her sharpened fingernail at Summer. "I just knew it!"

Summer shook her head. "I didn't. I don't—"

"Don't give me that!" Audriandra looked around wildly. The first thing she found was a plate. She grabbed it and hurled it straight towards Summer.

Summer yelped and ducked. The plated *whooshed* past above her, then shattered against the forehead of an influencer whose reflexes weren't quite as fast.

He fell backwards to the floor, out cold, and was lost among the feet of the tightly packed crowd.

A few of his fellow social media stars shuffled aside to avoid trampling on him, but otherwise, they paid him no heed. They were still all focused on Audriandra, and the epic meltdown she was in the throes of.

Summer's former best friend started to snatch up everything that was close to hand, and hurl it towards Summer and, to a lesser extent, Brad. She launched a vase of flowers, a chair, a silver candelabra, complete with burning candles that were blown out as it flew through the air in Summer's direction.

A chair came next. Then, running out of things to throw, Audriandra pulled the tablecloth from a table and began spinning it around her head like a lasso, *whumming* it closer and closer through the air towards where Summer stood.

Ducking, Summer searched the crowd. Lola and Hugh were still missing, and now Duncan had disappeared, too.

Summer got a flashback to that look of hurt and betrayal on Lola's face. Her heart broke for the little girl. She had to find her. She had to let her know that everything was going to be OK.

"Out of my way," Summer said, avoiding the swinging table-cloth and marching off in the direction of the door.

Brad caught up with her and grabbed her by the arm.

"It's OK, babe. Don't let her scare you. I'll look after you."

"No, Brad. Let me go," Summer seethed. "I have to go find Lola."

Brad frowned. "Who?"

Summer glared at him.

God, what had she ever seen in this eejit?

"Leave them, babe. Forget them. They're nobody. You've got me now."

Suddenly, from nowhere, Summer felt overcome by a sense of calm. After years of searching, she finally knew where she belonged.

And she knew what she had to do.

"No, Brad," she said, spitting out his name like it left an unpleasant taste in her mouth. "I do not have you. I do not want you! So, let me go!"

She tried to pull her arm free, but he kept holding it. He was still smiling at her, that same condescending grin, like she was a child just acting out.

As quickly as it had come, her calm left her. Anger swooped in to fill the void it had left.

"I said, let. Me. Go!" Summer roared, tearing her arm away and shoving him in the chest with both hands.

He wasn't a particularly heavy man, and the force of the

shove sent him sprawling backwards. He hit a table, flipped awkwardly over it, then landed in an untidy heap on the floor.

"I'm fine! I'm OK!" he cried, trying to retain some dignity. He sprang to his feet, all smiles and waves, and Summer once again felt the eyes of the world upon her.

"I don't want you, Brad!" Summer told him.

"Whoa," someone in the crowd cried before Brad could respond. "Check it out!"

Every camera swung toward the edge of the ballroom.

Summer's jaw dropped.

Oh, no, she thought as she watched Audriandra, who, having run out of things to throw, had somehow managed to detach one of the ancient and massive battle-axes from the wall. She was breathing hard through her nostrils, wielding the weapon like a warrior of old, albeit one in a silver dress and high heels.

"Summmmerrrrrr!" she roared.

The name rang out around the hall like some ancient challenge was being issued. Summer didn't have time for all this, though.

"I don't want him, alright? You can have him," she said, glaring at Audriandra while stabbing a finger in Brad's direction. "To be honest, I'm glad you stole him, because over the last few days here I've realised that, you know what? I don't actually like him."

She turned slowly on the spot, looking at the crowd around her. None of them looked directly at her, but instead smirked at the tiny version of her on their screens.

"In fact, I don't like any of you," she told them, her anger building, her hands flying around to emphasize the points she was making. "You're all horrible, judgmental, shallow, self-obsessed jerks! You think you're better than everyone else, even though none of you has ever had an actual real job, or contributed anything even remotely positive to society. What even are you? What's even the point in you people?"

She was in full-blown rant mode now, her eyes wide and wild, flobs of spittle flying from her mouth. She stamped her bare foot on the wooden floor, and fired one final remark at them.

"You all make me sick!"

She turned back to Audriandra to see that, thankfully, she'd dropped the battle-axe. In its place, she held a weapon she was much more comfortable with.

Her phone.

Like the rest of them, she had been recording Summer's outburst. She turned the phone so Summer could see it, and played back the clip of her ranting.

The version of Summer on-screen looked utterly demented, and the spit bombs spilling from her lips didn't exactly help matters.

Audriandra grinned in triumph. "Oh, Summer, this might be my most viral video yet. You make it so easy. You and your little meltdowns. When it comes to your total humiliation, I think this blows the *WAHHHHH! DON'T YOU LOVE ME?* video out of the water."

Summer just stared at her, at this pathetic girl she'd once called her best friend. It was hard to believe that she'd lived that lie for most of her life.

But she was over it now.

"You want to post it? Go ahead." Summer looked around at every one of them, most of whom were still filming. "Post it all you want. I don't care. Let it out. Let it fly free. Because it'll probably be the first real, honest thing you've ever put up on your channels."

She spun around, staring straight down the lenses of their

phone cameras, making eye contact with them through their screens.

"Because it isn't real. The stuff you post. You know it as well as I do. That isn't you in those videos, it's all filters and fantasy. You think you're living, but you aren't. You're not people, you're performers. You're actors trapped in a play..." She remembered who she was talking to. "I mean, trapped in a TV show. And one day, people are going to stop watching that show, and move on to something else. One day, they'll all stop noticing you. And what happens to you then? What good will all this have done? What will be the point of it all?"

She turned again, and saw that same sea of phones staring back at her.

"The people of this island welcomed me. They were nice to me, even though that wouldn't earn them any views, or likes, or new followers. Because none of that matters to them. Because they, unlike you, are real people. They live in the real world, not on a screen. Not hiding behind a filter."

She glanced around, and caught a few encouraging smiles and nods from the islanders that she saw.

"I don't care what you all think of this place. I really don't," she continued. "No, it doesn't have a spa. Yes, it's old. And maybe the internet doesn't work very often..."

Somewhere near the back of the crowd, the Barbie clone fainted clean away at the very thought.

"But I was made to feel like I belonged here. This was made to feel like my home," Summer said. She inhaled, and drew herself up to her full height. "And, if this is my home, then you are no longer welcome in it."

Silence hung in the air. A few of the influencers were still recording, but some had started to lower their phones. Summer liked to think she'd managed to get through to them, but that was unlikely, she knew. It was much more likely that they were starting to realise the free food and drinks were about to be cut off.

"You heard the lassie!" boomed Mick. He clapped his hands like he was trying to scare away a pest, and the echo of it raced around the ballroom. "Bugger off, the lot of you!"

"Aye," Isla Campbell cried. "And don't let the door hit you on the arse on the way out!"

"You can't just throw us out!" cried Audriandra. "We're guests!"

"No, you're freeloaders," Mick corrected. "And either you all leave quietly, or we release the haggis on you!"

Audriandra frowned. "What's a haggis?" she asked, her eyes darting anxiously around the room. "I thought you, like, ate those?"

"Oh, we do," Isla said. "But only after a long hunt, and a violent battle."

"Fearsome wee beasties, they are!" added her husband, hurrying over to join her. "Big, pointy teeth, and jaggy claws that'll have your eyes right out of your head!"

Audriandra swallowed, her eyes now frantically searching for the creature the islanders were describing. The other influencers were picking up the pace, too, rushing for the exit so quickly it was practically a stampede.

"Hark!" Mick cried, putting a hand to his ear. "I think I hear the pitter-patter of angry wee feet now! They're coming! I'd sling your hook, lassie, before it's too late!"

That did it. Audriandra turned on her expensive, ridiculous heels, and broke into a teetering run.

"Coming through! Out of my way! I'm more famous than you!" she screeched.

And then, they all thundered up the two stone steps, and silence filled the ballroom.

Summer turned to the islanders and smirked. "I thought haggis was all purple knobbly bits squeezed into a sheep's stomach?"

Mick grinned at her, then shrugged. "Aye," he said. "But some people will believe any old shite."

Summer heard a scuffling behind her. She turned to find Brad grabbing the influencer Audriandra had knocked out by the ankles.

"So, uh, if you ever change your mind and get tired of this place, my yacht's always open," he said, dragging the unconscious socialite towards the door.

Summer rolled her eyes, then shot him the thinnest of smiles. "Thanks, Brad. I'll keep that in mind," she said, before turning her back on him.

Forever.

With a final nod to the islanders, she set off running towards the door at the back of the room, where she was sure Lola had gone.

Barefoot, she slid out into a long hallway, and went racing along it, calling out as she ran.

"Lola? Hugh? Duncan?"

Nobody answered. Only the echo of her own voice bounced back at her off the thick stone walls.

She ran on, through parts of the castle she'd never seen before. Faces leered at her from dusty paintings. She caught glimpses of herself, all warped and deformed, in the dull reflections in ancient weapons and suits of armour.

And then, her heart thumping inside her chest, she stumbled around a corner and into absolute darkness.

Behind her, electric lights buzzed, illuminating the hallway.

Up ahead lay nothing but a vast pool of inky black.

She was about to turn when she spotted a shape moving in the darkness.

"Lola?" she called.

The figure who came stumbling out was not the little girl, but her grandfather. He looked old—much older than she'd ever seen him. The lines of his face had deepened with worry.

"Oh, Summer, there you are!" he wheezed, struggling for breath.

"Where's Lola?" she asked him.

Gasping, Duncan raised a hand and pointed off into the darkness.

"Down there," he whispered.

"What is that? What's down there?" Summer asked.

"It's the East Wing," Duncan told her, and what little colour was left in his face drained away. "It's not safe for her. It's falling apart. It's far too dangerous."

Summer moved to step past him, but he blocked her path.

"No! You can't! You mustn't!" he said. "Hugh's looking for her. It's too dangerous for you, you don't know the way!"

"Duncan, please! This is all my fault," she said, staring deep into his eyes. "I have to help. I have to try and fix this." She laid a hand on the forearm he was using to hold her back. "I have to."

Duncan didn't move. Not at first. Not right away.

But then, he lowered his arm, nodded, and stepped aside.

"Just... be careful," he told her.

"I will," Summer said.

And with that, she set off into Lachart Castle's dark and crumbling East Wing.

32

THE EAST WING

Summer fumbled in her bag until she found her phone, and turned on the flashlight. She almost screamed at the face she saw leering back at her, before realising it was yet another creepy portrait hanging on the wall.

Unlike the others, this one wasn't just dusty, it was being consumed by blooms of black mould. She quickly turned the torch away, aiming it at the floor as she pressed onwards into the gloom.

With each step, the surrounding air grew colder, making her shiver. The floor ahead of her was falling apart, loose floorboards having collapsed down into the foundations, the spaces they had left now filled with clumps of prickly, angry-looking weeds.

The corridor's stone walls were weeping, and water reflected the light of her torch. She could see more paintings on the walls, but these were so thick with dust and mould, that it was impossible to see what they depicted.

Thick cobwebs swayed like curtains in a draft. Shadows were

everywhere, playing tricks on her eyes, and the smell was more earthen and mouldy than in the main house.

"Lola! Hugh!" she called.

Nothing but echo replied.

Shivering in her light sundress, her arms bare, she stepped unsurely on the uneven floor. Puddles had pooled in those parts of the floor that hadn't collapsed. She could feel the cold, stagnant water against the exposed skin of her feet.

Another set of painted eyes bored into her through a gap in the mould, and she suddenly became afraid that there was something behind her, chasing her through the darkness, hunting her down.

She broke into a run, her bare feet slipping and splashing on the slick floor. There was a corner dead ahead, and her heart thumped wildly as she swung herself around it.

Thump.

She collided hard with a broad, powerful chest, and was about to scream when she realised that she knew who the chest belonged to. She'd woken up snuggled against it just the morning before, after all.

"Hugh!" she breathed, shining the light in his face. He looked tense and worried. "Where is she? Where's Lola?"

"I don't know," Hugh said, his voice trembling. He squinted in the torchlight. "Can you stop shining that in my face?"

"Oh! Yes! Sorry!" Summer said.

"What are you doing here?" Hugh demanded. "I thought you were leaving with that shower of clowns?"

"No," Summer said.

Hugh shifted his weight, and his kilt swished against his knees. "I thought your big wedding was back on?"

"No! That's what I wanted to tell you—"

Before she could say any more, there came a crash and a

scream from deeper in the dark corridor. Hugh stiffened, then took off running in the direction of the sound, calling Lola's name.

Summer broke into a run, following after him, her torchlight fending off the darkness ahead.

It didn't seem to matter to Hugh, though. Even here, in the condemned part of the castle, he seemed to know every inch. He bounded over collapsed beams, dodged holes in the floor, and skirted around fallen rubble.

Summer tried to keep up, but by the time she was nearing the end of the corridor, Hugh was already throwing open a door there and hurrying inside.

"Lola!" Hugh bellowed, and the panic in his voice gave Summer a burst of speed. She scrambled over the obstacles, and without looking where she was going, launched herself into the room like a bullet from a gun.

An arm like an iron bar hit her in the chest, stopping her dead in her tracks.

The light from her torch swung down to reveal a vast, gaping hole where the floor should have been.

The whole thing had collapsed into a basement room. Possibly even a dungeon, Summer thought, though she chose not to dwell on that.

There, several feet below them, surrounded by the years-old wreckage, lay the tiny, motionless body of a girl in a pretty blue dress.

"Oh, God!" Summer whispered. "Hugh?"

"Lola!" Hugh bellowed.

As his voice rolled around the room, there was a groan from below, and a creak from above.

Down in the basement, Lola's eyes fluttered open. Directly above her, the ceiling of the room they were in bulged ominously, like it was filled with thousands of gallons of water.

"Dad?" Lola wheezed. She coughed a few times, then sat up. "Dad, is that you?"

"Aye, it's me, Lo! It's alright! Don't move! Just you stay where you are. Dad's going to get you out."

Before he could make a move, Summer grabbed his arm and aimed her torch upwards.

"Look," she whispered. "It could come down any second."

Hugh's jaw tightened. "Aye," he said. "And my daughter's no' going to be there when it does."

There was no way they could see of climbing down, so Hugh dropped onto his belly, shuffled to the edge of the hole, and stretched down as far as he could.

"Grab on, Lo!" he urged.

"What do you think I am, a giant?" Lola called up to him, and Summer couldn't help but smile. Clearly, the girl still had her attitude, which meant she hopefully wasn't badly hurt.

"Try!" Hugh said.

Lola jumped, reaching up, but came nowhere even close to catching his hand. The impact of her landing made the bulging ceiling give another warning groan.

"Lo, stop. Just wait, alright?" her dad whispered. "No sudden movements. Just hold on."

"Hurry, Dad!"

"You need to lower something down to her," Summer said.

Hugh looked around, then felt at his shoulder for the sash he'd been wearing. He must've ditched it somewhere during the search, though, because it was no longer fastened across him.

"I've no' got anything to lower!" he whispered.

Summer looked down at the girl in the basement, then up at

the ceiling. Little cascades of plaster dust were falling from it now as it shifted. They were running out of time.

"Me," Summer told him. "Lower me."

"What? But…"

"Hugh!" she hissed. "Either you lower me, or I'm jumping in, and you can figure out a way to get us both out. Your choice!"

She propped her phone up so that the light from the torch continued to shine down into the hole below, then dropped onto her stomach beside Hugh.

"My legs. Hold my legs and lower me in," she instructed.

Hugh held her gaze for a moment, and then launched himself onto his feet.

Summer took a deep breath as she felt his strong hands wrapping around her ankles.

What are you doing? You're going to die! she thought, then she pushed that nagging voice away, silencing it just in time for Hugh to slide her towards the edge.

"You sure?" he asked.

She nodded. She was. She had never been more sure about anything in her life, even when she slid forwards and her stomach lurched as Hugh lowered her, upside-down, over the edge.

"Ooh, it's high!" she whispered. "Don't drop me! Don't drop me!"

"I'm not going to drop you," Hugh promised.

And she believed him.

"Lola, take my hand," Summer urged.

The little girl looked up, and her face was a mask of dirt and betrayal.

"No," she sobbed. "You said you would stay, but you lied. You're leaving. You're going to go marry that man with the stupid hair."

Summer found herself smiling at that. "It really is stupid hair, isn't it?" she said.

"Lola!" Hugh hissed. "Grab on!"

"I'm not marrying him, Lola," Summer said. "And not because of his stupid hair. Well, not *just* that."

Above them, the ceiling moaned in protest.

"But you're leaving, aren't you?" Lola whispered.

"No. If you'll all have me, I'd like to stay. For as long as you want me here. I told everyone that upstairs. That I love it here. I love the island, I love the castle, and I love the people."

Lola's lower lip trembled, and she drew it behind her teeth. "You do?"

"Yes. Of course. Two in particular." Summer smiled. "So, take my hand, Lola. I'm not going anywhere, I promise."

Lola eyed her, despair giving way to hope. A smile played on her lips, only to be swallowed by another sob.

"But how can you stay with us if we won't be here?" she asked. "It didn't work. The plan failed. We're going to have to leave the island. Our home."

The ceiling above gave a sharp, sudden creak.

"Get a bloody move on down there!" Hugh spat. "Talk later, climb now!"

"Please, Lola!" Summer pleaded, then she almost cheered when the girl stretched up and caught her hand.

Summer's fingers tightened around her wrists.

"Got her. Pull!"

Hugh didn't need to be told twice. She heard him grunt with the effort as he heaved them both back up out of the hole, and onto a more solid part of the floor.

And not a moment too soon. Thunder erupted overhead, and the ceiling gave way. Summer caught Lola and pulled in her close, shielding her from the dust and debris that came crashing past them.

And then, Summer realised, she was being protected, too. Hugh had his arms wrapped around them both, and was holding them close, hugging them tightly, like he would never let anything bad happen to either of them.

The noise seemed to go on forever. Wood splintered and snapped. Rock cracked and shattered. It wasn't water that had been pressing down on the ceiling, but the weight of the ceiling above that one, which had succumbed to rot a long time ago.

And then, finally, the chaos became still. Hugh kept holding them for a while, even after it had all stopped.

Then, slowly, cautiously, he unwrapped his arms from around them, and they all turned to take in the damage.

The weight of the debris had punched a hole in the wall of the basement room that Lola had fallen into. The old stone had collapsed into an adjoining chamber, which seemed to have been completely claimed by weeds and other foliage.

Summer froze as, through the cloud of dust, her eyes fell on something growing amongst the rubble.

Several somethings. A whole vibrant field of them, in fact, so beautiful that it stole Summer's breath away, so she could only point down at them, speechless.

Lola and Hugh followed her outstretched finger and gasped.

"No way," Hugh muttered, shaking his head. "No way those are—"

"Lachart Lilies!" Lola screamed, and her voice was so piercing that both Summer and Hugh looked up in case she was going to bring another ceiling crashing down on them.

To their relief, the one overhead looked solid enough.

"They're Lachart Lilies! Millions of them!"

"Aye," Hugh was forced to admit. "Looks like it!"

"I knew it! I knew we'd find them!" Lola cried. She leapt into the air with glee.

Panicking that she was going to fall back into the hole again, Hugh and Summer both grabbed her and pulled her back. They tripped on a pile of rubble behind them, and tumbled into the corridor, a tangle of flailing body parts.

When they finally finished rolling, Summer found herself wrapped in Hugh's arms, her face close to his, his chest heaving beneath her.

Breathless, their eyes locked, and this time, he made no move to pull away. She didn't either. Instead, she lowered her head to his, and—finally—their lips pressed together in a kiss.

They were lying in a puddle in a filthy, crumbling castle, but Summer didn't care. She was floating somewhere, lost in the moment, and yet at the same time, racing ahead to all the potentials of the future that awaited them.

Until, that is, Lola loudly cleared her throat.

"Ew. Guys. Come on. Get a room," she grouched, but when they looked at her, she was smiling from ear to ear.

And behind and below her, the Lachart Lilies grew.

33

LOVE, LIFE, LACHART

Ten minutes later, the islanders were all gathered in the dining room, watching the procession of jet skis and yachts trailing off into the last rays of the sunset.

Lola sat atop the long wooden table, bouncing like a jumping bean in her now-filthy dress. "This was the best party ever!" she cheered. "We should do this more often. I had so much fun! Did you all have fun, too?"

The islanders all answered as one. "No," they said. "No, not really."

"Well now, lass, I enjoy a good knees-up as much as the next man!" Duncan said. "But I think I aged about ten years since this morning. Good riddance to that lot, I say!"

He raised a two-fingered salute to the window, but Lola, thankfully, didn't notice the slightly inappropriate gesture, as she was now wrestling with her father's attempts to apply a sticking plaster to a tiny scrape on her forehead.

"Hold still, will you?" Hugh said. He applied the plaster, then leaned back, admiring his handiwork. "There. And don't go poking at it. Let it heal."

"Aye, sir!" Lola said. She saluted, and then immediately prodded at the site of her injury.

"She never listens," Hugh said.

"No, she does not!" Duncan said, turning back to her. His face was firmly set, his eyes narrowed. "But you need to, lass. We can't have you running off and getting into trouble like that again. Something terrible could've happened."

"But, Grandpa! It was good that I did it! It was worth it!"

"But Grandpa nothing!" Duncan said. "You are worth more to me than anything, Lola. More than this castle. More, even, than this island. If anything happened to you..."

He turned away to the window. The boats and jet skis were just dots in the distance now.

"It doesn't matter that we're losing our home," Duncan said. "We'll have each other. That's the main thing. That's the *only* thing that matters."

Summer gently cleared her throat. "Duncan?"

"It'll be hard, aye," Duncan said, tucking his hands behind his back. "Adjusting to life out there. But we'll manage. Somehow. Between us, we'll manage."

"Duncan?" Summer said again, a little more forcefully this time.

"Yes, of course, Summer," the old man said, still not turning. "If you want to come with us, you'll be more than welcome."

"Dad, will you stop you havering and just turn around?" Hugh barked.

Surprised, Duncan did as he was told, only to find himself staring directly into a bunch of beautiful blue flowers with crisp white edgings.

The old man's hand flew to his mouth. His eyes shimmered, tears swelling in them.

"Is that...?"

"It is," Summer confirmed. "Lola found them."

"Millions of them!" the little girl added.

"Hugh climbed down and picked some," Summer continued. "But there's plenty more where this came from."

She smiled, watching his reaction. It turned out that the secret to saving Lachart Castle didn't lie somewhere out there beyond the island. Everything it needed had been right here within its walls, all along.

"Do you know what this means?" Duncan whispered.

Lola jumped up on the table and threw her clenched fists into the air.

"An annual share of a three billion pounds of botanical tourism!" she cried. The way she said it made it sound like she'd been waiting her whole life to shout those words.

And maybe, in a way, she had.

Duncan let out a *whoop* that made all the islanders except Lola jump in fright. He launched himself up onto the table beside her, and they both danced a jig, laughing and hugging each other in delight.

And then, as suddenly as he had started, Duncan stopped dancing. "Wait! I need to make a phone call!" he announced, then he raised an index finger like he'd just had a big, important idea. "Make that *two* phone calls! One to those eejit investors, telling them that Lachart Castle is no longer up for sale!"

He crouched, like he was thinking of jumping down from the table, then common sense got the better of him, and he carefully climbed down instead.

"And then, I'm going to phone the newspapers and get the word out there," Duncan said. He held up his hands, like he was visualizing the headline now. "World's Rarest Flower Found," he announced, then he winked at his grinning granddaughter. "By the Lady of Lachart Castle."

Lola giggled, and jumped into his arms. He caught her, spun her around, and then his eyes went wide as she whispered in his ear. "One of the ladies."

Duncan looked from his son to Summer, and back again. Then, holding Lola tightly to him, he beckoned to the other islanders.

"Come on, folks, let's go have a quick sweep of the grounds, and make sure none of those buggers are still lingering around!"

Taking the hint, everyone followed him out through the doors of the dining hall, leaving Hugh and Summer alone, at last.

Off in the distance, the final boat was just disappearing, along with the last rays of the sun. It was the biggest boat of all —the large, expensive yacht that carried with it the remnants of her old life.

They both watched until only the moon and stars remained, glimmering over the mirror-calm sea.

"Will you miss them?" Hugh asked.

She shook her head. "No," she said, honestly. "I won't."

"I think you might," Hugh said. "Living here, it's no' easy. It can be hard work sometimes."

"Ah well," Summer said. She slid an arm around his waist, and he wrapped one his around her shoulder. "As a wise man once told me, a little hard work never hurt anyone…"

And, as the moon shone brightly on Lachart Isle, they fell into each other, and kissed.

THE END

RETURN TO LACHART ISLE

Meet a whole new couple - plus some familiar faces - in Isle Be Home for Christmas.

Printed in Great Britain
by Amazon